kittens
& kisses

Berry Lake

CUPCAKE
POSSE

friendship • romance • cupcakes

BOOK THREE

USA TODAY BEST SELLING AUTHOR

MELISSA McCLONE

Kisess & Kittens
Berry Lake Cupcake Posse
Book Three

Cover and Photography by Cover Me Darling
Cupcake from SAS Cupcakes

ISBN: 9781944777647 (paperback)
ISBN: 9781944777630 (eBook)

Published by:

Cardinal Press, LLC
June 2022

get a free read

To receive a free story,
join Melissa's newsletter.
Visit subscribepage.com/w9w0y1 to sign up.

dedication

In memory of my brother
Randy

Hi! Thanks for picking up Kittens & Kisses. I love the characters in this book (and series) so much! I hope you do, too.

The Berry Lake Cupcake Posse series is a women's fiction friendship saga and will be best enjoyed if the books are read in order.

Can you read this one before the first two? Of course, but please understand the stories are not standalones. There are also cliff-hangers, so I wanted to let you know about that, too!

Happy Reading!

chapter one

THE CHEERY WOODEN sign on the roadside read, *Welcome to Wishing Bay, your home away from home on the Washington Coast.* The cute seashells and anchor surrounding the words should have brought a grin to Bria Landon's face. She wasn't crafty, but Aunt Elise would have loved the quaintness and stopped to take a photograph.

If only Bria was there to sightsee…

Goose bumps covered her arms.

She shivered.

Not from the air blowing through the vent of Dalton Dwyer's car as they drove west toward the Pacific Ocean. No, the chill came from the conversation with her father. That had been hours ago, but the aftereffects lingered.

She rubbed her forearms. As soon as she stopped, another round of goose bumps prickled her skin.

Dalton raised his right hand from the steering wheel and patted her thigh. "Almost there."

"Thanks." Gratitude tipped the corners of her lips when smiling was the last thing she imagined doing. But without Dalton, she would be driving to the coast alone.

And lost.

Not literally.

Though possibly. Bria could have easily taken a wrong turn somewhere. She appreciated Dalton not forcing a conversation. The silence made the drive seem longer, but Bria couldn't concentrate. Nothing stopped the flow of Dad's words.

I didn't want you to hate me. Please don't hate me.

Go to Wishing Bay, and you'll see. Don't wait. Go today. And pay. Please pay what I owe.

I love you. I didn't always show it, but everything I did… I love you, baby doll. And I hope you can forgive me.

From the moment he'd spoken in the county jail's visitor room, his sentences had played on an endless loop in Bria's head.

He'd made no sense.

Not that anything had since an arsonist destroyed the Berry Lake Cupcake Shop. But if an impromptu trip to Wishing Bay proved Dad's innocence, the drive would be worth it. And if sending them to the coast was another one of his schemes…

Not going there.

Dad couldn't be guilty of setting fire to Aunt Elise's legacy and nearly killing Missy Hanford, who'd worked late and decided to sleep in the upstairs office.

Please let me find his alibi here.

Bria blew out a long breath. Too bad her suspicions wouldn't be exhaled as easily. Even though she *wanted* Dad to be innocent, a part of her thought he'd done it.

The worst part?

She wasn't alone.

Most of Berry Lake, including Sheriff Dooley, had judged Brian Landon as guilty. They were just waiting for the trial and the jury to pass the verdict so the judge could sentence him.

She was a CPA, not an attorney, but even to her, it appeared to be a slam-dunk case.

Dad had the motivation.

Greed.

He'd had the means.

Keys to the bakery.

Except one thing kept popping up. In her mind, at least.

The fire had destroyed much of the building's value. That was the true worth of their inheritance from Aunt Elise, not the bakery itself.

Why would Dad have set the fire and risk lowering their potential profit from a sale?

He'd brought that up himself.

A red herring?

Had Dad not thought his actions through, and only after the fire realized his mistake?

So many questions, and no answers.

Bria shook her head, as if that could transport her to a place where she knew everything and stop the churning in her stomach, which must be filled with three pounds of butter by now.

Oh, Aunt Elise, if only you hadn't believed in your brother and rewritten your will.

Dalton lowered his hand from the steering wheel and reached across the middle console for her arm. "You okay?"

His touch was warm and gentle, the perfect combination.

"Just thinking how things would be different if Aunt Elise hadn't left my dad and me each fifty percent of her bakery."

"She had her reasons."

Sentimental ones about reuniting an estranged father and daughter. Ones Dad had encouraged for all the wrong reasons. "Yes, but she had no idea he'd want to sell."

When Bria didn't.

Only two things remained—a charred shell of the bakery and Aunt Elise's notebook containing her recipes and ideas. "And now, being sent to Wishing Bay... I'm more confused than ever."

"Let's hope you find some answers."

Not trusting her voice, Bria nodded. If she didn't get any...

No, she didn't want to think about that.

Bria glanced out the passenger window, where water stretched to the horizon. "I haven't seen the Pacific since I left San Diego."

"It hasn't been that long."

"Last month." It felt longer. "I used to see the ocean every day on my drive to work."

"Do you miss living there?"

"No." The rapid-fire answer shot out like cars speeding to beat a freeway on-ramp metering light. She didn't want Dalton to doubt anything, especially her. Them. As she stared at him, warmth balled at the center of her chest and flowed out.

"Southern California's no longer my home. I prefer being in Berry Lake and with you."

He sent her a sideward glance and grinned. "There's the smile I love."

"I love yours, too."

His cheeks reddened. "Thanks. Stare all you want. Just don't drool on the leather seats."

"When have I ever drooled?"

"High school."

Okay, he had her there. "That was a long time ago."

They'd been so young and made many mistakes, but the past was behind them. They were moving forward after more than fifteen years apart.

Dalton turned into what appeared to be the commercial district of the small town. A wood-plank sidewalk was in front of shops and cafés with nautical and beachy names. A three-story, brightly painted Victorian sat past those buildings, with a white picket fence that looked out of place except for the Wishing Bay Dress Shop sign. It was decorated with flourishes and seashells.

"Is this the kind of themed town your boss had in mind for Berry Lake?" Bria asked.

"Yes, and Tanner's still pursuing his options there. My mom thinks Sal should sell the art gallery to Mitch."

"That's…" Bria struggled for the right words. "The Berry Lake Art Gallery has been on Main Street for as long as I remember. I mean, everyone goes there to take a selfie with Squatchy."

The Bigfoot sculpture at the gallery had its own website and social media.

"Sal hasn't said yes."

That didn't make her feel any better. Not that Bria was against change, but Squatchy was part of town lore.

"Sal's never told your mom no." Including firing his daughter, Sheridan, to hire Dalton's sister, Remy. "Will Sal this time?"

"No idea, but Berry Lake has the potential to be as commercially appealing as Wishing Bay." Dalton pointed to his left. Cars filled a parking lot, but the boxy building appeared worn, needing a paint job and a new sign. "If I were in charge here, I'd demolish that monstrosity and build shops that fit better."

Bria took a closer look. "Ice rinks aren't known for their aesthetic design."

He nodded. "Didn't expect to find one in a town this size. Though Berry Lake might end up with a rink when Logan and Selena move there."

"Elias Carpenter mentioned installing a portable rink in the park this Christmas. Selena brought it up to his grandmother, who's on the Winter Extravaganza committee, and Mrs. Carpenter loved the idea."

"I'd rather skate on the lake."

Bria enjoyed skating there, but… "You can't do that if you're on a date at night, but the park's rink will have lights. I've never skated outdoors at night."

"Is that a hint?"

"Maybe."

"I'll make a note of it."

What Dalton was doing hit her like the ice against her bottom when she fell. He was trying his best to distract her when they were minutes away from discovering Dad's alibi. "Thanks for getting my mind off my father."

"Anytime."

The affection in his voice told Bria he meant it. "I only hope he didn't send us on a wild goose chase."

"Even if he did, there's still a bill to pay."

Dad hadn't explained why he owed money for a room at some place on the coast. She'd been afraid to search on the name. Afraid of what she might find. "This all seems so crazy."

"It does, but we're together in a quaint coastal town. Can't complain about that." Dalton flipped on his right blinker. "Cliffside Manor is up ahead. See the sign."

Below the name read: An Assisted Living Center.

Why would Dad own them money? Bria clutched the armrest. Not that she could hold on to it once they got out of the car, but she clung now. "Here we go."

Dalton parked in the paved lot. The lines, white and bright, appeared newly painted. "Not what I was expecting."

He'd shown patience when Bria's nerves got to her during their drive. But those feelings had quadrupled in the seconds since he parked the car. She tried to tamp down the extra nerves as to not stress him out, too.

"Me either." Cliffside Manor looked more like a new hotel than an assisted-living center. "I have so many questions."

Dalton removed the keys from the ignition. "That's why we're here."

"What was my dad doing here on that Thursday night? I thought he might have been involved in something sketchy, but now that I see this place, I'm not sure. Not saying anything to the police or his lawyer makes no sense unless he was trying to swindle retirees."

"People do strange things sometimes." Dalton's voice remained steady, the way it had been since they'd left the jail. "Let's find out how your dad's involved with this place."

Even though Bria wanted to know what was going on, her insides trembled with uncertainty. Still, she got out of the car.

Why was prison a better option than her father mentioning someone at an assisted-living home as his alibi?

Bright flowers grew in neatly manicured beds. Someone had mowed the strips of green lawn recently. Not one weed was in sight. Bria took a closer look. "The landscaping is nice."

"The facility is high-end. You can tell from the architecture."

Dalton worked in commercial real estate, so he saw buildings and businesses through that lens.

"Well, if the residents are wealthy, that explains why my dad was here." Brian Landon was always searching for the pot of gold at the end of the rainbow. Rainbow was synonymous with a get-rich-quick scheme. "He might need investors."

Dalton reached for the front door. "No matter what we find inside, I support you, and I love you."

Bria brushed her lips against his. "I love you, too. But—"

He placed his fingertip against her mouth. "No buts, okay?"

She loved this man, but her practical side had to get this out. As soon as he lowered his hand, she had her chance. "I don't have a 'but.' It's more of a what-if."

"Go ahead."

"If my dad is being made a scapegoat by the Berry Lake Sheriff's Office and Fire Department, it means the real arsonist is still out there. They might blame Missy or me."

"If—and I'm emphasizing the word *if*—that's the case, we'll deal with it. Together." Dalton laced his fingers with hers. "I lost you once because of my family. Nothing—and no one—will drive us apart again. I promise."

As she nodded, contentment flowed through her. A strange emotion given the day, but a welcome one. "Good, because I don't want that to happen again."

He squeezed her hand and opened the door. "It won't."

His confident voice spurred her forward. She approached the receptionist. "Hi. I'm Bria Landon. My father, Brian, asked me to pay for room three thirteen."

"Oh, hello. I'm Lauren." The woman appeared to be around the same age as Bria. Lauren's business-casual clothes would have been right in style at Bria's old accounting firm. "We've been expecting you."

This was bizarre.

The only thing missing?

The theme song from *The Twilight Zone* playing.

She'd watched reruns of that show when she was younger with Aunt Elise. "My dad said he was here a few weeks ago on a Thursday night."

Lauren nodded. "I'm sure Brian was here. Thursday night is date night."

Date night? Bria met Dalton's gaze, and he shrugged slightly.

"Could we..." Words failed her.

"Of course, go up, and then I'll have you meet with our business manager to pay." Lauren didn't miss a beat. "It's so wonderful to finally meet you. I see the strong family resemblance."

Bria didn't look like Dad, but maybe Lauren saw something Bria didn't.

Lauren motioned to a clipboard with a pen attached. "Please sign in. Put room three thirteen for the resident."

So he'd visited someone. Someone in the room he was paying for. That was more than they knew before. Except...

This felt too easy, which gave Bria a sense of foreboding. Weird when this place was light and cheery. Clean and welcoming. She signed the form before moving out of the way for Dalton to do the same. She handed him the pen.

He filled out the line below hers. "Do you keep the sign-in logs?"

"Yes." Lauren took the clipboard from him. "Management keeps paper records for a minimum of seven years and video for ninety days."

That meant they would have proof—evidence. But that begged a question.

What was her father hiding?

Brian Landon looked out for one person—himself. If Bria thought Dad had changed, the way he'd convinced her aunt to leave him half the cupcake shop showed her he was the same as always. Acting in his best interest was his priority.

Lauren handed over two badges, and they each clipped them to their shirts. "I'll buzz you through the double doors. Take the elevator to the third floor. Follow the signs to room three thirteen. Enjoy your visit."

"Thanks." Bria only hoped they left with more answers than questions.

A few minutes later, they stood in the elevator. The doors closed.

"How are you doing?" Dalton asked.

She inhaled deeply. "I'm not sure."

He placed his arm around her and pulled her against him. "The good news is there's a log with his name and the time he signed in and left. There might even be video of him being here."

Bria nodded. "But this place... It makes so little sense. Aunt Elise never mentioned my dad coming to Wishing Bay. This facility is newer. It wouldn't have been built when I came here with him on vacation."

The elevator dinged. The doors opened.

"Third floor." Dalton motioned for Bria to exit first. "The sign says the room is on the left."

As they headed in that direction, the room numbers went down from 320. Fall wreaths and autumn-inspired swags hung on several doors. Other doorframes were strung with orange, yellow, and red leaf garland. Skulls, bats, and skeletons graced a few.

Did the residents pick which holiday or season they wanted, or did someone else?

She reached room 313. No decorations and no nameplate. Talk about anti-climactic, except the door was ajar.

The soundtrack in her head switched to a game show count-down. Bria would have preferred silence.

"You can do this." Dalton's gaze held only strength and love.

She needed every ounce he had to share.

With a nod, Bria tapped lightly on the door. "Hello?"

No one answered.

She knocked again. That pushed open the door more.

"Go in," Dalton encouraged.

Bria took a tentative step inside, as if she were entering an alternative universe or a black hole.

The room was bland except for a pretty bouquet of mixed flowers in a glass vase on the nightstand. A chair sat near the wall on the far side of a hospital bed.

Someone was asleep in the bed and covered with a quilt.

Wait. Bria recognized the quilt.

A shiver ran along her spine, coiling at her tailbone, like a Western Rattlesnake ready to hiss and bite.

She peered closer, trying to remember where she'd seen the pattern and fabrics before. Her mind went blank, but she recognized it. The question was why.

Bria took a step and then another.

A woman—at least Bria assumed the person was a woman—with brown and gray hair faced away from her.

Seeing anything was difficult from this distance, so Bria moved to the side of the bed. It was impossible to tell whether the woman was actually asleep. Waking her wouldn't be polite, but curiosity got the best of Bria. "Hello?"

The woman turned toward Bria.

Bria gasped. Her face. It was like staring in a mirror. Well, if Bria added twenty-five years to her own age.

The woman's gaze narrowed before she grinned. "Hi."

She trembled. "I'm Bria."

"Pretty name." The woman sounded almost childlike. "Mol."

A lump scorched Bria's throat. She struggled to breathe, afraid she might throw up. "Molly?"

The woman nodded.

No. This wasn't happening.

Molly.

Bria hadn't heard the name in years, but she knew it, even if she hadn't met this woman or remembered her.

"Your name is Molly?" Bria asked again, unsure what she wanted the answer to be.

Another nod.

Her blood turned to ice. She dug her fingernails into her palms. *Why, Dad? Why?*

But suddenly, everything made sense.

From not wanting to give himself an alibi to asking Bria not to hate him.

Questions rammed into her, one after another until she wanted to scream.

Who else knew? Did Aunt Elise?

Tears stung Bria's eyes. Hot tears. Bitter tears. Sad tears. Regretful tears.

This wasn't her fault.

Selena, Juliet, Nell, and Missy would tell Bria that.

Dalton came up behind her and placed his hands on her shoulders.

A million thoughts ran through Bria's brain, but she couldn't string any words together.

The woman's gaze sharpened on Dalton. Her lips parted. "Paul?"

"Dalton," he said.

Molly shook her head. "My love. Paul."

Air rushed from Bria's lungs.

"Do you know who this is?" Dalton whispered.

"Yes." Bria wiped her eyes. Needing his strength, she leaned back against him. "Molly is my mother."

Dalton gasped. "She's…"

Molly's face scrunched. "Don't touch me."

"We won't." The words flew out. More instinct than anything because Bria's insides reeled.

Why didn't Dad tell me?

She'd grown up without a mom. Sure, Aunt Elise had been the perfect surrogate mother, but a part of Bria had blamed herself for Molly leaving.

Why else would a mother leave her child and never come back?

Molly grew more agitated, fisting the blanket. Her face reddened, and the lines on her forehead deepened.

Eyes dark, she stared at Bria. "Want a gift."

It wasn't a question, more like a demand.

The woman was in her fifties, but she sounded like a young child. Bria had spent little time around kids other than Briley Hanford, a walking burst of sunshine with a wide smile and open arms for giving hugs.

Honesty was the best policy. At least for this Lanford. Bria held out her empty hands. "I have nothing for you."

"Get out." Molly thrashed in the bed.

Bria glanced at Dalton, whose expression was weary. "We're going."

Molly's mouth tightened. "You go. Paul, stay."

The woman mistook Dalton for his late father.

So not good.

"I'll be back." Dalton's calm tone always soothed Bria. "We both will."

Molly screamed, the piercing sound bouncing off the empty walls. She kept screeching.

Bria stood frozen.

Dalton placed his hands on Bria's shoulders and backed her away from the bed.

A nurse, whose nametag read *Lisa*, sauntered past them, not rushing like this was an emergency. "Don't worry about Molly. She gets upset when her routine is broken."

Bria had no idea what to say to that, so she nodded. A ridiculous response once she had done it.

Facing away from Molly made the most sense, but Bria's practicality—her strength—was nowhere to be found, so she continued to let Dalton lead her out of the room backward.

Molly's screaming intensified as if every horror movie killer towered over her.

The nurse tsked. "Another tantrum, Molly? We talked about this."

Before Molly replied, Bria was in the hallway on the left of the doorway. She sagged against the wall and exhaled, the slowest exhale in the past week.

Dalton ran the edge of his finger along her jawline. He kissed her forehead.

She closed her eyes. "My questions keep growing. So does my confusion."

"Mine, too. But you... we'll get through this."

She nearly laughed. "Are you sure about that? Because everything I thought about my mother—my family—appears to be a lie. I have no idea who knew the truth and who didn't. Or what's even happening with..."

She pointed to the door. Molly Landon had given birth to Bria, but she was a stranger. A woman who must've suffered some sort of injury or had a mental illness.

No matter what had happened to Molly, her father had kept it a secret from Bria. Why had he done that? And what about Aunt Elise?

If she'd known about this...

Bria closed her eyes, picturing her aunt's smiling face. Her world might implode if Aunt Elise had lied to Bria, too.

chapter two

AS JULIET PACED the length of the living room, Butterscotch purred on the couch, comfy and cozy as usual. The only difference was that the cat curled on a cushion, not along the top. That was because of Lulu…

The air rushed from Juliet's lungs, and her heart squeezed tight. The back of her eyelids burned.

Do. Not. Cry.

She'd cried enough.

Lulu would be okay. She had to be.

The vet said wanting to observe the dog overnight was a precaution, nothing more, and in Lulu's best interest. The Berry Lake Animal Clinic was the best place for her. Still, Juliet craned her neck as if she could hear the tiny paws across town.

"She'll be fine."

The words didn't loosen the knot of unease in her gut. Still, one of Selena T's most recent podcasts had discussed the problem with worrying and why it was a useless pursuit. Thoughts were better aimed elsewhere.

True.

And at this moment, Juliet wished part of her was a cat.

Because Butterscotch didn't appear to notice Lulu was gone.

The cat hadn't looked up when Juliet spoke. Maybe males of all species had selective hearing. Or perhaps he was used to ignoring people.

Butterscotch had belonged to Elise Landon and then lived with Charlene Culpepper, who returned the cat when Juliet moved into Elise's—well, now Bria's—house. He wasn't the biggest fan of their canine roommate, especially since Juliet had used his cat bed to transport Lulu to the animal clinic, but then again, it might just be his personality. If Butterscotch got fed and a few rubs each day, he acted chill.

Maybe the cat could teach Juliet how to be chill.

That was the vibe she wanted—needed.

Stop worrying!

Dr. Goya had sounded hopeful about Lulu's prognosis. Dr. Roman Byrne, her next-door neighbor, also a veterinarian and her *new* friend—that latter part would take some getting used to—had sounded positive about Lulu's condition when they'd spoken. Both vets had assured Juliet someone would be at the vet clinic overnight, so Lulu wouldn't be alone. But this would be the first night since the dog had come to live at the house that Juliet would be without her.

Goose bumps covered her skin.

This isn't about me.

Juliet rubbed her arms. "It'll be okay."

It had to be.

She hadn't called Mrs. Vernon, Lulu's former owner, yet. The woman had a heart issue and moved out of her home in Berry Lake to an assisted-living center an hour west in Vancouver. Until Juliet learned more about Lulu's condition, she wouldn't say a word to Mrs. Vernon or anyone.

Including the Posse.

Only the clinic's staff, Sabine Culpepper, and Selena Tremblay, who was paying for the dog's treatment, knew about Lulu's health issue. Juliet didn't want Bria to know, not until she got home from her date with Dalton.

It must be going well.

Juliet had expected her roommate to be home earlier from her brunch date and visit to her father, but it was well into the evening.

A grin spread across her face. She rubbed Butterscotch. "Not all of us are lucky in love, but I'm glad Bria's fortune has changed."

Maybe after Juliet's divorce was finalized and she had some time on her own, she would want to date again. But that wasn't now or any time soon. If she'd doubted that was true, her experience with Roman had shown her she wasn't ready for a relationship.

Butterscotch stretched, taking up another cushion on the couch.

Juliet laughed. Something she hadn't expected to do tonight. "You just want belly rubs."

The cat exposed his stomach.

"Okay, okay. I can take a hint."

As she rubbed his belly, he pawed at the air.

"Silly kitty."

But Juliet was so relieved he was here. Pets provided so much entertainment. Butterscotch was funny without trying to be.

"Enjoy being a couch hog while you can, big guy. Lulu will be home tomorrow."

Her cell phone buzzed. Bria's name lit up the screen. Juliet picked up the phone and read the message sent to the Cupcake Posse's Group Chat.

> **BRIA:** *I'm in Wishing Bay on an errand for my dad.*
> **BRIA:** *Staying the night.*

The date must have been going better than Juliet imagined, given Wishing Bay was hours away on the Washington coast. She was curious how Bria had ended up there on an errand. What would her father need while in jail?

But if there was a problem, Bria would have told them.

That meant this trip to Wishing Bay must be a good thing. Given enough time, Juliet could make a happy ending out of most scenarios. She didn't want to ever give up on having a happily ever after of her own.

In this case, Bria and Dalton seemed to go well together, and Bria needed something in her life to work out after all she'd been through these past two months.

Juliet typed.

> **JULIET:** *What about your interview at Brew and Steep?*

Three dots formed.
Bria must be replying.

> **BRIA:** *Moved it to Tuesday morning.*

NELL: *Have fun.*

Leave it to Nell to focus on the most important thing—having fun—because Bria deserved to have fun. Elise's death, inheriting the cupcake shop with her dad, reuniting with the guy who'd broken her heart in high school, the fire, and losing her job in San Diego. The list of what had happened during the last few weeks was relentless. The only bright spot in Bria's life had been Dalton reappearing and the Posse reuniting.

But even with those good things, the others had sent Bria Landon's carefully planned life into a tailspin. All the changes since September would have been difficult for anyone to adapt to, and Juliet wasn't sure how Bria coped. Sure, the CPA's middle name might as well be *practical*, but each day Bria impressed Juliet. And not only because she was a friend.

Juliet's cell phone buzzed. A second buzz followed right after. The other members of the Cupcake Posse must have jumped on the group chat.

> **MISSY:** *Call if you need anything.*
> **SELENA:** *If you want me to drive over tomorrow morning, Seattle's only a couple of hours away.*

Leave it to Missy Hanford to offer help, but nothing she did surprised Juliet. The baker had a heart of gold, especially with her friends. And, of course, Selena would drive to the coast if Bria needed her there. Her Selena T public persona might even rent a helicopter. Selena Tremblay wasn't a quieter version of that life coach who was larger than life, but she seemed to be more down to earth, a loving wife to her hockey-playing husband, and a loyal friend to Juliet and the Posse. One who hadn't minded Juliet's texts earlier when she'd needed help to pay Lulu's vet bill.

The Posse had been there for Juliet when her marriage disintegrated in September. The four other women were still there for her a month later. All five of them would be there for each other. Juliet hadn't been confident of that before. She was now.

Zero doubt.

Friends forever.

That was what Elise would have wanted for them.

And if they'd stayed in touch as Elise had recommended, their lives might have been completely different.

Never look back with regret. Unless you meant to eat more than one cupcake. That's easy to remedy.

Their former boss's cupcake wisdom had brought both eye rolls and inspiration during the summer they worked for Elise at the Berry Lake Cupcake Shop. What all of them would give to have five more minutes with their late friend now.

Juliet stared at the cell phone.

She should tell her friends about Lulu. They weren't supposed to keep secrets from each other.

Juliet's thumbs hovered over the phone.

Another notification sounded.

She startled, nearly dropping the phone. But she took that as a sign to wait. If only a few more minutes.

> **BRIA:** *Thanks. Dalton's here, so I'm not alone.*
> **BRIA:** *I'll be in touch tomorrow. Take care. xoxox.*

Good advice. Juliet would wait until tomorrow to tell them about Lulu.

She placed the phone on the table. Selena knew since she was paying the vet bill, but no one else needed to know. Especially Bria. She would worry about the dog, which would ruin her impromptu trip to the coast. Yes, Selena T was right about worrying being a waste of time and energy.

Juliet wouldn't say a word. She hoped the trip brought Bria and Dalton closer.

A knock sounded at the door.

The clock on the fireplace mantel showed seven o'clock.

Not that late, but most things in their small town closed at five on Sunday nights.

No worries.

Berry Lake was a safe place to live, but years of living in the L.A. area had trained Juliet to be cautious. Danger could come from anywhere, unfortunately.

She peered out the front door's peephole and did a double take.

Roman stood on the front porch.

What's he doing here?

She'd seen him only a few hours ago at the clinic.

Still, the neighborly thing to do was talk to him. Maybe he was starting their *new* friendship off with a visit tonight.

She unlocked and opened the door.

Roman wasn't the only one on the welcome mat.

Katie, his twelve-year-old niece, stood in front of him. She wore a hoodie over her leggings and held out a medium-sized pumpkin. "I went to the pumpkin patch with Chloe and Alexis. I got a pumpkin for us to carve, and this is for you and Bria, since I didn't see one on your porch."

Juliet took the pumpkin. "Thank you. It's a lovely pumpkin. Almost too pretty to carve."

Katie bit her lip. "I-I've missed you."

Juliet's heart bumped.

Roman inhaled sharply.

She focused on Katie, shifted the pumpkin to rest on a hip, and one-arm hugged the girl. "Oh, sweetie. I've missed you, too."

Relief filled Katie's expression. "Uncle Roman said we're all still friends."

"We are friends." Not true between Roman and Juliet until he'd brought it up to her at the clinic earlier. She and Katie... "I've always been your friend."

Roman touched Katie's shoulder. "One pumpkin delivered. You need to go back inside the house so I can get to the clinic."

Adrenaline shot to Juliet's toes. Her stomach rose to her throat. She clutched the doorknob. "Lulu—"

"Lulu is fine." Roman's words rushed out. "The vet on shift tonight had a family emergency, so I need to cover until the third shift person arrives."

"Oh, sorry. I'm..."

"Worried." He gave her an encouraging smile. "That's what dog moms do."

"You're the best dog mom ever." Katie stared up at Juliet. "Lulu's so lucky to have you."

Juliet's heart overflowed with joy. "I feel the same way about Lulu being in my life. And you. So lucky."

Katie beamed. "If you need help carving the pumpkin..."

"We could do it now." Juliet didn't like the house being so quiet with Lulu and Bria away. "If your uncle doesn't mind."

Roman's gaze bounced from Juliet to Katie. "Homework finished?"

Katie nodded. "Please, Uncle Roman."

"I can walk her back after we finish." Juliet hoped she didn't sound desperate for the company.

Katie rolled her eyes, a move she appeared to have practiced since her recent birthday party that Juliet hosted. "I'm twelve now. Old enough to walk next door by myself."

Roman appeared to be holding back laughter. "You can stay. But Juliet needs to make sure you get home safely."

Katie blew out a breath. "Fine. You can go. We'll be fine here."

He held up his hand. "I know when I'm not wanted."

Juliet motioned Katie inside.

Roman remained on the step. "I'll check on Lulu for you. If you don't hear from me, she's resting and doing well."

"Thanks." Juliet didn't know what else to say to the man she'd spent the past few weeks falling for until it all came to a screeching halt the night her soon-to-be ex-husband's mistress had rear-ended her.

She nearly laughed. That sounded like lyrics from a country music song. "Good night."

She closed the door without waiting for a reply.

A new her.

Independent and strong.

#goals

With her friends' support, Juliet would get there.

Katie made a beeline for Butterscotch and rubbed the orange cat. "Does he do anything but sleep?"

"Besides eating and drinking?"

Katie laughed. "He should come over to my house and play."

"One of these days."

Juliet had a feeling the cat was still processing his person dying. She'd searched the internet and discovered that animals grieved. Elise had spoiled Butterscotch. She had called him her baby. Maybe he needed time to get used to Elise being gone and Juliet and Bria living in the house with him now.

"Ready to carve the pumpkin?" Juliet asked.

"Yes!" Katie ran to the dining room table. "Mom and Dad always put down newspaper."

"Hmmm." Juliet thought for a minute. She headed to a kitchen drawer and removed a box of wax paper. "We don't have any newspaper. But this should work and make cleanup a snap."

Katie took the wax paper and spread long strips of it on the table. "We also need a marker, a knife, and a bowl."

The last item brought memories of growing up at the Huckleberry Inn and filling a metal bowl with pumpkin seeds and pulp. She felt a pang. No regret because she'd done nothing wrong. But being disowned by her grandmother still hurt.

Who wanted their granddaughter to stay married to a man who treated her more like a maid and had an affair with a much younger woman, a woman who claimed to be pregnant when she wasn't?

But Penelope Jones was more concerned about appearances than loving Juliet.

As Selena and her friends had said, it was Grandma's loss.

Not Juliet's.

If Grandma rewrote her will and left everything to Ezra, so be it. The only thing Juliet had ever wanted from Grandma was love. Ezra didn't care about the Jones's legacy in Berry Lake. He would sell the inn once it was his and not look back. But whether or not Grandma realized that wasn't Juliet's concern.

Tonight should be about having fun, nothing else. She gathered the supplies and placed them on the table. "I don't suppose you like roasted pumpkin seeds."

"I do!" Katie's shoulders sagged. "But Uncle Roman doesn't know how to make them."

"Then you're in luck because I do."

Katie jumped up and down. "Yes! I knew it. I asked Fleur's mom if she knew how to, but she scrunched her face and said no."

Fleur's mom.

Heather Kirkpatrick.

The woman had treated Juliet and most of the other girls in their high school class horribly. Heather had returned to Berry Lake after her divorce. Like other single women in town, she had been blatant with her interest in Roman.

Juliet had cleared out of the way for whoever came next. Still, she hadn't thought Roman would move on so quickly. They'd just ended things on Wednesday...

None of my business.

She handed the marker to Katie. "You and I will roast them. You can bring over the seeds from your pumpkin, too."

"Thank you." Katie studied the pumpkin. "Do you want a scary face or a smiley one?"

"Whatever you decide." Juliet made a mental note to buy candy for trick-or-treaters. The upcoming holiday had slipped her mind. "Bria and I are just happy to have a pumpkin."

Otherwise, they would have forgotten to buy one themselves.

Katie spun the pumpkin around, examining it from all angles. "I'll draw. You carve."

"Sounds like a plan."

A few minutes later, Katie had finished her design with triangular eyes and a smirk for a smile. She placed the pen on the table. "What do you think?"

"Looks like a perfect jack-o'-lantern."

"My dad always cut the top first." Katie's gaze remained on the top. "He said that made cutting the other parts easier."

Juliet picked up the knife and cut the top.

Halloween would be yet another first for Katie without her mom and dad. Been there, done that at age ten, and no words would make the grief easier. Twenty-five years had passed since her parents had died, but Juliet still missed them. After the mess with Grandma and the divorce, she was truly alone for the first time in her life.

Juliet's eyelids heated.

"It does make it easier." She lowered the knife and blinked. "You can clean out the pulp and seeds before cutting the other parts."

"Mom said it's less messy."

"Yes, but less is relative. Pumpkin carving can be messy if you want it to be."

"I do."

"As long as you help me clean up."

"Of course."

Juliet finished cutting out the top and lifted it from the pumpkin. "Time to get messy."

"Yay!" Katie dug in. A handful of pulp went into the bowl. "Are there any boarding schools nearby?"

"Not that I know of. Why?"

Katie focused on the pumpkin.

Juliet didn't want to force a conversation, but the question had been odd. "Are you not happy in Berry Lake?"

"What? No! I love it here."

She should probably drop it, but she couldn't. "So boarding school…?"

"Fleur said after her mom married my uncle, they'd send me off to boarding school."

The words floated in the air before slamming into Juliet like a freight train. She struggled with what to say. Struggled and failed.

Katie pulled out more pulp. "I guess boarding school would be better than being forced to live under a staircase or in the attic."

"Your uncle loves you. He would never allow any of those situations to happen, including boarding school."

"Mr. DeMarco fired his daughter from her job at the art gallery. Gave her apartment to his stepdaughter."

All true, but… "Your uncle isn't anything like Sal DeMarco."
Thank goodness.

"But if something happens to Uncle Roman, I'll be left with an evil stepmother or step-aunt."

Katie's shoulders slumped. Her arms went to her sides, getting pumpkin all over. It didn't matter. The way her eyes gleamed tore at Juliet's heart.

Katie sniffled. "I don't like Mrs. Kirkpatrick. I'd be worse off than Cinderella. She wouldn't let me sleep by the hearth. I'd be in that big doghouse in the backyard. And Fleur is so mean to me. She made fun of me when we were supposed to be playing before dinner. And it's worse at school."

"Have you mentioned it to your uncle?"

"No, I was hoping he and…"

You was implied but not spoken.

"I'm sorry if we gave you the wrong impression." Juliet wiped her hands and touched Katie's shoulder. "You two haven't been in town long. I doubt marriage is even on your uncle's radar."

"He thinks I need another mom. Which means he needs a wife."

"Oh." Well, that would explain why things had moved so quickly between them. Still, Juliet felt out of her lane discussing this with Katie.

"I don't want another mom. Not yet. Maybe never."

Juliet had lost both her parents, so a new mom hadn't been an option. She'd been grateful to have Grandma. And now... Juliet shook it off. This was about Katie. "Talk to your uncle. He might not know how you feel. I'm sure he's only trying to do what he thinks is best for you."

Katie's lower lip thrust out. "Boarding school isn't it."

"No, it isn't." Heather and Fleur weren't best for Katie, either. However, that might be Juliet's emotions talking. "But he won't know what you're thinking or vice versa unless you tell him."

"I will. Thank you." Katie looked at her hands and clothes covered in pumpkin. Her mouth gaped. "Oops. I made a mess."

Juliet grabbed a handful of pulp out of the pumpkin. "I'll show you a mess."

She threw the pulp at Katie's arm.

Katie laughed. "Pumpkin fight!"

The pulp and seeds flew. This was more than a mess. It was a total disaster, but Katie's smile and laughter would be worth every minute of cleanup.

Though, it was probably a good thing Bria wouldn't be home tonight.

☕ chapter three ☕

SUNDAY NIGHT WAS Missy Hanford's least favorite
time. While friends prepared for the week ahead and hung
out with their families, she sat at home by herself on the
couch, feeling more lonely than usual.

Her life could be worse, which was why she shouldn't complain, but sometimes, she forgot.

Missy held her cell phone. A cozy fleece blanket covered
her lap. October meant colder temperatures, but she was nice
and warm.

See, things aren't that bad.

Okay, the quiet rattled her, more so than usual. Her cats' paws
against the hardwood floor and an occasional ice cube dropping
in the freezer were the only sounds in her sister-in-law's guest
cottage where Missy lived.

Not untypical.

She shifted positions to get more comfortable. But something
was different tonight.

Missy had whittled her fingernails to nothing in the last ten minutes, and the gnawing in her gut wasn't typical.

That meant one thing…

Eating a cupcake, or three, would come next.

Vanilla with white buttercream frosting. She'd made them earlier for herself.

Not a bad way to go.

She half laughed.

You bake cupcakes for a living. Vanilla shouldn't be your favorite flavor.

Her late boss, Elise Landon, used to lecture Missy about loving "vanilla" each time she ate one at the cupcake shop.

The spot over Missy's heart hurt. The ache of grief, as familiar to her as her shadow for the past nine years, sharpened.

Missy rubbed it. *Seriously, though…*

A thirty-two-year-old could have far worse vices than nail-biting and sugar-binging. And she would be doing both things for a reason.

Her knee bounced, a result of spiraling anxiety.

Again, not untypical.

Missy placed her hand on top of her thigh to keep her leg still. The only positive? For once, she wasn't worried about herself.

She reread the messages sent to the Cupcake Posse's chat group eleven—make that twelve—minutes ago.

> **BRIA:** *I'm in Wishing Bay on an errand for my dad.*
> **BRIA:** *Staying the night.*
> **JULIET:** *What about your interview at Brew and Steep?*
> **BRIA:** *Moved it to Tuesday morning.*

NELL: *Have fun.*
MISSY: *Call if you need anything.*
SELENA: *If you want me to drive over tomorrow morning, Seattle's only a couple hours away.*
BRIA: *Thanks. Dalton's here, so I'm not alone.*
BRIA: *I'll be in touch tomorrow. Take care. xoxox.*

Bria's words weren't ominous. Far from it. An overnight stay in a quaint beach town on the Washington coast could mean nothing other than a break from the usual.

Yet something about the sudden trip niggled at Missy, given Bria's dad was in jail for arson and nearly killing Missy.

What kind of errand did Brian Landon want done?

She didn't want Bria getting herself in trouble trying to help him. And the more Missy thought about it, the more the bone-biting distress deep within her intensified.

She rubbed her fingers along the edge of the fleece blanket. The action did nothing to decrease her unease. Sighing would be another useless gesture.

Ugh. Her sky-is-falling attitude sucked.

She tried hard not to be the millennial version of Chicken Little, but her glass hadn't been half-full since Rob's death.

A widow at age twenty-three.

The thought bristled like it had since she'd first said the words to herself nine years ago. No matter how much she tried to be the bubbly optimist she'd once been, she couldn't shake the one-knock-on-the-door-can-change-your-life mentality.

Because one knock *had* changed her life. Ruined her life. Made her want to press fast forward and skip to the end of her life.

Bria's not you.

Her life is different.

So were Bria's priorities.

Bria had focused on her grades and getting into a good college as a teenager. Now, a super-smart CPA, she'd returned to their hometown after ten years in San Diego and was opening her own accounting firm. She was also the definition of nice.

Okay, most people called Missy nice, too, but she hadn't a clue about the math stuff Bria used daily. Trigonometry might as well be a four-letter word. Converting a recipe was the only math Missy wanted to do—or could do if she were being honest—besides reconciling the cash register after closing.

Bria would freak out if she discovered Missy's checking account hadn't been balanced in years.

Face it. Bria oozed practicality and common sense, which meant...

Missy didn't need to worry about her friend. She let go of the blanket and blew out a breath, letting her exhale carry away her concern.

Bria was fine.

A well-deserved vacation, especially an impromptu one for a person who rarely acted spontaneously. A chance to watch the sunset or see the sunrise was reason enough to go to the coast. An errand for her dad that might take more than one day was another.

Yep, Missy had been thinking the worst for no reason.

As usual.

Add that to her list of flaws.

Not that she had to hide her true self from anyone. She lived alone and would for the rest of her life.

Mario meowed.

Oops. Not completely alone.

The cat couldn't read her mind, but she didn't want to hurt her fur baby's feelings. Make that fur babies' feelings.

"Sorry. I'm not alone. I have the two of you."

Peach and Mario were Missy's life, but they cared only about her opposable thumbs and her ability to feed them at this time of night. The cats paced across the living room with an attitude and matching steps.

Silly, adorable cats.

"Slow down. It's not dinnertime yet. You'll wear yourselves out."

Both cats stopped, sat, and glared at her—their way of alerting her to their imminent starvation.

On the living room wall, a clock featuring twelve different breeds of felines meowed. The cats scurried to the doorway of the kitchen. They recognized their dinner bell.

She stood and didn't grimace.

Progress.

Oh, her foot twinged, a dull throb reminding her of the burn she tried to ignore.

The cats stared at her with narrowed gazes.

Missy laughed. "Your bowls will be ready in a minute, your highnesses."

She walked into the kitchen. Her limp wasn't as noticeable, but a sharp pain shot through her burned foot and up her leg with each step.

Missy gritted her teeth.

At least her foot didn't hurt as much as yesterday.

Dr. Whiting was correct about her recovery.

Good, because she needed two healthy legs—er, feet—to rebuild the cupcake shop.

Wait.

Not "the" shop but "her" shop.

A firework-grand-finale thrill shot from Missy's head to the tips of her ten orange-painted toenails. After working at the Berry Lake Cupcake Shop since she was fifteen, she would soon own the place.

Okay, not only her.

Tingles danced across her skin.

That was the best part.

Once Elise's probate closed and Brian sold them his share, Missy, Bria, Juliet, Nell, and Selena would co-own the cupcake shop. The bakery would finally flourish the way Elise wanted it to.

Missy shimmied her shoulders and glanced at Peach. "Mama's a small business owner."

That change in her title might explain why she worried about Bria. Missy wanted everything to go perfectly for her and her four best friends. Soon, they'd be partners in the bakery where they'd worked together for one summer fifteen years ago.

She glanced up, imagining Heaven with fluffy white clouds and angels in white with golden halos and wings. "I hope this makes you happy, Elise."

Face it. Owning the bakery was Missy's dream. Sure, it meant living in Jenny's guest house for another year or two. Perhaps longer. Her sister-in-law didn't mind, which enabled Missy to use her house down payment savings to buy her share of the cupcake shop. Talk about a no-brainer decision.

All Missy needed was patience.

For her foot to heal.

For Elise's probate to close.

For the Posse to implement plans for the new cupcake shop.

For happiness to become Missy's new normal.

Missy filled the cats' food bowls and placed them on the floor. "Eat up."

She yawned, stretching her arms over her head. The day had worn her out, but in a good way, until Bria's text arrived.

Still, Missy wouldn't mind more days when her smile came naturally, and the sky in her world remained sunny even when clouds moved in. "Time for bed."

Both Peach and Mario stopped eating to glance her way.

Missy's heart swelled. The cats were the touchstones in her life—the closest thing to babies she would ever have. They'd kept her going when she might have given up otherwise. "Don't rush on my account. Enjoy your dinner. You know where to find me when you finish eating."

A noise from the living room sent the cats jumping.

She stood in the kitchen doorway and glanced into the living room. No other noises sounded.

Okay, no reason to be afraid.

She went in there.

Nothing appeared out of place, except…

One of Rob's medals had fallen to the floor. That usually happened when Mario had been doing his parkour routine. But the cats had gone into the kitchen before her.

Weird. Missy picked up the medal. "I need to get a shadow box for these."

Except she enjoyed touching them whenever she wanted.

As she returned the medal to the mantel, Rob's photo caught her attention. Okay, photos.

The mantel wasn't a shrine to her late husband, no matter what Jenny called the collection, but the pictures and items comforted Missy like a soft, worn quilt. They kept Rob with her.

She picked up one of the framed photos and stared at him. Dashing and handsome in his full Marine uniform.

His eyes reminded her of Jenny's and Briley's. Rob lived on in his older sister and the niece he never knew. He would have been the best uncle and an even better dad, given how he'd doted on the cats.

Cold glass covered Rob's face.

Missy traced her fingertip over it, along the side of his face. "Come back to me. One more time."

Liar.

One more time would never be enough. She wanted him to come back and stay. Or to take her with him this time.

A familiar heaviness bore down on her chest. Something she hadn't been able to shake except during her dream in the hospital. It had to be a dream, right?

The only thing she was sure about was the longing in her heart. "I miss you."

She returned the photo to its place, next to the Purple Heart. She ran a fingernail over the ribbon. One ridge, two, three…

Missy stopped at nine. Nine ridges for the nine years he'd been gone.

Might as well be ninety.

Her heart wept, but no tears fell. She waited for the darkness to come, but…

Nothing.

She blew out her breath and lowered her hand. "I'm not alone."

Peach and Mario were all Missy needed—all she dared to need.

Once upon a time, when she was a teenager, she'd been the one with a boyfriend. Now, she was alone, and everyone else was part of a couple.

Jenny and Dare.

Hope and Josh.

Selena and Logan.

Sheridan and Michael.

Bria and Dalton.

Nell and Gage.

Juliet and… Well, not Roman. But Missy had a feeling it would happen, eventually.

Missy's sister-in-law and her friends deserved to find love. Nothing was greater in life than love.

You have a whole life to live. All those things we dreamed about together. They're yours for the taking. But you have to believe they can be yours.

Rob's words from her dream echoed in her head.

"I want that life, but I want it with you."

Holding her breath, she waited for something to happen, but unlike when she'd been unconscious in the hospital, nothing did. It was her and the cats. The same as every night since Rob left on that fateful deployment. "Maybe tomorrow."

Mario meowed.

He must have devoured his food. "I know. It's time for bed."

Her phone rang.

Sabine Culpepper's name lit up the screen. That was odd for her to call at this hour unless something was up at her animal rescue.

Missy pressed the green button. "Hello?"

"It's Sabine." The words rushed out. "I hope I didn't wake you."

"You didn't." Missy's nerve endings twitched. "Is everything okay?"

"Max and I are in Portland. Sheridan and Michael's flight was delayed, so we ate dinner with them. I just got off a call about someone dumping a box in the market's garbage bins. A cat jumped out, but there might be more in there. I'm an hour and a half away and—"

"I'll go."

"No, your foot." Sabine's words came too quickly. "But do you mind calling around to see who can check it out? I forgot my charging cord, and my battery's dying."

"Almost healed." Missy used to go on these calls all the time for Sabine. "I'll head over there now."

"Are you sure?" Concern dripped from each word.

"Positive." Missy held her breath.

"Let me know what you find. I'll conserve my phone's battery. Max has a little juice left if we can't handle what we find ourselves and need to call the emergency clinic."

She exhaled. "Will do."

Missy didn't change her clothes. She slid on one boot. Her injured foot could only handle a slipper. She would drive there, find the empty box, return home, and go straight to bed.

Peach sat next to Mario. Both stared at her.

"I'm sorry to disturb your evening," Sabine said.

Missy glanced at Rob's photo. "You didn't. Happy to help. I'll let you know what I find."

She disconnected the call before grabbing her purse and keys. "Sorry, babies. Mommy must see if any animals need help. If we have company tonight, be nice and get along. They won't be here forever."

She patted each cat's head, left the cottage, and got into her car. The drive wouldn't take long.

On the way to the store, Missy tapped her thumbs against the steering wheel. Clouds hid the moon and stars, but the night might as well be clear and bright. She couldn't wait to make herself useful again.

Missy pulled into the Berry Lake Market's parking lot and drove around the building to where the trucks unloaded in the back. A single light above a set of double doors illuminated the area.

She gripped the steering wheel. Tension sharpened between her shoulders. "Only a little creepy."

At least the soundtrack from *Psycho* or *Jaws* wasn't playing. And Brian Landon was in jail. If he were the arsonist, he couldn't set fire to anything...or her.

Missy parked and got out of the car. She sniffed the crisp autumn air. "Smells like rain. Better hurry."

She'd left the headlights on. That provided enough light so she didn't turn on her phone's flashlight. "Any kitties here?"

People who got in over their heads with animals or didn't want more pets figured dumping them was an easy way to get rid of them. Not easy, but extremely cruel. Unfortunately, she'd seen it happen too many times.

"Meow." A tabby—based on the size, less than a year old—who appeared to be lactating stood near a container.

Missy came closer. "Are your babies in there?"

The cat placed her paws on the blue industrial-sized container as tall as Missy.

"Let me find a way to look inside."

Missy shined her phone's light around the area. Something white flashed. Torn box flaps. Nothing she could use. But...wait.

Missy peered closer.

A stack of plastic milk crates. Those might work. She carried one to the bin.

Mewls, not meows, sounded. Young ones.

Not good.

Missy needed to hurry. "I'm coming, kittens."

She climbed onto the milk crate, ignoring the jagged slice of pain the weight put on her foot.

Suck it up.

Rob would tell her that.

Missy ignored the pain.

The flashlight illuminated the inside of the container. A stack of compressed cardboard formed cubes, but tons of spaces were in between and around those.

Where were the kittens?

She kept searching. "Hey, little ones. I can't hear you."

Missy hoped they'd fallen asleep and not...

The beam of light caught something.

Wait. Holding her breath, she retraced the light's path.

A box, haphazardly on its side, contained four, maybe five, kittens. "There you are."

She took a closer look. Young. Maybe only hours old.

She hit the call button. "Pick up. Pick up."

"Missy?" Sabine asked.

"Some jerk dumped newborns. I'm pretty sure the mama cat is here waiting for her babies. I'll get them, but we should have them examined."

"I'll give the clinic a heads-up you're bringing them in."

"Thanks." Missy tried to figure out the best way to get in and out of the container.

"Watch your foot." Sabine used her mom tone.

"I'll be careful."

"Call me from the clinic."

Overprotective much? Missy held back a laugh. Sabine Culpepper was one of a kind, a mama bear who cared for animals and humans alike. Missy appreciated having the woman in her life. "Will do."

"I can hear you want to get them out. I'll leave you to it. Bye."

The line disconnected.

Missy placed her phone in her sweatshirt's pocket. On the side away from the kittens, she stacked a second milk crate on the first one before grabbing a third one to use as a step.

"Coming, kitties." Not that the newborns could hear or see. She climbed up, ignoring the pain. Her waist hit the top of the recycle bin, and she bent over.

Thud.

She glanced at her cell phone lying on the asphalt.

The throbbing inching up her leg told her not to climb down. She clutched the edge, swung her burnt foot over the side, and straddled the bin's edge. "Here goes nothing."

Missy brought her other leg around and lowered herself onto a bale of cardboard.

Her foot, however, found only air between the boxes inside. She fell.

Fast.

Thud.

She hit another bale and a few boxes, her arms and face scraping against them, before landing on her side.

In the dark.

Her phone rang.

Sabine? Jenny? Nell?

It could be anyone.

Except her phone lay on the ground out of her reach.

Please be Sabine. She'll know something is wrong if I don't answer.

Missy blew out a breath. The ringing stopped.

No big deal.

So what if her face burned as if scratched? Or her foot hurt? Or her bottom ached?

No reason to think the worst or panic.

It's just dark.

Night dark. Not smoky dark.

Her eyes would adjust, and she had plenty of air to breathe.

Find the kitties and get them out of here. That was all she had to do. It shouldn't be that hard.

"Get moving, Hanford."

Carefully, slowly, she made her way toward the other side of the recycle bin.

This was better than crawling through garbage. Except for— she scrunched her nose—the smell.

"Don't think about that."

The tabby cried from below.

"Hang on, Mama. I'm getting closer."

Her phone rang again, but she could do nothing about it.

Missy reached forward, searching for a box with kittens inside. She used a light touch to keep from pushing anything over. She didn't want the wee ones to fall out.

"Ugh! I need a flashlight." She inhaled and then exhaled, trying to calm her spiraling pulse rate. "Don't panic. I can do this."

She crawled over the uneven terrain. Her knees took the brunt to keep her foot protected. Her slipper would be toast after this.

The mewling became louder.

"Getting closer."

She reached out again, and her fingertips brushed a box's flap. *Yes.* The tension in her shoulders eased.

She ran her hand along it until she found the interior. Her fingers brushed something soft—a kitten. "I've got you."

Missy leveled the box to keep all of them inside, but she couldn't see if any others had fallen out.

"At least I have you." The kittens couldn't hear her, but she needed to talk to them. "I'll check for any brothers and sisters when I get my phone."

She clutched the box and stood, unable to see out of the bin. Her heart dropped.

"So maybe I didn't think this all the way through."

Missy didn't want to let go of the box, but moving the bales of boxes was impossible without two hands.

"There has to be a way."

Water splashed on her face.

Oh, no. She glanced at the night sky, only to be hit with large raindrops.

Missy's heart lodged in her throat. She fumbled, trying to close the flaps on the box so the kitties wouldn't get wet, but she had to make sure they had air, too.

The rain pelted, running down her face like tears. She wanted to cry, but she had to help the kittens.

"Guess there's only one thing for me to do." She breathed in and then yelled, "Help!"

☕ chapter four ☕

AT CLIFFSIDE MANOR, Bria sat in the business manager's office. The framed artwork hung on the taupe-painted walls did nothing to soothe her twitching nerve endings and aching heart over what she'd discovered on the third floor.

Her pulse sputtered, matching the irregular beat of her heart.

If only Dalton was with her, but he needed to call his boss and Dad's attorney.

She wrung her hands to keep from fidgeting in the upholstered chair.

It didn't help.

A two-ton imaginary weight pressed against Bria's shoulders.

She glanced at Kenna, who sat on the opposite side of the desk and tapped on the computer keyboard.

Kenna tucked a wavy strand of auburn hair behind her ear. "I've applied payments for what Brian owed and credited the account for three months of rent and services. Thanks for making the drive from Berry Lake to take care of this on the weekend."

"Well, you're here on a Sunday."

"It's my weekend. The managers rotate in case residents need anything."

Bria didn't want to know what anyone might need there. "How long has Molly Landon been a resident?"

Kenna's smile wavered until the curve of her lips slid into place. "I'm sorry. Even though Molly's your mom, HIPAA prevents me from answering questions about her. I can give you a release form for Brian to sign."

Bria wanted a lot of things—answers being one of them. But she didn't want to wait until visiting hours at the county jail.

Frustration burned in her veins. She clenched her hands. "I'd like the form. Is it something I can scan and email?"

"Yes, especially since you don't live close and Brian's..."

"In jail."

Kenna swallowed. "Email or fax the signed copy."

That was something. Only Bria would be left waiting. Still, that wasn't Kenna's fault. "Thank you. The situation isn't your fault."

"It's no one's fault."

Bria hoped that was the case. But call her skeptical because she couldn't explain what was happening there. And she needed to know.

"I can tell you that Molly has received the best care possible. Your dad's seen to that. His sending you here tells me he has her best interests at heart."

Bria froze. Every nerve ending froze, and her blood turned ice-cold.

Her best interests.

The woman upstairs.

Molly.

Not Bria's.

Her eyes stung, and she blinked.

No matter her feelings about the resident in room 313, Dad had an alibi now.

"My boyfriend's outside making calls. One of them is to my father's lawyer, Marc Carpenter. I'm sorry to involve Cliffside Manor in a legal matter, but my dad needs an alibi."

"We'll cooperate. We all believe your father isn't capable of arson or any other crime. His devotion is relationship goals for most of us who work here."

The admiration in Kenna's voice bristled and sank to the bottom of Bria's stomach like the bowl-sized stone paperweight a coworker had kept on his desk at her old accounting firm.

Nothing in Wishing Bay made sense.

Dad wasn't a man to admire or like. He wanted to sell his sister's bakery—her legacy—to make a quick buck.

Bria pressed her lips together.

Kenna handed Bria two pieces of paper. "Here's your receipt. I also emailed one to Brian. The release form so that we can discuss Molly with you is there, too."

Bria's fingers tightened around the pages. She loosened her grip so she wouldn't crease them. "Thanks."

She stood and hurried out of the office.

Dalton sat in the lobby. As soon as his gaze met hers, he stood. "How'd it go?"

"All paid up thanks to Selena loaning the money to my dad with his share of the cupcake shop as collateral." Bria waved the papers in the air. "Once my dad signs the top sheet, I'll get some answers."

"Until then?"

"They can't tell me anything. I ask questions, but then someone mentions HIPAA."

"They have to follow the rules."

"Yes, but all I want is a crumb of information. I mean, I'm her…" Bria couldn't bring herself to say daughter. Not yet. Perhaps never. Thinking the word brought a bitter taste to her mouth. "Should I not want to know?"

"You have every right to know everything."

"Thanks."

"I booked rooms at a local inn. They recommended a place that is open late on Sundays for dinner."

Her mouth gaped. "Is your boss okay with you missing work tomorrow?"

"Doesn't matter if Tanner is okay with it or not. I'm staying with you. I ran over a few things with him for a call, so he won't need me there tomorrow."

Affection swelled, overflowing from her heart. "Thank you. For being here. For making us reservations for tonight. For taking me out to dinner."

"We're in this together." He laced his fingers with hers. "I'll keep saying it until you believe me."

"I know." And she did.

But her mom hadn't loved Bria enough to stay. Okay, Bria didn't know when Molly had been injured, but it had to be after she left or others in Berry Lake would know, right? And Dad only cared about making money, which meant dumping her with Aunt Elise. Could she trust Dalton to stick around?

Bria wanted to. They hadn't been together that long, but so far, so good, including today. "I'm so happy you're here."

"Nowhere else I'd rather be." Dalton squeezed her hand. "Though I wish it were under different circumstances, we could have done some sightseeing."

"Selena T would tell us not to worry and make the most of being in Wishing Bay. It's a cute town."

"We can see a little of it on the way to the restaurant. You need to eat."

Food was the last thing Bria wanted, but Dalton hadn't eaten since brunch either. "And so do you. Let's go."

Maybe some distance from Cliffside Manor would do her good. She sure hoped so.

The restaurant was delightful, but Bria's mood sucked. Forget her entrée. Not even the bread with the honey butter appealed to her. She pushed the delicious-smelling shrimp scampi around her plate with a fork.

Dalton sat across from her. He'd been eyeing her plate for the past five minutes.

Bria didn't want him to worry more about her. She shoved a shrimp into her mouth, forced herself to chew, and swallowed. "I'm sorry."

Since they'd left Cliffside Manor more than an hour ago, she'd apologized to Dalton so many times. Not even the quaint wood boardwalk or shops and cafés decorated with gold, red, and hunter-green to mark autumn got her out of the funk she feared would take permanent residency inside her. "You found us this lovely restaurant, and I'm sitting here moping."

"Not moping. Contemplating. Perhaps pondering."

A grin tugged at her lips. That was unexpected but welcome. "How do you do that?"

"What?"

"Make me want to smile instead of cry?"

"I only told the truth." Dalton raised his water but didn't sip. He stared over the glass. "You needed to hear the words."

She needed him. "I did. I prefer anything to moping."

"There you go." He raised his glass as if toasting her and then took a sip. "You have a lot to process. No one would blame you for moping."

She swallowed a sigh and placed her fork on the plate. "Except I don't mope. I didn't after Aunt Elise died or when I lost my job. I can't start now."

"You're doing great." Dalton covered her hand. His warm skin and gentle touch comforted Bria. "And you have every right to mope or be frustrated. Even annoyed."

"I'm not annoyed. At least not yet."

"Then you're doing better than me because I'm ready to withdraw money from the first ATM I see and start bribing people, which is totally my mother's MO, not mine. Which tells you my state of mind."

"I appreciate that, but bribing is unnecessary, though…" Bria half laughed. "Deena would so do that."

"Believe me, she has." His tone was resigned, not angry. "We'll figure this out."

Bria nodded, not sure she believed they would. That made the situation seem even more hopeless. She stared at her plate but didn't pick up her fork. Forcing herself to eat more wasn't the answer.

"Let's ask them to box up your dinner," Dalton said. "The inn should have a microwave if you get hungry later."

"Sounds good." Dalton was the perfect boyfriend. She'd been so focused on herself she hadn't considered his situation. She might be a mess of confusion, but she didn't need to drag down Dalton. "I've been thinking about what you said. How Selena T might frame this."

He stared out the window before returning his gaze to Bria. "We could be somewhere far less picturesque."

"And let's not forget we're at the beach." Bria glanced out the window. A spotlight beamed at the shoreline. "I love Berry Lake, but..."

"There's something about the ocean. Waves crashing against the shore. Scent of salt in the air. Gulls flying overhead. Oh, and saltwater taffy."

Her jaw dropped. There was no way he'd know that. "When have you ever seen me eat taffy?"

"I haven't, but you love sweets and candy. Am I wrong about the taffy?"

"No."

A smug expression formed on his face. So handsome.

He raised her hand to his mouth and kissed it. "Knew it."

Bria nearly laughed. "You get me."

Dalton placed her hand on the table, but he didn't let go. "Yes, but I can't take too much credit for that."

His look of pure adoration sent her pulse speeding up.

"It took me over fifteen years to get to this point," he added. "Because let's face it, I was clueless about you and myself in high school, but I'm learning more every day. And I can't wait until I have my Ph.D. in you."

"Is that a thing?"

"No idea, but it should be. I want you to tell me everything. What you love, hate, all your secrets."

"I don't have any of those."

She glanced around the restaurant, which had cleared out since they'd arrived. Not surprising given the hour, but she couldn't help but wonder if Aunt Elise had ever eaten there? Visited Wishing Bay? Bria might never find out the answers.

"But the same can't be said about the rest of my family." This time, a sigh escaped.

He squeezed her hand, the gesture filling her with the comfort she needed.

"One day at a time," he said. "And let's not get started on my family. Ian's the only normal one."

"Besides you."

"Do you want to check into the inn?" Dalton asked.

"I want to see how she's…"

"Whatever you want."

He paid the check, drove to Cliffside Manor, and parked. Lights illuminated the landscaping and entry, making the facility look even more like a hotel than earlier.

As they entered the lobby, he placed his hand on the small of her back. "Should I call Juliet? Tell her we're staying?"

Bria headed to the elevator. Each step wanted to speed up to get her to the third floor faster, but she kept pace with Dalton. "I messaged the Posse earlier."

"Should've known you'd do that."

"I didn't want anyone to worry. I didn't…tell them."

"Good. You need to process this first, and your friends aren't known for holding in their opinions."

"True, but I do the same with them."

After Aunt Elise's death, the Posse had reunited, but the years apart hadn't changed their friendship. If anything, being older had made them appreciate each other more.

"Lots of time to tell them why I'm here," she added.

"Get the answers you need, and when you feel comfortable telling people, your friends will understand. But I'm sure the Posse said stuff about you being in Wishing Bay."

"They did." Thinking about their group text made her laugh. "Nell wants us to have fun. Selena offered to drive over. Juliet's worried about my interview. Missy wanted me to let her know if I needed anything."

"You're lucky to have those four women in your life again."

"I am." She pressed the elevator's up button. "But I'm lucky to have you, too."

The elevator doors opened. They stepped inside.

Bria pressed the button for the third floor.

As the doors closed, her heart rattled against her rib cage.

Breathe. Just breathe.

That was what Selena would tell her.

Dalton smoothed Bria's hair. "You'll get through this, and someday we'll look back on this in utter amazement."

Someday. She liked the sound of that. "I hope so."

The elevator arrived. The doors opened.

She should have chosen checking into the inn before returning to the third floor. Too late. "Here we go again."

He laced his fingers with hers. Holding hands, they headed to room 313.

The door was ajar.

Bria peeked through the crack.

A different nurse stood by the bed. The woman under the quilt wasn't moving.

Not just any woman.

The mother Bria hadn't seen since she was two but only knew that from what Dad and Aunt Elise had said. No memories of Molly emerged, and Bria tried hard to remember.

Her breath sped up, becoming shallower by the second, in a race with her pulse to see who would cross the finish line first or leave Bria lying face-down on the floor.

She closed her eyes to see if that helped.

"Hey." Dalton's arms wrapped around Bria, and he pulled her against his chest. "Take a deep breath."

She did, filling her lungs with much-needed air.

He brushed his lips over her hair. "Another."

Bria inhaled again. "Don't let go."

His arms tightened, pulling her closer. "I won't."

She leaned against him. "I thought the time away would put me in a better mindset to handle this. But one look and... My mind goes blank. Each time I think I've figured it out, everything blows up."

"There's no playbook for a situation like this. No timetable."

"Guess not."

"You wish there was."

"Of course. I'm a planner. But none of my plans have worked out the way I expected. If they had, I'd still be working and living in San Diego."

"If that were the case, we wouldn't be standing here together. I much prefer being together than apart."

"Me too." And she did. Dalton was everything she hadn't known she needed. "It's a lot to handle."

"You're handling it better than many would. All you can do is take things day by day."

"Is that how you got over your dad's death?" she asked.

"Honestly, you don't get over it, but I got through it, which I count as a win."

He made a good point.

"Obviously, my dad was a part of"—Bria glanced around the hallway and pointed to room 313—"her being here. But I can't believe he's known where Molly was and kept it hidden from me. We never had the best relationship, but for him to lie about my...her."

"You'll have to ask him."

Bria did and would. She needed answers. So many answers. "The next visiting time."

The county jail had a set visitor's schedule. That meant she would have to wait.

The nurse headed toward the door. "She's asleep."

Unable to shake a chill, Bria crossed her arms over her chest and leaned against Dalton. "Will Molly remember..."

Me?

Hannah's gaze softened. "She doesn't remember the staff who work here. I'm sorry."

"What's wrong with..." The words died on Bria's lips. "Wait. You can't discuss her with me."

Hannah nodded. "I can't and appreciate you understanding that. Not everyone does."

"I do." Even if Bria didn't like it.

"You just returned, but there's no reason for you to stay," Hannah said. "Molly will sleep until morning."

Dalton rubbed Bria's arm. "We can head over to the Wishing Bay Inn."

A smile spread across Hannah's face. "Oh, that's a lovely place to stay. Gorgeous views of the bay."

He squeezed Bria's arm. "Ready to go?"

A part of her wanted to stay there, but that made no sense. "Yes, it's been a long day."

But she wasn't sure sleep was possible.

He hugged her as if knowing what she needed at that moment.

She wrapped her arms around him, not wanting to let go of him. "Thank you."

"Let's go."

A few minutes later, they walked to his car. She inhaled the salty air. In the distance, a foghorn blared. Strange, the night sky appeared overcast but not foggy. "I wish I remembered coming here with my dad, but it had to be twenty-five years ago. Nothing looks or smells familiar."

"That was a long time ago."

"A different life." When her dad had been Bria's hero.

"It's difficult to be patient, but your dad is probably the only one who knows everything."

Bria nodded. "I'd like to visit in the morning before we drive home."

"Of course." Dalton kissed her forehead. "We can stop and buy her something. Like a gift."

"I'd like to do that. Thanks."

The man was too good to be true. She remembered the hurt he'd caused in the past when he picked his family over her and broke Bria's heart, but she didn't want to look back. That was all she'd done today. With her family, that was okay, but not with Dalton. Or she would ruin…everything.

chapter five

*S*WISH, *SWASH. SWISH, swash.*

The wipers cleared the water from the SUV's windshield, but Nell Culpepper thought the pounding rain was winning the battle. The rain fell harder as if angels in heaven dropped marbles onto the SUV's roof.

If Elise was one of those angels, she must be giggling her butt off at what Nell was doing. But chances were Elise was still in the training or probationary phase of becoming an angel. Getting wings and a halo probably took more than a month, right?

Swish, swash.

Nell glanced around the driver's seat and could barely see out of the windshield. She would be more worried if Gage Adler didn't appear to have control of his vehicle in the torrential rain and darkness.

"I should have you home in a few minutes." Gage didn't take his gaze off the road. "Then we can eat dinner."

"No rush." And she meant that. Years of working in the emergency department had exposed her to the brutal injuries and deaths from car accidents. Arriving later and in one piece was better than faster and on a gurney.

Welles Riggs, riding shotgun, pressed the radio's scan button. "Well, I'm hungry, and the smell of burgers and fries has me ready to drool. Usually, that's reserved for the lovely ladies."

Typical Welles. "We'll eat as soon as we get to my place. Remember, though. Patience is a virtue."

Nell wouldn't skip a chance to rib Welles.

"Oh, I can be patient." Welles winked. "Like Job when it comes to getting what I want."

His you'll-be-mine-someday grin implied he wanted her.

Nope. Not going to engage. The handsome paramedic asked out Nell each time he saw her at the hospital. It was a big joke between them, but she didn't want to involve Gage in Welles's silly game. Because that was all she was to him—a way to pass the time between calls and runs to the emergency department.

Nell lifted her toes to stretch her sore legs.

That didn't lessen the pain.

Focus on the fries.

Cupcakes were her favorite scent, but the combination of grease and flavored seasoning made her mouth water. Too bad asking for a couple of fries was out after telling Welles to be patient. She needed to think before she spoke.

Still, the thought of junk food as her reward for surviving their earlier hike made ignoring her aching muscles easier.

And the dirt…

Not even the darkness hid the gritty feel of her skin and the smell of her clothing.

She grimaced.

So much dirt. But no mud, thankfully. They'd arrived at the car before the skies opened.

Focus on dinner.

A long, hot shower would wash away the grime and feel so good after another day off spent traipsing in nature.

Why was she doing this again?

"What's something you've been patient with, Welles?" Gage asked.

Oh, right. The reason for today's hike sharpened in Nell's mind. Gorgeous, athletic, addicted to risk-taking Gage.

The dashboard lights gave her a decent view of his eyes in the rearview mirror. A smile tugged at the corners of her tired mouth.

Hanging out with Gage had stopped her mother from meddling in Nell's dating life. Her mom believed they were a couple, and Nell would happily let Mom think that for as long as possible.

Yes, this was working out well.

Given Nell hadn't worn a climbing harness and clung to rocks like a lifeline as she had last week, she would even call today a win-win.

Three wins, actually.

Four, if she counted the fast food they'd be having for dinner. Albeit a late one.

Welles Riggs glanced over his shoulder. "Nurse Nell tries my patience whenever I see her at work."

"That's not my fault." She needed to tell Welles to step it up. He was supposed to be Gage's new adventure buddy, so she wouldn't have to risk her legs or lungs in the great outdoors. She preferred dates where kisses, not almost dying, got the adrenaline pumping. At least Welles made Gage take a slower pace, so there was that.

But she'd rather be inside on a date, cuddling on the couch and watching TV with enough sweets to induce a sugar coma. Someday, she hoped. And if Gage decided he wanted to be her cuddle buddy, she wouldn't say no. Yes, he was that yummy.

"You two know each other well," Gage said.

"Yes." Welles spoke up before she had the chance to answer. "Nell is four years older than me, but we grew up together."

She shook her head. "Had to bring up my age, didn't you?"

"What?" Welles feigned surprise. "A four-year age gap in school was a big deal. It's nothing now."

"People put too much emphasis on age," Gage agreed.

Welles flashed her his most charming I-told-you-so smile.

It was a good thing she was immune to the firefighter, but age wasn't the only reason she kept turning him down. "I'm happy you agree, Gage, since I'm older than you."

"As I said, age doesn't matter." Gage stared out the windshield. "You keep up like you're ten years younger."

Nell flinched. That didn't sound like the best compliment. But then again, who knew how Gage thought of her? That might mean something coming from a guy friend. And Selena would say whatever Gage said had nothing to do with Nell and everything to do with him.

"Nell's on her feet all day long at the hospital." Welles barely took a breath. "I doubt many teenagers or twenty-somethings could keep up with her."

Okay, that was sweet of him to say. She should give Welles more credit for being such a good guy.

"She does great on the trail," Gage added as if he didn't want to be left out of the give Nell compliments party.

Not that she would shut it down. Nell had barely dated since returning to her hometown five years ago, after being dumped by the man she thought she would marry. She deserved this, whether from friends or a potential boyfriend.

Gage turned into the parking lot of the condo building where she and Welles lived. They were next-door neighbors with units that shared a wall.

Gage parked illegally in the loading zone, but no one would mind or notice in this weather.

"I hope the rain lets up by the time we finish dinner." He lived across the Columbia River in Oregon. "But I've driven in worse if it doesn't."

In the front seat, Welles maneuvered to get his stuff and the food. Nell guessed he didn't want to do it standing in the pouring rain because she didn't want to get wet either.

He handed the drink carrier to Gage. "My guest bedroom's yours if you don't want to drive home."

"Thanks, but I'm sure Nell would put me up," Gage said in a flirty tone.

In her guest room, yes. But that didn't seem to be what he was implying. She struggled to find the right words.

"Nell has to get up early for work." Welles shifted the food bag from one hand to the other and pocketed his cell phone. "By early, I mean, before the sun. Even the birds are still asleep."

"I do," Nell confirmed. Welles knowing her schedule surprised her, but she appreciated him speaking up.

Yes, she found Gage uber-attractive. Sure, he kept her mom off Nell's case. Thirty-seven wasn't too old to be single. If that made her a modern-day spinster, so be it. But she didn't know him that well. What she knew told her they were opposite in every way. Sure, opposites attracted, but she wasn't about to rush into anything with Gage...or anyone for that matter.

"Let's play it by ear." Gage glanced at her. "I'll pop the back. We'll have to make a run for it in the rain."

As the rear opened, they slid out of the car into the falling rain. Drops streamed down Nell's face. She ducked under the hatch for a moment's reprieve, grabbed her pack and hiking boots, and ran toward her front door. Her thighs burned, but the rain kept her moving faster than she thought she could go.

She unlocked the door, and they poured into her living room.

Mr. Teddy sat on the couch. He glanced at Nell and then turned his back to her.

Typical cat.

Gage and Welles were like models rocking the wet look. How come the ends of her hair never curled like theirs when damp? "I'll grab some towels."

Welles carried a bag of food. "Do we need plates?"

"Not when I'm ready to eat the paper." Gage set the drinks on the table. "I'm starving."

"Same." Nell checked Mr. Teddy's water and food bowls, grabbed a stack of towels from the linen closet, and passed them out. "Though the calories from dinner will wipe out all the ones I burned off today."

Gage wiped his face. "You can burn more off when we go out again."

"You don't have to burn off anything," Welles said a beat later, drying his hair.

The damp towels went onto the island, and the three sat.

Nell bit into the burger. The cheese was melted goodness. "Oh, I needed this. Not used to eating dinner this late, but the burger place was a great suggestion, Welles."

"I ran out of snacks. Didn't want to get hangry." Welles shoved French fries into his mouth. "So good."

"Pack more food next time." Gage finished his hamburger.

The next time. Nell's sore shoulders slumped. "I'm going to be fully transparent. If it keeps raining this week, I'm not climbing. The two of you go without me."

"Come on, Nell." Gage wagged a fry at her. "A little rain never hurt anyone."

"The three of us can go to the climbing gym in Hood River," Welles suggested. "Then we won't get wet."

"I prefer outdoor climbing, but I don't want Nell to be uncomfortable," Gage agreed.

So much for transparency.

She swallowed a groan.

The rain didn't make her uncomfortable. She'd grown up in the Pacific Northwest. Rain didn't slow kids down, whether it was Halloween or any old day of the week. The climbing, however, was totally out of her wheelhouse. Hiking, too. Yet she hadn't been honest with Gage. She was more likely to win a gold medal for channel surfing than by doing any kind of sport. She and athletics were distant acquaintances at best.

She stared at her half-eaten cheeseburger.

Was it finally time to admit to Gage she wasn't an outdoor-loving adventurer like him? She'd let him assume things about her, so he'd want to go out with her.

A lump of guilt lodged in her throat.

Welles placed his drink on the table. "What do you say, Nell?"

She blew out a breath. So much for Welles becoming Gage's new nature buddy. They'd become a weird trio, which meant she was falling behind on binge-watching her favorite shows. And if she were being honest, Nell wasn't sure how much she enjoyed what they'd become.

Gage kept pushing Nell out of her comfort zone. That wasn't a bad thing, except he needed to see the real her, not suggest they take a trip to Alaska to go climbing. The only way she wanted to see Alaska was from the deck of a cruise ship that had a never-ending buffet, drinks, and live entertainment. Oh, and a hot tub. She'd never been on a cruise, but a hot tub should be required for all vacations.

Nell squared her shoulders as if preparing for battle. Perhaps this wasn't the time to spill about her lack of thrill-seeking DNA, but she had to say something. "How about we skip the climbing and stay in this week? Watch a movie?"

Or two. Even three.

She'd provide the popcorn, drinks, and snacks.

Rom-coms with handholding and forehead kissing were her favorite. Besides, not climbing would give her a chance to get to know Gage better without her breaking a sweat and worrying about dying. Plus, Mom wouldn't know it wasn't a romantic date.

"I'm in," Welles said.

He would be. She blew out a frustrated breath. But it was her fault for mentioning a movie in front of him. Welles was only supposed to join them on outdoor outings, but he hadn't got that memo yet.

Gage shrugged. "I might be tempted, depending on the movie."

Welles grinned. "Whatever you want to watch is fine with me, Nell."

Gage's gaze bounced between her and Welles. "I don't really care what we watch. I just want you to be happy, babe."

Babe? Her jaw stiffened.

Gage hadn't called her that before. Because…friends.

Nell should be happy, right? Endearments were a good sign that he was attracted to her, except her ex used to call her babe. Then and now, the word made her feel more like a barnyard animal than a girlfriend—or a potential one in Gage's case.

Stop. That was what Selena T, a life coach and podcaster, would tell her. She would say Gage wasn't her ex, so don't dump that baggage on him.

And that was one hundred percent the truth.

Being tired and grimy was causing Nell to overreact.

Her cell phone rang.

Nell pulled out the phone from a backpack pocket. *Jenny* lit up the screen.

That was weird. Jenny usually texted.

Nell answered. "Hey. What's up?"

"Have you talked to Missy?" The sentence came out sounding like one long word.

"No, but Missy was in our group chat earlier."

Welles leaned over the table. "Is Missy okay?"

Nell waved her hand to shush him. "Is something wrong?"

"Yes. No. I don't know." Jenny sounded worried.

Not unusual where her sister-in-law was concerned, but Missy had been doing better—healing.

"What's wrong?" Nell asked.

"I noticed her car was gone. The cottage's front door is locked. The cats weren't meowing, so she must have fed them before leaving. But where would she go at this hour?"

"Nowhere."

Since the fire, Missy was the definition of a homebody. Way worse than Nell, who was mainly there for the ease of snacking and not having to exert herself too much. Missy wouldn't leave her cats and head out in the rain on a Sunday. At least not without a good reason.

"I tried calling her." Footsteps sounded, suggesting Jenny was pacing. "It rang a few times before going to voice mail. She's an adult, but..."

"It's Missy." Who'd been through so much. She hadn't been the same since Rob died. That was why people worried about her at the best of times. "Have you called Juliet?"

"No, I went by last names. Culpepper came before the others."

"Bria's out of town. I'll call Juliet," Nell offered.

"Thanks." But Jenny didn't sound relieved. "Dare's driving around looking for Missy."

Nell drew back. "In this rain?"

"He's a former Army Ranger. My husband can handle anything." The love in Jenny's voice was the definition of relationship goals. "He also knows I won't go to bed until I know where Missy is."

Nell didn't blame her. Jenny and Missy were sisters-in-law, but closer than Nell was to her younger sisters. "I'll call now and let you know."

"Thanks so much."

Nell disconnected from the call.

"What's going on?" Lines formed around Welles's mouth and on his forehead.

Nell understood. He'd risked his life and career to save Missy's life during the cupcake fire. "Jenny's being overly protective, as usual. But this time, she has a reason. Missy's car is gone."

Welles stiffened. "Missy rarely goes out."

"At night or at all?" Gage asked.

"At all," she and Welles answered in unison.

"She an introvert or something?" Gage asked.

"Widow," Nell answered a beat before Welles. "Her husband was a Marine. Killed while deployed. She was twenty-three when that happened. And she's had a hard time moving on. She worked at the cupcake shop that caught fire last month. She's been recovering from her injuries from that, too."

"Do you want me to call anyone?" Welles offered.

"Let me talk to Juliet first." Nell pulled up her contacts. Her dinner could wait. "I don't want to sound the alarm for no reason. That would upset Missy."

Nell pressed Juliet's name. Two rings...

"Nell?" Juliet's voice still sounded like one of the theme park princesses she used to play over a decade ago. "Looks like you survived another weekend adventure."

Not a question but Nell felt like answering. "Just barely."

"Sore?"

"You have no idea."

Juliet laughed. "You're working out and getting in shape. At least that's what Selena T would say."

"I gave up on that stuff years ago. Pass the cupcakes, please."

Welles cleared his throat.

Oh, right. "Jenny's looking for Missy. Have you seen her?"

"No, but she should be at home. Missy doesn't go out much now that the cupcake shop has closed."

"She did tonight." Nell noticed Welles eavesdropping while Gage added ketchup to his fries. "Her car's gone."

"I wonder…"

"What?" Nell asked.

"Maybe Missy took one of her cats to the animal clinic. If one was sick, she wouldn't stop to call anyone."

Missy was a crazy cat lady. Nell loosened her grip on her phone. "You're right. She babies Mario and Peach like they're her kids."

"They are, as you know."

"I don't have a cat."

"Mr. Teddy."

She glanced at the well-fed cat who'd claimed her couch as his own. "A foster cat."

"Your stepmom is infamous for her foster failures."

Wait. Sabine had mentioned those, but… "She wouldn't set me up like that."

"Wanna bet?" Juliet laughed.

"I'll ask Sabine about that, but I need to call the animal clinic now."

"Text me that Missy's okay, please."

"Will do. Bye."

Nell had the animal clinic's number in her contacts. A precaution in case Mr. Teddy had any troubles. That was what a responsible foster parent did—take care of their foster animal.

Welles said nothing, but he wasn't eating. Instead, he stared at her.

"I saw you eavesdropping, Paramedic Welles," she said.

Gage kept eating, but he seemed to be watching them.

"Hard not to hear the conversation sitting next to you at the table, Nurse Nell. You better call the clinic."

Nell did.

On the third ring, the line connected. "Berry Lake Animal Clinic. This is Kyrene. How can I help you?"

"This is Nell Culpepper. Is Missy Hanford there?"

"Hey, Nell. Missy isn't here yet, but I'm expecting her any minute. She's bringing in a litter of kittens someone dumped."

Relief flooded Nell. "Thank you. Have a good evening."

"No problem. Bye." The line disconnected.

"Is Missy there?" Welles asked.

"She's on her way with kittens someone dumped. I'm not sure how she got involved, but I assume Sabine needed help."

Welles shook his head. "What is wrong with people? Dumping helpless kittens."

"They don't want to deal with the medical expenses and finding homes for them." Gage glared at Mr. Teddy. The two didn't get along from the first time Gage had picked her up. "And let's face it, cats aren't the nicest creatures. Especially the one over there who keeps giving me the stink eye."

"Mr. Teddy isn't used to you yet." That wasn't the cat's fault but Gage's. He hadn't spent enough time there for Mr. Teddy to get to know him. "I'm going to text Jenny, so I don't wake her daughter, Briley."

Nell typed on her phone and hit *send*.

Welles sat taller. "Cats are great. Mr. Teddy loves me. That's one cool cat."

Nell sent a text to Juliet, too.

Gage glanced at Welles. "You seem more of a dog person. Aren't firefighters required to have a dalmatian or something?"

"You watch too many movies. I don't mind dogs, but I work for my dad. People think dogs scare away Sasquatch, so I've never had one."

Gage burst out laughing. "You don't have a dog because of Bigfoot?"

"Laugh all you want, but Sasquatch Adventure Tours put me through college and has supported my family for decades. Bigfoot hating dogs could be an urban legend, but people, namely tourists, have certain beliefs about sasquatches, so no dogs are allowed on our tours."

Gage snorted. "Whatever works."

Nell's cell phone buzzed with Jenny's reply. Nell read the entire exchange to make sure she didn't miss anything.

> **NELL:** *The animal clinic said Missy's bringing in a litter of kittens, so she must be picking them up.*
> **JENNY:** *Thank you. Dare didn't find her.*
> **NELL:** *She might be a while.*
> **JENNY:** *I'll stay up. Missy shouldn't be out with her foot. But at least I'll be able to write now.*
> **NELL:** *Hope Ash saves the world again.*
> **JENNY:** *World? Universe? Still debating which for this book.*
> **NELL:** *Have fun writing everyone's favorite book boyfriend.*

Nell lowered her phone. She ate a fry.

"All good now?" Gage asked.

Nodding, she picked up her drink. "Yes. Though, I'm sure Missy will get an earful when she arrives home."

"Missy told me she missed volunteering at the rescue when I visited her at the hospital." Welles hadn't finished his burger. "If I'm not at the station, I'll offer to go with her."

"Not at the station or guiding for your dad." Nell appreciated Welles's offer. That gave her an idea. "I'll ask Dare if he can do the same until Missy's foot heals. I'm sure he would if only to keep Jenny from worrying."

Gage leaned forward in his chair. "I thought Hood River was a small town, but it's got nothing on Berry Lake. Everyone knows everybody's business here."

"It's true." Nell's mom was the hub of town gossip. "But as much as people are nosey, they care. And that's something I missed when I lived in Chicago and Boston."

"I moved from New York, and I miss the city," Gage said. "Don't you?"

Welles stared at her.

"Not as much as I thought I would." Nell missed the life she'd imagined having with Andrew, being his wife and the mother of his children. But he was living her dream with another woman he'd married after only knowing her for two weeks when he'd strung Nell along for over ten years. "I love living in Berry Lake."

"Do you plan to stay here?" Gage asked.

She considered the question. "Why would I want to leave when everything I want is here?"

Welles raised his drink. "You left before."

"For the wrong reasons," she admitted.

"Why wrong?" Gage asked.

"I was in love and followed a guy to two different states. Yet here I am alone. But I learned my lesson and won't do that again."

Nell...couldn't. Her heart would never survive.

She went into the kitchen, picked up a box of cupcakes Missy had made, and carried them to the table. "And if that isn't reason enough to stay in town, these sweet treats will keep me here until my last breath. No one makes anything as delicious as these."

And one dayell and the Posse would become co-owners in the Berry Lake Cupcake Shop. She couldn't wait.

🧁 chapter six 🧁

AN EMERGENCY AT the market on a Sunday night? Sam Cooper didn't grip the patrol car's steering wheel. No apprehension tightened his muscles. He hit the lights—red and blue reflecting in the puddles on the road—and made a quick U-turn on Main Street.

Not that he needed the lights with no one out in the downpour, but some habits were ingrained.

He reached to switch on the siren and then lowered his hand. It was late enough for some people to be in bed. Something he'd never considered in Seattle. But Berry Lake had different rules.

Perhaps *courtesies* might be a better word.

He'd only been in his hometown for a week. Long enough to know working in Berry Lake as a sheriff's deputy was nothing like what he came across in Seattle as a police officer.

Face it. Not much happened in the small town.

Sam didn't hate it.

He rubbed his shoulder. The wound had healed months ago, but the rain made the joint ache. The doc had warned him and added the scar would fade but always be visible.

Sam didn't ask about the invisible scar. The shrink he'd been referred to was overworked, apathetic, and counting the days until retirement.

He'd thought about leaving the force, but Sam didn't want to leave anyone with a green partner, so he'd stayed to train the rookie taking Richie's place, sweating every domestic abuse call, but then again, Sam hadn't been happy before the shooting. Things spiraled downward into misery from there. It surprised no one when he quit, especially the chief who encouraged Sam to start over where there weren't so many bad memories.

As if a new location would make him forget his best friend and partner.

Yet, he had a new job in a town he could navigate with his eyes closed.

But darkness and rain made it hard enough to see with his eyes open. No reason to close them when the dispatcher's "an emergency" was too vague.

No code—which reaffirmed how lax the sheriff's department was.

His best guess?

A raccoon had gotten into something at the market.

That would count as an emergency in Berry Lake.

Those suckers were messy when hungry.

A raccoon being his first guess told Sam how far he'd come since leaving Seattle. But his Berry Lake calls had involved a fender bender on Main Street, a lost ferret who'd somehow found his way into the attic, a noise complaint, a high school kegger at the lake, and a stolen bike.

Not that he kept track.

The skills learned at the academy and his years on the Seattle force weren't necessary in Berry Lake. At least, not so far. Common sense, a steely gaze, and manners became his tools of choice.

Yep, a big difference from his old job.

He checked the intersection and drove through the red light. The town needed to upgrade to automatic lights, so first responders always got green lights.

Sam, however, counted the number of nights he'd stayed at his parents' house.

If he didn't move out of their house soon, he would lose it.

Oh, Mom and Dad were great. Supportive. Wanted to pay for everything.

Sam appreciated them. He did. They still saw him as the youngest of their three children, the baby of the family, even though he was thirty-one-years-old and could pay for himself.

That wasn't the worst part, however. His folks asked about everything he did, and only a minute-by-minute recap satisfied them from work to where he stopped on the way home and how long he slept.

He clenched his teeth, wishing he'd rented a place before moving. Each morning—or night, depending on his shift—they asked what he'd been doing. Sam understood. His older brother, Josh, had struggled with alcoholism, and whether they asked out of habit or an abundance of caution, it was growing old.

His sister, Ava, and Josh had each offered up guest rooms at their houses, but Sam turned them down. Moving in with an older sibling was a half step up from being at their folks' house.

He needed to lease a rental or buy a place. Something that had been unaffordable in Seattle, but real estate was more reasonably priced in Berry Lake.

He turned into the Berry Lake Market's parking lot. The place appeared deserted, but he made a slow pass in front of the entrance—no flashes of light or movement inside.

Better check the other side.

He rounded the corner and slammed on the brake.

A car was parked haphazardly. The doors were closed, but the headlights shone toward the recycle and garbage bins.

Not a raccoon.

A thief wouldn't announce their presence, unless they weren't very smart, so dumpster diving, perhaps. But that didn't count as an emergency. And he saw no one around the bins.

Sam typed the vehicle's plates into the mobile data computer and waited.

Information popped onto the MDC's screen.

He did a double take. Rubbed his neck.

Missy Hanford's car.

What was it doing here? And where was she?

His pulse kicked up a notch. Sam surveyed the area but saw no movement. Sure, the headlights didn't illuminate everything, but nothing moved.

A band around his chest tightened. He closed his eyes and counted to ten. That loosened the pressure.

Sam opened his eyes.

He hadn't seen Missy in years. Nine, if he were counting, which he wasn't. But he'd avoided her whenever he returned home for the holidays and later to watch Josh during his first year of sobriety. Sam never went into the cupcake shop.

It wasn't Missy's fault.

His silly schoolboy crush on her was to blame.

Not that she even noticed him.

Nope.

Her heart belonged to Rob Hanford, Sam's teammate on the wrestling team. Great guy, but Sam used to tease Rob endlessly about being crazy in love with Missy. The guy never denied it, which sucked then. Man, jealousy had burned badly. Sam would have traded places with Rob in an instant.

And then an IED killed Rob.

Instantaneously, according to Charlene Culpepper, who knew most things that happened in town.

Sam's first thought hadn't been about the loss of his friend. Nope. He'd wondered how long to let Missy grieve before he made his move.

Pathetic.

No, disgusting.

One thing had been clear to Sam.

He didn't deserve Missy.

Which was why he hadn't stepped foot in the cupcake shop. He'd never sought her out. He hadn't even sent her a condolence card. And now…

Had her vehicle been stolen? If so, he wouldn't have to see her. Though Berry Lake was small, so he might not be able to put that off forever.

"On location, Unit Three?"

The radio sprang to life, the dispatcher's voice shaking Sam out of his head and the past.

"On site," he called in. "Missy Hanford's car is here. But no sign of her."

"Sabine Culpepper called it in. She lost contact with Missy, who's on a rescue mission."

"Repeat that?"

"Sabine asked Missy to go to the market for an animal rescue. Someone dumped kittens."

"Knowing that would have helped."

"Sabine's first call dropped after she said there was an emergency at the market. Got more information after she bought a phone charger, but you beat us there."

Life in a small town.

That didn't keep him from touching his revolver. Sam never wanted to have to draw a gun on anyone again.

He swallowed.

"Copy that." Sam parked his patrol car and shrugged on his rain jacket. "Exiting the vehicle now."

He slid out of the car. Rain poured off the brim of his hat.

"Someone out there?" a shaky voice asked from either the recycle bin or the garbage can.

Not any voice.

Missy's.

He'd recognize it anywhere.

Sam ran. Three milk crates sat in front of the recycle bin. A phone lay in a puddle. "Missy?"

"Help." Her voice sharpened, cracked.

His heart slammed against his rib cage. "It's Sam Cooper. Deputy Cooper. I'll get you out."

He peered over the edge. Rain had soaked Missy from head to toe. Shivering, she leaned the upper part of her body over the top of a cardboard box she clutched.

"I-I found kittens. T-They're wet." Her teeth chattered. "Need to get them to the animal clinic fast."

"You're freezing." Sam removed his raincoat and covered Missy with it. Raindrops pelted him, but his vest would keep him from getting drenched. "We need to get you to the hospital."

"The animal clinic."

They would discuss where Missy would go after she was out of the rain. He rearranged the milk crates and stacked them to be sturdier. "Are you injured?"

"No. Not really. The kittens..."

Not really didn't tell him much. Climbing into the bin in the dark was dangerous.

He stepped onto the crates and peered down.

Missy covered the box, he assumed full of kittens, with his coat.

Of course, she did. She'd loved animals in high school and volunteered for Sabine then.

She lifted the box toward him. "Put them in your car. I need a flashlight to make sure no kittens fell out of the box."

"I need to get you out first."

"They're only hours old. Fragile."

Her pleading tone blanked him, tugging at his heart as if trying to wake the organ after a winter hibernation.

What is going on?

After all these years, he should be over her.

Wait. He *was* over her.

"Please," she added.

Grrrr. Sam handed her the flashlight from his belt, took the box, ran to his car, and put the cats in the back seat. He turned the heater on full blast, grabbed the raincoat, and sprinted to the recycle bin.

He was back at the dumpster in a split second, and he wasn't even winded. His brother might be the famous jock in the family, but Sam held his own, which had helped him graduate second in his class at the police academy.

He scooped up the phone from the puddle and tucked it into his pocket. "The kittens are in the car where it's warmer."

"Thanks. There aren't any other kittens in here." The same green eyes that had haunted his dreams since he was fourteen met his.

His heart thudded.

Hold it together, Cooper. You still have a job to do.

Training kicked in. Her face was scratched, covered in blood and water unless she'd been crying.

His gut twisted. He covered her shoulders with his coat. It would keep her from getting wetter. "Let's get you out of here."

She shivered again. "T-Thank you for coming. I didn't think anybody would hear me."

"Sabine called it in." He searched for the easiest way to get her out. "Can you reach up so I can lift you?"

"You'll hurt yourself."

Sam couldn't see Missy fully, but he likely dead-lifted more than she weighed. "I'll be fine."

Missy shook her head. "Hand me a milk crate. I'll climb out."

"You might fall." The words rushed out, rapid as bullets shot from a Glock 17.

Arguing in the rain was stupid.

"Please. We need to take the kittens to the animal clinic." Yep, he would play the kitten card if that's what it took to get Missy out of the rain.

"Fine, but if you hurt yourself—"

"You can make me cupcakes. Deal?"

"It's your sciatica." She raised her arms, and Sam lifted her. Even soaking wet, she was lighter than he expected her to be.

Thin.

A way he didn't remember her being.

With her in his arms, cradled against his chest, he stepped down from the milk crate.

She'd lost a shoe. She also wore pajamas.

Water streamed down her face. She squirmed. "You can let me down."

He carried her to the patrol car. She wore one boot. "You're missing a boot."

"Slipper. It's still in the recycle bin. Probably where it should stay."

"A slipper, a boot, and pajamas. Your usual animal rescue uniform?"

"Depends on the situation." She glanced around. "Did you see the mama cat when you drove up?"

"No."

Missy blew out a breath. "I'll set a trap after dropping off the kittens."

Not on his watch. "You need to go to the hospital."

"I'm fine." Her teeth chattered. "A little cold, but I just need to warm up."

His car would be toasty now.

She pushed against his arms. "I can stand, Sam."

He startled. "Didn't think you recognized me."

"Well, Juliet told me you were at her car accident, but I would have recognized you even if you hadn't introduced yourself."

Oh, right. He'd done that.

"I can drive myself to the animal clinic," she said.

Except she was missing a shoe, bleeding, and who knew what else? He carried her to the patrol car. "Humor me."

"Why?"

He didn't want to let Missy out of sight, but he didn't dare tell her that. "I'm not a cat herder, but I can get you to the animal clinic faster."

That seemed a legit-enough reason. One she might buy.

"Sirens and flashing lights?" she asked.

Whatever it took. "If you want."

"I want." The corners of her mouth curved upward. "Us cat herders like to make a splash sometimes."

Was she joking? He couldn't tell.

Sam held her tighter as he opened the back door. He had a feeling she'd want to sit with the kittens. He tried not to think about how she felt in his arms, even though she fit perfectly against him. But this was work, not...

He shook the thought from his head.

They weren't teenagers or even young adults. His crush had ended when he realized she deserved better than him. She still did.

He gently placed her in the car. "There you go."

She opened the box.

Of course, she did.

"Fasten your seat belt. I'll turn off your headlights and grab your keys."

"Would you mind leaving one window cracked in case Mama cat needs a dry place?"

"Your car will get wet."

"It'll dry." Missy didn't glance his way. She focused on the kittens. "Thanks."

He got into the driver's seat. Water dripped everywhere.

Part of the job.

Sheriff Dooley wouldn't care. The guy had a soft spot for Missy because she'd worked for Elise Landon. Supposedly, the sheriff and the baker had an on-again, off-again thing for years.

Sam turned on the lights and sirens. If neighbors complained, he'd send Sabine after them. No one messed with her rescue animals. "That work?"

A glance in the rearview mirror showed Missy's bruised face. Still, she smiled. "Yep. Thanks."

His stomach fluttered as it had on his first day at Berry Lake High School when he saw her in the hallway wearing an oversized sweatshirt—one he later learned belonged to Rob Hanford.

Stop. Now.

Rumor had it—okay, Mom and Ava had told him—Rob's death changed Missy. Sam hadn't been able to compete with the guy when he was alive. No way would he take on a ghost. That would only end in heartbreak.

Mine.

If only that were possible...

Missy wasn't glamorous like Juliet Jones Monroe or synthetic like Remy Dwyer, but Missy's goodness shone through. Always had.

She had the prettiest eyes he'd ever seen—hazel that turned greenish in the light. The color reminded him of the stones he used to find on the shore of Berry Lake, the ones too nice to skim across the water, the ones that ended up in his pocket and then in a shoebox under his bed.

Stop thinking about her like that.

Hard not to while she sang and cooed to the kittens.

Each word mesmerized Sam. He forced his attention on the road.

"You're going to be okay. Each one of you is perfect," she said to the kittens. "I'll find your mama, and you can live with me until you're big enough to go to a forever home where you'll be loved and spoiled rotten."

A forever home sounded…nice. Home had been a studio apartment in Seattle. Not the best area, but he'd been saving money. Now, he slept in his childhood bedroom.

Not home.

Not any longer.

His family struggled to recover from Josh's alcoholism. Now that Josh was sober and married to Hope, things were slowly returning to normal, but Sam doubted things would ever be the same.

That was why he needed his own place.

He'd come to Berry Lake to start over, not fall back into borderline codependent patterns.

Guess he learned something from that shrink after all, even when the guy only wanted to check off boxes and circle diagnosis codes to keep payments coming.

Sam pulled into the animal clinic and parked near the front door. He shut off the flashing lights and siren.

She gathered the wet box onto her lap. "Thanks for the ride."

Carrying her wouldn't go over well, but… "Let me help you inside. That box is wet and ready to fall apart. And you only have one shoe."

She hesitated. "Thanks."

He hopped out of the car, opened the door closest to him, and took the box. "You're welcome."

She got out on her side.

The rain hadn't let up, but they were both soaked at this point. As he hurried toward the clinic's double glass doors, he glanced over his shoulder. Missy limped, favoring her sock-covered foot badly.

"It's not too late to call an ambulance," he said.

"Told you, I'm fine." She caught up to him and opened one of the clinic's glass doors so he could enter.

He stepped inside.

She followed him into the lobby and made a beeline for the receptionist standing behind the counter. "These kittens are young. Two have respiratory issues."

Sam's mouth dropped open.

How had she figured that out in the dark?

A tech rolled out a cart. "Put the box on here. We'll take care of these babies."

Relief rolled off Missy. "Thanks."

Sam did as he was told.

Leaning against the counter, she kept the weight off her injured foot.

He forced himself not to reach out to touch her cheek. "Your face is bleeding."

She touched her chin. "Must have scratched it when I fell in the bin. Nothing soap and water and some antibiotic cream won't fix."

That explained the cuts and bruises. "You should be checked out."

"I need to call Sabine." Her face fell. "My phone."

He pulled the device from his pocket. "Found it in a puddle."

She tapped on the screen. Nothing happened. "I needed a new one anyway."

"Sometimes putting the phone in rice helps."

"I doubt anything will help this."

"I'll try." The words popped out.

She handed him the phone. "Thanks. I'll use the clinic's phone for now."

Sam stood there, holding her dead cell phone, unsure of what to say next.

"Thanks for helping me with the kittens," she continued. "Sorry you got wet, and your patrol car is drenched, too."

"It's part of the job." Sam didn't know what else to say.

"You do it well. Oh, welcome back to Berry Lake, Sam."

The way his name rolled off her tongue would have made his younger self do a happy dance and think he had a chance. Adult Sam knew better. "Thanks."

Missy Hanford was an adult, a widow, nothing like the girl he'd crushed on through high school and beyond. Sam had never heard her say no to anything Rob said or asked. The Missy of Sam's fantasy had been sweet and demure and the perfect girlfriend. That Missy would have let Sam take her to the hospital, not put the health of a kitten litter ahead of her own. She was different than he'd expected, but he preferred the stronger, more self-sufficient Missy than the one in his head.

Sam should have known she wouldn't be the same. He'd learned daydreams were a long way from reality. Especially teenage ones. Best to forget about them.

Still, Rob had been a friend. If Missy needed Sam, he would be there for her now that he was back in town.

Sam straightened. "If you need anything..."

"I'm good. After I call Sabine, who must almost be home by now, I need to track down the mama cat. And I'm sure Jenny must be freaking out if she noticed I'm gone. One of them will give me a ride to my car."

That wasn't what Sam had meant, but he got the point. He was being dismissed. That shouldn't bother him as much as it did. "Take care of yourself and those cuts. See if they have dry clothes you can borrow."

Man, he sounded like his mom. But something about Missy brought out Sam's protective instincts, which went beyond doing his duty.

"Will do." Her soft, closed smile shot straight into his heart. "Be careful out there. And take care of yourself."

"Always." Sam would, but he didn't have to worry.

The most dangerous call he'd faced, other than the one in Seattle that changed his life, was tonight's with her. That meant the safest thing he could do was stay far, far away from Missy Hanford in the future.

And then Sam remembered what he held in his hand—her cell phone. He'd offered to stick it in rice.

So much for staying away from Missy.

Now, he would have to return her phone at some point.

At least it shouldn't take long, right?

☕ chapter seven ☕

AN ALARM BLARED, slamming into Missy's brain like a sledgehammer.

Forget opening her eyes. Instead, she squeezed them tighter. It was the principle of the matter. She needed more sleep after such a late night.

With her eyes still shut, Missy reached for the nightstand. She'd done this enough times to know exactly where her phone would be. Her palm hit wood.

Where was her phone?

And then she remembered.

Kittens. The rain. Sam Cooper.

He had her phone. It hadn't turned on, and he'd mentioned some trick with rice to see if that would dry it out.

Well, that explained the earsplitting noise, which continued blaring. The alarm clock was much louder than her phone alarm.

A headache erupted, as if the sledgehammer had left a bruise right in the middle of her forehead.

Not how she wanted to start her morning.

She tapped her hand around the nightstand to find the clock.

Her palm hit Elise's journal. Missy's box of tissues. And...
Something plopped against the carpet. Most likely a pen or nail
clippers.

The alarm continued. Battery-operated bunnies weren't the
only thing that kept going and going.

Enough. Missy opened her eyes and zeroed in on Rob's
old-school digital clock, which sat on the opposite end of the
nightstand at the edge. No wonder she hadn't found it.

She glanced at the green numbers.

Whoa. Missy did a double take. After nine?

She was usually up by six. If not, the cats would paw or knead
her until she woke, unless they were tired, too.

Two tired cats and one exhausted cat mom who set the alarm
wrong would explain what had happened.

Not surprising when she relied on her phone to wake up.
Unlike Rob, who used to set three different alarms to make sure
he was never late. She couldn't remember the last time she'd used
his clock before last night.

But man, that noise was killing her.

She hit the off button.

"Meow." Lying on the dresser, Peach stretched, looking more
like Cleopatra than a domesticated feline. A spoiled one at that.

"I know. Mommy slept in. And you're ready to eat." Her cats
were always hungry, except for the few minutes right after they ate.

Missy pushed herself up. The sheet and the blanket fell onto
her lap. Her muscles tightened—ached.

She stretched her arms over her head. *Ouch.* That hurt, too.
What was going on?

The fall into the recycling bin shouldn't have made her that sore, but her body wasn't used to physical activity. She'd been taking it way too easy since the fire. That was what the doctor recommended, and Jenny made sure Missy complied.

Jenny would ground Missy if she could.

Missy swung her feet over the edge of the bed. A neon-green sock covered her burned foot. That wasn't the one she'd worn last night with her slipper. She rubbed her temples.

She didn't remember putting on a clean sock last night. Dare had picked Missy up at the clinic, driven her to her car, and followed her home. She'd checked the cats, showered, and changed into new pajamas. She must have put on the sock right before crawling into bed.

Peach meowed again.

"Patience, your highness."

Missy's sore body needed to catch up with what her mind wanted her to do. She took a breath, held it for five seconds, and exhaled. She repeated that exercise five times. Selena had told Missy to do that each morning, but she'd forgotten why.

"I'll get your breakfast now."

As she stood, a familiar pain ripped through her foot. Not as bad as it could have been after the night Missy had and definitely better than when she'd first come home from the hospital in September.

She would take it as a win.

Mario stood in the doorway, using his ninja stealth skills to seemingly appear out of nowhere. His thick tail stood upright, and his jade-green eyes met hers. He didn't meow, but he beamed "Feed me now, feed me now before I waste away to nothing" vibes.

"On my way."

His whiskers twitched as if he didn't believe her.

A smile tugged at her lips. No matter how down she got, her two fur babies made life better. They also ruled the house. Missy didn't mind. "I promise. You won't starve."

A few minutes later in the kitchen, the cats gobbled their breakfast. Missy brewed coffee. The caffeine would help her wake up.

"We're going to have company later today or tomorrow. I told the kittens I would foster them. You two might get jealous, but they'll only be here for a few weeks, so be nice."

Both cats meowed.

Her stomach growled. Food would be good, except cooking didn't interest her. A glance around the kitchen provided the perfect solution.

She looked at the ceiling. "This is for you, Elise."

Missy removed a vanilla cupcake from the plastic container where she'd stored the latest batch, peeled the liner from one side, and bit into the white buttercream icing.

Yum.

Missy closed her eyes.

Her tongue did a happy dance thanks to the sugary goodness of the buttercream frosting tickling her tastebuds.

So good.

"And vanilla." Elise would be swearing if she heard Missy.

She finished the cupcake and considered eating another.

Peach tilted her head with an I-see-what-you're-doing expression.

"Stop. You don't get to judge me."

Missy faced enough judgment from others. Oh, they didn't think she heard the "crazy cat lady" or "depressed widow" or "pathetic loser living off her rich sister-in-law" mumbled comments, but she did. Okay, the last one may not have been words so much as glares she'd interpreted.

"Cupcakes share the same ingredients as many breakfast dishes. Flour, eggs, milk…"

The thought brought a rush of warmth, reminding her of how each year Mom had let Missy have cake for breakfast on the day after her birthday. Back before she'd disappointed them by marrying Rob. Still, those birthday cake memories were good ones. The rest…

Their loss.

Mario rubbed against her leg.

She rubbed under his chin. "I love you, sweet boy. But it's too soon for a treat."

And she should save the second cupcake until after lunch, or she would crash from the sugar high.

Missy poured herself a cup of coffee. The kitchen was still spotless from after the inspection. She wanted to keep everything clean for when they were approved for the cottage food permit.

When, not if.

The certificate from the state of Washington to allow her to bake cupcakes in her kitchen and sell them to customers should arrive in a few weeks.

Selena T was rubbing off on her.

"See," Missy said to the cats. "Mommy isn't too old to learn new things. I'll drink my coffee and then prepare the office for the kittens."

The office, the cottage's second bedroom, fit a desk and a twin bed. Well, if she needed a guest room, which she didn't. So only a desk was in there. That was where she'd worked when she'd been Jenny's PA. Dare had taken over that job when Missy became manager of the cupcake shop.

She kept the room clean in case Sabine needed a place for a foster animal, but that didn't stop her from wiping every surface and vacuuming. In the past, she'd put an X-pen around the desk, but she didn't use the desk much these days. A furniture-free space would be safer for the kittens. She had room for it in the living room if she rearranged stuff.

With a plan in mind, she placed the computer and this month's bills on the chair and rolled everything into the kitchen. She returned to the desk and lifted one side.

Well, tried.

She could only lift it an inch if that.

Missy glanced at her stupid foot in the green sock. *Okay, so this might be a problem.*

Except she had no phone to call Jenny and Dare for help.

Suck it up, Hanford.

Rob's voice circled in her head, giving her the willpower to try.

She moved one side a few inches. Okay, three. Then she went to the opposite side and did the same. Back and forth, inch by inch. It might take time, but this would work, albeit slowly.

A knock sounded.

Relief poured off her like the sweat dripping down her back. "Must be Jenny. She can call Dare, and we'll have this thing moved before Sabine arrives with the kittens."

Missy limped to the living room and opened the front door. Her mouth gaped.

Not Jenny.

She stared in disbelief.

Sam Cooper stood on her front porch. Not Deputy Cooper in his tan uniform and raincoat like last night. This Sam wore a burgundy Henley, faded jeans, and a brown jacket. His hair was damp, suggesting it was raining. And he looked better than a cupcake. "Hi."

The one word swirled around her like a big hug. That was weird. Missy clutched the doorknob. "Um, hi."

His gaze narrowed. "Did I wake you?"

She glanced at her pajamas and one sock.

Oops.

Heat pooled in her cheeks. "No. This is how I dress at home. I stayed with Jenny and Dare after I got out of the hospital, so they're used to it."

He glanced at her foot. "I heard about the fire. Should you be on your foot?"

"I'm okay. I usually take it easy, but last night..."

"The kittens."

"Exactly, but I change when I go out."

"Except for last night."

Right. She nodded.

"I like it," he said. "Pajama chic."

She laughed. "Not so chic but definitely pajama comfy."

"Beats my uniform."

"Don't say that. You look...er." Missy caught herself.

She was about to say how attractive he looked. One hundred percent true, but he left her feeling off-center. She didn't want him to take the compliment the wrong way. Not that he would, but...

Is it hot in here?

She would try again. "The sheriff's department uniforms look great on...people."

That was better, but what was happening? Sure, Missy said the wrong thing at times. Everybody did. But she'd never been tongue-tied like this.

"Thanks." A slow grin spread across his handsome face. "Too bad the uniforms are the antithesis of comfy."

"Yeah." His smile put her at ease. "But the bad guys wouldn't take you seriously if you wore PJs."

"That's true." Sam held up a shopping bag she hadn't noticed before. As he removed a plastic bin with a lid, something rattled inside. "This is for you. Your phone's covered with rice. Might take a couple of days before you know whether it dries out enough, but worth a try?"

Sam Cooper was Mr. Unexpected today. Missy appreciated his thoughtfulness. And it wasn't only because she couldn't afford to replace her phone, which had been a gift from Jenny for Missy's birthday last year. "Thanks."

"Do you have a landline?"

"Nope."

He pulled out a box and handed it to her. "Good thing I brought this for you."

For her? Missy took a closer look. Her gaze shot to his. "You bought me a cell phone?"

With a wry grin, Sam rocked back on his heels. "It's a Tracfone. Cheap and practical. You need something in case of an emergency and to keep in touch with your friends until yours works again or you replace it."

Missy's vision blurred. She didn't want to cry, so she glanced up and blinked. Twice. She opened her mouth to tell him how sweet he was, but the lump in her throat kept her from speaking. She swallowed and tried again. "Thank you."

"You're welcome."

Their gazes met again. His eyes were so blue, not dark like Berry Lake, but lighter like an aquamarine. Only this time, something passed between them. Something she'd felt with only one other man, whose birthstone happened to be an aquamarine.

Rob.

Oh, no. She shouldn't be thinking about another man's eyes like that.

Missy focused on the box to keep from staring at Sam Cooper.

"It doesn't have a lot of features," he said.

"This is all I need." The space behind her eyelids heated. She blinked. "But you didn't have to do this."

"I wanted to. Ava and Hope would be lost without their phones."

His sister and sister-in-law. That clarified the situation. Missy was reading way more into his kind gesture, a brotherly gesture. Sam was the youngest of the Cooper siblings, so not a big brother. If Missy remembered correctly, he was younger than her, too. But a deputy would have a protective instinct given his job. Buying a phone for her made sense in that light.

Of course, it did.

Someone as gorgeous as Sam wouldn't be interested in…

Missy smiled at him. "I appreciate it."

"Good."

"Yes, good. Berry Lake got lucky when they hired you. And I got lucky when you responded to the market."

I got lucky…

She cringed. Heat flew up her neck and flooded her face, which must be beet red. "I mean—"

Laughter lit his eyes, and at that moment, her breath caught. "I know what you mean."

That made one of them. She wanted to bolt. Except where would she go since she was home, in her pajamas, wearing one sock, with tangled hair because she hadn't dried her wet hair before falling asleep?

She clutched the phone box to her chest as if it were a shield to protect her. Not from Sam, who meant no harm, but from herself. "I'd invite you in, but I need to get the office ready for the kittens. Sabine's dropping them off with the mama cat."

"You found the mom?"

"Sabine and Max did. They used a trap. I'm so relieved because I won't need to do round-the-clock feedings, but I'll have to make sure all the kittens get enough. Runts often don't."

"Sounds tiring."

"It can be, but the kittens are so cute." Missy held back a sigh. "Though they almost always try to get into trouble. That's why I'm kitten-proofing my office right now."

"Need help?"

She did, but... "Don't you have to go to work or be somewhere?"

Like to his girlfriend's place or home to his wife... A glance at his finger showed no ring or tan line. That only ramped up her tension.

"I work the swing shift. I have time."

Turning him away now would be rude, so she opened the door wider. "I've been moving the desk out of the office, and it's going so slow."

"I can get it myself."

Missy eyed his biceps. Even though his jacket covered them, she remembered his muscular arms holding her last night.

That was something she couldn't recall when she'd been unconscious and rescued from the fire by a paramedic in September. She guessed Welles Riggs must have nice muscles like Sam.

At least, she was batting two for two. Two different rescues. Two different rescuers who had both been good-looking knights, though instead of shining armor they each wore uniforms.

"Yes, but it'll be easier with both of us." She didn't want someone else having to take care of her.

Sam opened his mouth as if he wanted to disagree.

Missy wouldn't give him a chance. She squeezed through the opening between the office's doorframe and the desk. "I'll take this side."

He said nothing, but the expression in his eyes spoke volumes.

"Got a question?" she asked.

"Where do you want the desk?"

Oh, right. She hadn't thought beyond out of the bedroom. "In the living room. Wherever it won't be in the way."

"Got it."

She hoped so since his side would reach there first.

"On three," he said. "One, two, three."

Missy lifted her side. Oh, man. The thing was heavier than she imagined.

"Okay?" Sam asked.

Don't drop it. Do. Not. Drop. It.

She nodded, fighting the urge to grimace and groan. Moving the desk with his help took more effort, but it also went faster. They got the desk out of the doorway.

Missy set her side down to push the hair out of her face. Her muscles cheered at not having to hold the weight.

"Do you need a break?" he asked.

Yes, but she wouldn't dare admit that. "I'm good, and we're just about done."

"We should find a place for the desk." He motioned to her foot. "You're still recovering."

"I am, but I'm not an invalid."

His hands shot up. "Didn't say you were, but last night couldn't have been easy on your burns."

No doubt his family had filled Sam in on the fire. It seemed to be on everyone's mind. "It wasn't, but sometimes you must do the hard thing. Elise always used to say that when trying to pick between her favorite cupcake flavors."

"She was a character."

Not trusting her voice, Missy nodded. Her pulse sped up.

Sam studied her and went into the living room.

She used the moment to take a deep breath. As soon as her breathing settled, she followed him.

"If you move the couch, you won't be able to see the TV." He walked around the coffee table. "I'd move the chair. Put the desk in its place."

Missy was aware of his every move. She needed space. That meant getting the desk moved and Sam out of there. "Sure. Let's do that."

They did.

Surprisingly, the desk fit in the space, and the chair looked good sitting at the corner of the throw rug.

He pointed to the couch. "Sit for a minute."

"I'm fine."

"You're breathing a little hard."

That most likely had more to do with him than exertion. But she didn't want him to know that. Missy sat.

"What else do you need?"

Besides him to leave? Except that wasn't what he meant. "There are boxes of supplies on the closet shelf. Oh, and a cat bed. I have a step stool—"

"I'll get them." With that, he went into the office.

Her foot throbbed. She placed it on the coffee table.

That was better.

Sam returned to the living room. "Everything's ready for you."

"Thanks. I really don't know how to repay you."

"Cupcakes."

She startled. "Excuse me?"

"You make the best cupcakes around."

"You haven't been into the shop." Missy tried to remember the last time she saw him there. "It's been a long time."

"I moved to Seattle after I graduated college."

"It was before that."

He shrugged. "My mom always bought a dozen whenever I came home."

Mrs. Cooper loved talking about her kids, though Josh's drinking problem had aged the woman ten years. "She was one of our best customers."

"And will be when you open again."

From your mouth to God's ears. Missy crossed her fingers.

"So…?" Sam asked.

She enjoyed seeing Sam so playful. That wasn't how she pictured police officers. He'd been more serious last night.

Probably because he was on duty then. "What flavors would you like?"

"Surprise me."

"You realize that's a dangerous option to give a baker who's been spending her days brainstorming new ideas for the menu. Some of which aren't as good as others."

His lips slid into a lopsided grin. "I trust you."

She nearly laughed. Whether or not Sam Cooper realized it, he'd issued her a challenge. Missy would not disappoint him.

chapter eight

THE NEXT DAY, Bria stood at the door to room 313. Once again, the door was ajar. Unlike yesterday, when she hadn't known what to expect, her heart lodged itself in her throat. Where it had been since realizing who the woman in the bed was. Bria's fingers clutched the gift bag handles.

"We don't have to go in," Dalton whispered. "She doesn't know we're here."

True, but... "I need to say goodbye."

Something two-year-old Bria had never gotten the chance to do. Oh, she might have said the word, but a child wouldn't have understood the meaning at that moment. Bria had trouble understanding it now.

She peeked through the crack in the door.

Molly sat with her legs crossed on the bed.

Aunt Elise had called it crisscross applesauce whenever Bria sat on the carpet that way.

Molly didn't appear to notice them. She focused on whatever was outside her window.

Bria knocked lightly on the door. "Can we come in?"

Molly swiveled toward the doorway, but she said nothing. She ran her thumbs over her fingertips.

Back and forth. Back and forth.

Bria took a cautious step toward the bed. "Hello."

Molly stared.

That was a good sign, right? "I'm Bria."

"Pretty name."

Molly didn't appear to recognize her. The nurse had said that would be the case, but Bria had hoped she would be different.

She swallowed around the lump in her throat. "What's your name?"

"Mol."

"Nice to meet you."

Molly's gaze zeroed in on the gift bag. "For me."

It wasn't a question. Bria came closer to the bed. "Yes, it's for you."

Dalton came up behind her.

Molly's gaze flicked up to him, but she didn't appear to recognize him either. Her calling him Paul seemed to be forgotten, too.

Bria handed her the bag.

Molly tore into the tissue paper, sending pieces flying. She pulled out a rainbow-colored unicorn with a shimmery silver horn. "Pretty."

"I hope you like it."

Molly clutched the stuffed animal to her chest. "Mine."

Her childlike actions and words broke Bria's heart even more. But she kept a smile on her face. "Yes."

"It's all yours," Dalton said a beat after Bria.

Molly's gaze narrowed on him. "Who you?"

"I'm Dalton," he said.

Bria glanced at him and then looked at Molly, who had an unreadable expression on her face. "Dalton helped me pick out your unicorn."

"Oh." Molly touched the unicorn's horn, scrutinizing the stuffy like a scientist analyzing a slide under a microscope. She completely ignored them, making Bria wonder if she had forgotten they were there. "You go. I play." Molly didn't glance their way.

The lump in Bria's throat quadrupled in size—burned.

"Okay." She forced the word out. "Nice to meet you."

Molly moved the unicorn across the bed.

If Bria expected a thank you, it wasn't happening.

What had happened to Molly? Possibly a brain injury or illness of some sort. Bria didn't need a release form to realize that. She only hoped Dad had done all he could for the woman who'd given birth to Bria.

Molly bounced the unicorn on her pillow. She giggled like a toddler or preschooler, not a woman in the prime of her life like Charlene and Sabine. No matter what Molly Landon had done to end up there like that, Bria fought a wave of sadness.

"Let's go home," Dalton whispered.

Bria nodded, but she had one more thing to say. "Goodbye, Molly."

Molly continued playing as if she were in the room alone.

Bria hurried and headed straight to the elevator. "That went better than last night."

"Much better. No screaming."

Bria glanced over her shoulder toward the room. "She didn't remember us. The nurse warned us, but I hoped…"

"You'd be different."

She nodded, and her chest tightened. "We were here less than ten hours ago. I thought maybe she'd remember… What kind of mother forgets her daughter? Though I didn't remember her."

"You were two years old. I barely remember elementary school."

She nodded, but that didn't erase the hurt. "I'm not sure which is worse. Believing my mom walked away from me and never cared enough to contact me or that she was injured and *couldn't*, and Dad knew but kept that from me."

Her eyes stung. No crying. Not over this. At least not until she learned more.

Bria punched the elevator's down button. "I need a minute."

"Take however long you need."

The silence in the lobby didn't help. Bria wasn't sure how she was supposed to feel—angry, disappointed, frustrated, numb?

On the way out the door, Bria stopped at the receptionist's desk, where Lauren sat.

"Can I give you my phone number?" Bria asked. "I'm not a contact, but my father's unavailable if you or Molly need anything."

Lauren handed her a sticky note and pen. "Once the release form is signed, I can add your number to Molly's file."

Bria wrote her name, number, and email address. She returned both the note and the pen. "Thanks."

Lauren beamed. "I hope we see you and Brian soon."

"Thank you for taking care of Molly."

"That's our mission here at Cliffside Manor. To care for our guests like they're family members." Lauren didn't hesitate to answer. "Moving into an assisted-living or care facility is so difficult, but it can be the best decision in the long term. We're here, so families don't have to worry about their loved ones."

"Thank you." Bria didn't know what else to say. Because Molly might be family on paper, but not in real life. Molly Landon was a stranger, someone Bria felt sorry for, but no hidden memories had surfaced; no love came to the forefront that made her want to stay. She wanted to leave and never return.

What did that say about her?

Bria didn't want to know the answer.

Dalton laced his fingers with hers. Hand in hand, they walked out to the parking lot. "What's on your mind?"

"How did my dad deal with seeing Molly and not being recognized? If every date night, he had to introduce himself to her all over again?"

"More questions you can ask him when you visit on Thursday."

"Unless they drop the charges sooner." She hoped they would so she could talk to Dad before that. A coincidence, but it was strange how the staff mentioned his date nights with Molly and visiting day at the jail were both on Thursdays. If he needed money for Molly's care, that would explain what he did to Aunt Elise with the cupcake shop, but he had so much to explain. "Can we go home now?"

"Yes." Dalton brushed his lips over hers. "And I want you to sleep on the drive home. I doubt you got much sleep last night."

"I must look awful."

"You're beautiful. But every time you yawn, I yawn. It's got to stop, or I'll need a nap halfway through the drive home."

"So you want me to sleep for you?"

"For you," Dalton admitted. "I was using reverse psychology."

"Tricky, Mr. Dwyer."

"I learned from the best." Dalton winked. "My tricky and sly mom."

The drive back to Berry Lake went faster than the one to Wishing Bay yesterday. Bria was thankful for that. Despite Dalton wanting her to sleep, she couldn't. Too many thoughts about Dad and Molly kept her brain from slowing down.

Bria typed a message to the group chat. She wasn't ready to discuss what had happened, but she wanted to tell her friends. She reread it.

> **BRIA:** *On my way home from Wishing Bay. My dad sent me to pay for a room at an assisted-living center for Molly Landon, my mom. It looks like she has a TBI. She didn't know who I was. Today, she didn't remember me. I'm silencing my phone. Be in touch tomorrow.*

Bria hit *send*.

It was done.

She silenced her phone and tucked it inside her purse.

"Tell your friends?" Dalton asked.

"Yes, but I said I wouldn't be in touch until tomorrow."

He held her hand. "You decide the timing. Wait until you're ready."

"I will." She slid her fingers between his, not wanting to let go of him for a second. She would rather hold his hand than sleep.

"Are you hungry? Thirsty?"

"I'm fine." Thanks to him.

Could Bria have survived the past thirty-odd hours without him?

Yes, but she wouldn't have wanted to. "I've thanked you…"

"A hundred times."

"More like twenty."

He raised her hand to his mouth and kissed the top of it. "Twenty-eight if you want to get technical."

"You did not count."

He laughed, lowering her hand. "No, but I appreciate every single one. Next time I'll keep a tally."

"I hope we never go through something like this again."

"Same."

Aunt Elise's one-story house came into view. Warmth washed over Bria. "Home."

If she'd ever doubted where home was, she no longer did.

Dalton pulled behind Bria's car in the driveway. His car idled. "Want me to come in?"

"Thanks but go home." She tried for a kind tone but wasn't sure she succeeded.

Bria had an interview tomorrow and wanted to touch base with Marc Carpenter about the alibi and ask if he would get Dad to sign the release form ASAP. She also wanted to give Dalton a break. Her emotions kept wanting to drag her out to sea like one of the coast's infamous sneaker waves. Time apart would be good for both of them.

"Tanner let you off today, but you don't need to waste another vacation day."

"Not a waste."

"No, but my guess is the Posse wants to get together."

"You need your friends."

"I need my friends and *you*." She emphasized the last part. "Besides, if you go now, you might miss the worst of the rush hour traffic."

Portland was a little over an hour and a half from Berry Lake. Afternoon traffic across the bridges backed up for miles. He'd driven enough the last two days.

"Call me later," he said. "If you want me to come back—"

"I'll call you tonight." Bria didn't want him to make plans to return later. She appreciated him being with her, but he had a life to live. One beyond them being in love. "I will want you with me when I talk to my dad."

"Of course." Dalton squeezed her hand. "Do you want me to talk to my mom?"

"Not yet. Let's see what my dad has to say first. Your mom might not know what happened back then."

"I'd like to believe that's true, but my mom is as connected to the rumor mill as Charlene Culpepper. Except I believe Mom's the one who starts them. What happened with Sheridan clued me in on that."

Bria hadn't seen Deena in decades, but the woman seemed to have gotten worse over the years. And what she'd said about Sheridan, her new stepdaughter... "All lies."

"Ones that hurt Sheridan."

"True, but she landed on her feet and is now engaged to a multimillionaire. Your mom lost big time with how that one turned out."

"Mom reminds me of a cockroach. Nothing can kill them. And they'll be the last ones standing long after we're all gone."

Poor cockroaches. Some might be offended to be lumped in with the infamous Deena currently-DeMarco. "That's the perfect analogy."

"Have everything?"

She grabbed her purse. The inn had given them each a toiletry kit, so at least she'd been able to brush her teeth, shower, and comb her hair. "Yes."

Dalton reached behind his seat, pulled up a small paper bag, and handed it to her. "You forgot this."

She glanced inside. Laughed. "Saltwater taffy. Thanks."

"I hope each bite is as sweet as your kisses."

"Keep it up, and you'll be giving Aunt Elise a run for her money with your sayings." Bria leaned over the console between the seats and kissed him. "I'll talk to you later."

"I love you."

"Love you." So much. Affection overflowed from her heart.

"Get inside, or we'll spend an hour saying goodbye."

Dalton wasn't wrong. Purse and taffy in hand, Bria slid from the car and closed the door. She waved.

He blew her a kiss.

She caught it, touched her lips, and headed to the porch. As soon as she opened the front door, Dalton backed out. She waved again before entering and shutting the door behind her.

She took two steps and stopped. "Lulu?"

No bark or paws against the hardwood floor sounded.

A glance at the sofa showed Butterscotch on one cushion. Not the back where he usually slept so the dog wouldn't disturb him.

Bria placed her purse and the taffy on the coffee table. "Hey, Butterscotch."

The cat didn't raise his head. Not untypical, but...

Bria glanced around. "Juliet?"

Footsteps sounded.

Bria released the breath she'd been holding.

"Hey." Juliet came into the living room. She wore a pink skirt and coordinating jacket, but her feet were bare. "I saw your message. When you're ready to talk, I'm here."

"Thanks. I'd love a hug."

"That's a given." Juliet hugged her. "We're all here for you."

"Thanks." Bria stepped away. "You're pretty in pink."

"Baby shower. It's a girl. And the mother-to-be loves pink." Juliet laughed, a melodic cartoon princess laugh. "She said I looked like a real-life Barbie doll."

Bria studied her roommate and friend. "You do. Especially if you wore pink pumps."

"I did. However, I prefer Princess Barbie. Should have worn one of my tiaras."

The two laughed.

Bria realized someone was still missing. "Is Lulu outside?"

Juliet's smile disappeared.

Oh, no. Bria recognize the lines around Juliet's face. "What?"

"Lulu's been at the Berry Lake Animal Clinic since yesterday. They thought she'd be ready to come home today, but the vet called and said they wanted to keep her for one more night."

The vet? Talk about a worst nightmare. Bria reached out to Juliet. "Roman?"

"Dr. Goya. Roman said Lulu was in capable hands." Juliet glanced at Butterscotch. "The cat's the only one who's happy about the quiet."

Bria's chest hurt. She'd fallen in love with the little dog. "Is there a prognosis?"

"Disc space narrowing. Lulu will need to rest and be on meds for pain relief and inflammation. It might take time to show improvement, but Dr. Goya didn't recommend surgery. At least not yet."

"That's a good sign."

Juliet blew out a breath. "Yes, but I haven't called Mrs. Vernon. I should, but I wanted to make sure I had all the info, or she'll worry. Selena's paying for everything, so Lulu is getting the best possible care, but—"

"You feel as if you let Mrs. Vernon down."

Juliet's lips parted, and her eyes widened. "How did you know?"

"Because that's how you are." Bria loved how Juliet showed her emotions now that she was free of Ezra. "Am I wrong?"

"No."

"Well, I'm not a vet, but you haven't had Lulu that long." Bria wanted to put Juliet at ease. "She's also old, and disc narrowing sounds like something that happens over time."

"You're not wrong."

"But waiting until you have all the information to call Mrs. Vernon is smart. There's nothing for her to do now except worry." Bria hoped Juliet didn't feel bad." Which you've probably done enough for all of us."

A contrite expression crossed Juliet's face. "That's why I didn't post to the group chat. I didn't want any of you to worry. I thought you were on a romantic beach getaway, not…"

"We were both protecting everyone else."

Juliet nodded. "It made sense yesterday. But now, I want to spill everything, including Roman telling me yesterday he wants to be friends."

"Wait." Something didn't make sense. Bria rubbed her temples. "He lives next door. I thought you were friends, and that's how things started."

"Me, too. But apparently, Roman put me directly into the girlfriend slot, but we can save that discussion for later. Nell knows because she called last night, but I'm still processing it all."

"I get it." It was time for Bria to come clean. "That's why I didn't post to the chat until the drive home."

"You might need more time."

"Like the rest of my life." Bria laughed because that was better than crying. "I'm ninety-nine point nine percent sure my mother wrote the letter we found. She was in love with Paul like the author of the letter was. He got Deena pregnant and agreed to marry her like the letter mentions. It all fits."

"I have so many questions, but I'll wait until the Posse is all together."

"Thank you."

Juliet picked up her cell phone. "I'm taking your lead and posting about Lulu and Roman, but I'll tell everyone we can talk tomorrow."

"Be sure to silence notifications."

"I will." Juliet fiddled with her settings. "And then, I have an idea."

"Should I be afraid?" Bria tried to lighten the mood.

"Not really, but your waist and hips won't be happy."

Bria perked up. "The Burger Barn?"

"My treat." Juliet rubbed her chin. Her eyes lit up. "We're splurging on onion rings *and* French fries. And we'll eat in front of the TV and watch *Enchanted*."

Bria pointed to the bag on the table. "And have saltwater taffy for dessert."

"Perfect."

They might not forget their troubles, but they would escape them together for a few hours. Bria couldn't wait.

"Put on your shoes, Princess Barbie." She picked up her purse. "If you're buying, I'm driving."

chapter nine

AT THE ICE arena in Seattle, Selena waited in the family room with the wives and girlfriends of the other players. The women stood or sat in small groups, talking but sending judgmental smiles and glances at others not in their circle.

Selena nearly laughed.

The Seattle Volcanoes were no different than any other team in the league. Oh, to the public and press, everyone was one happy family, but behind the closed doors, in here, the cliques were as strong as in middle school cafeterias.

But one thing drew them together, even if some would never admit it—what it meant to love a professional hockey player. And now, they each waited, wanting a few minutes to say goodbye to their loved one before the team left on an extended road trip.

Again.

Something inside her chest ached.

She shook it off.

Her life was...

Not perfect.

That wouldn't happen until Logan finally retired, something that kept getting pushed off. Each year he'd said this was the final season. But the older he got—and he was one of the oldest players in the league—the better he seemed to play. Tonight's game had been no exception for the defenseman, who'd managed two assists.

But soon, Selena would have everything she'd been dreaming about—a house on Berry Lake, more than the off-season with her husband, and co-owning the cupcake shop with the Posse. She couldn't wait for it all to happen.

None would interfere with her personal development business. She loved being a life coach, but she'd stopped taking on new one-on-one clients in preparation for slowing down when he left the game. It had worked out in her favor. Launching classes and workshops at a variety of price points to help women get what they wanted out of life brought in new and more followers. And she would be eternally grateful for them trusting her to help them. They'd pushed her from making seven figures a year to eight. More than Logan's salary.

A baby cried.

Selena stiffened. She hadn't seen anyone with a little one in there.

Maybe they'd let her hold the baby.

Oh, she'd resigned herself to no kids in her twenties and moved on. But that didn't mean she didn't like babies. And seriously, holding one and then being able to give it back without taking on all the feeding, diapering, and sleepless nights was perfect.

She wandered farther into the room, saying hi to those women who caught her eye, and then...

In the far corner, as far away from the others as she could possibly get, stood a young woman who couldn't be more than twenty. She rocked a baby bundled with a Volcanoes blanket and wearing a tiny set of blue headphones. No doubt ear protection for the infant. The woman was pretty in a fresh-faced sorority girl kind of way and had long, straight brown hair. Her attention was focused on the baby as if no one else were around.

Not that anyone approached the pair.

The other women kept their distance.

That was awkward.

Selena moved toward the woman. Someone touched Selena's shoulder and stopped her.

"You don't want to go over there," Echo whispered, lowering her arm. "Puck bunny."

Puck bunnies were the bane of WAGs. But the groupies would probably say the same thing about the wives and girlfriends of the players. But this was the first puck bunny Selena had seen show up with an infant in tow. "Haven't noticed her before."

"Grable's fiancée. She's come to a couple of games, but she's never ventured down here. Takes some nerve to act like one of us."

"If they're engaged, she's one of us." Selena was only stating the obvious, but a sour expression crossed Echo's face.

"She trapped him." Echo was a supermodel who'd graced the cover of this year's swimsuit issue. She was forward Alek Ransom's latest girlfriend. "Can you believe Grable fell for it? Thought he was smarter since he went to one of those Ivy League schools."

"Grable *is* smart." Logan liked the guy, for what that was worth. "He owns a few businesses and—"

"He left his wife and kids for a baby who probably isn't even his and a woman who would have happily slept with any player on the team."

Talk about a lot of judgment to unpack. More on Echo than anyone else.

Grable wasn't as old as Logan, but he had to be a decade older than his fiancée. "If he didn't ask for a paternity test, I'm sure his agent and attorney did."

"Whatever." Echo rolled her eyes. "But he shouldn't have proposed and put that gigantic rock on her finger. Groupies will think getting pregnant is the way to steal our men."

Being one of the world's most beautiful women hadn't stopped Echo's insecurity. It was triggering her. Badly. But Selena didn't dole out soft and cuddly advice. That hadn't worked with her, and it didn't give her clients the results they needed. Hearing the bitter truth worked the best.

"Hate to break it to you, Echo, but groupies have been doing that from the beginning." Not just puck bunnies, but a few wives standing near them, too. "But not all ended up with a ring on their finger."

She didn't mention Grable's fiancée because she didn't know the story. And there was always a story, one from each party involved, so in this case, there would be three. Not that it was Selena's business or Echo's or anyone else's here.

But Selena wanted a closer look at Grable's baby. A boy if the blue headphones were anything to go by.

Echo flipped her hair behind her shoulder with a practiced flair. "Well, I'm going to have a no-cheating clause in the prenup. Any cheating negates the contract terms."

Selena startled. "I didn't know Alek had popped the question. Let me see the ring."

Echo's left arm swung behind her back. "Oh, Alek hasn't proposed yet, but it's only a matter of time. We're the perfect couple. Everyone says so. Imagine how cute our babies will be."

Echo sounded like Missy had when she was dating Rob in high school. Those were the days.

Unfortunately for the supermodel, Echo wasn't the first to believe she'd found true love with the forward, who was pretty-boy gorgeous. Selena understood Alek's appeal from an aesthetic point of view, but she preferred Logan's rugged handsomeness. He wouldn't win any sprints, but her husband was all muscle and pure strength, not to mention a hottie in and out of his uniform.

"Alek is a catch." Selena, however, didn't think the player was ready to be caught. "Logan loves the guy like a little brother."

Alek had stayed at their house a few times. So had other players, including a couple of them who'd been kicked out by their wives. It was funny how Logan didn't want any plants, pets, or kids, but he brought home enough stray hockey players that the house felt empty when it was only the two of them.

She'd gotten Logan to agree to let her have a succulent. Those were low-commitment plants, and she had a dozen of them now. Maybe they could discuss adopting a cat. Cats were lower maintenance than dogs, and a pet would make the house feel less empty when Logan was away. And she could bring a cat with her to Berry Lake when she visited. Selena stayed with Juliet and Bria. They wouldn't mind.

Players drifted into the room, some taking their significant others elsewhere for privacy.

Alek strutted up and kissed Echo on the lips. "I was on fire tonight."

Echo practically purred. "You always are."

"Your guy had quite the night, too. That's why the media have him surrounded. Logan will be a few," Alek said to Selena. "I loved the way the D-man handled the biscuit tonight. Now for him to light the lamp."

Echo's nose scrunched. "What?"

She must be new to hockey. Selena hoped Echo stuck around. The two made a stunning couple and would have gorgeous babies.

"Biscuit is another word for puck," Selena explained. "Light the lamp means to score a goal."

Realization dawned on Echo's face. "Oh, the light on the net goes on when that happens."

Alek tapped her nose. "Exactly. Come on, gorgeous."

Selena waved goodbye. The others left quickly.

Soon only she and the young woman with the baby remained.

Not saying anything made Selena feel like a mean girl. She hated cliques. Even though the Posse had been tight fifteen years ago—and now—they didn't exclude others. "What's your baby's name?"

The woman glanced up with wide eyes. "Murphy."

"Great name. Sounds like a future hockey player."

She nodded. "I'm Roxy."

"Selena."

"Everyone knows Selena T." The woman's voice wasn't as soft. "I've listened to your podcast a few times."

Selena didn't know if Roxy was complimenting the show or not, but that was Roxy's issue, not hers. "Thanks. I enjoy doing them. Can I see the baby?"

"You can hold him if you want."

"I'd love that." Selena took the infant and cuddled him against her chest. She inhaled the baby scent. This was...

Nice.

That was all it could be.

Murphy slept. She studied his little nose and pouty lips. "He's sweet."

"He has his moments." Roxy raised her chin. "I'm not a homewrecker."

Selena's gaze snapped up. "Did someone call you that?"

"No. I just... You're the only one who talked to me tonight. I didn't want you to think..."

"I don't know you, Roxy. And I'm not one for gossip." Murphy stirred. Selena rocked him back and forth. Something about this...

Do. Not. Go. There.

"I'd hoped the others would be like that. They don't say anything, not to my face, but I see it in their eyes. They whisper about me and Murphy like we don't belong."

"You have every right to be here."

"That's what Grable says." Roxy's slumped shoulders, however, didn't match her confident tone. "What is it with these guys wanting to go by their last names?"

"Just hockey players."

"I guess, or he likes Grable better than Clovis. But he's so smart. He should know a name doesn't make a man. His actions do."

"Maybe." Roxy was young, but Selena recognized an old soul.

"Give the others time," Selena said. "The season just started."

"You're as kind in real life as on the podcast. I wasn't sure if you would be."

"Thanks." Again, Selena wasn't sure if that was a compliment, but as long as Roxy allowed her to hold Murphy, Selena was content.

"Those other women will never accept me. I see the questions in their eyes, but they're too afraid to ask, too terrified of what I might know."

Selena had no idea what Roxy meant. "Know what?"

"If Grable is the only one on the team I've been with. Or if I've seen their husbands and boyfriends with other *puck bunnies* at the bars and clubs."

That would explain the hostility. "I never once thought about asking you."

"I know. I could tell." Roxy smiled, and her face lit up. Not pretty—beautiful. "You're also the only one brave enough to talk to me."

"Just being friendly, no bravery involved." Selena fought the urge to sing the lullaby Mom had sung to her. Man, she needed to ask Jenny and Dare O'Rourke if they needed a babysitter. Selena would need another baby fix soon.

"I'm not surprised you approached me."

"Why is that?"

"You're one of the few women who have nothing to worry about. Tremblay gets hit on all the time when the team goes out, but he never looks twice at anybody. He's a good guy. But you know that."

Hearing Roxy say that was...not unexpected. Selena trusted Logan. If she didn't, she wouldn't have stuck around. "I do, but it's nice to have the trust confirmed."

"Thanks for talking to me. It gets a little lonely."

The emotion in Roxy's voice hit hard. Selena struggled not to pull the young woman in for a group hug with Murphy. "Well, now you know someone who goes to the games."

Roxy's eyes gleamed. If she went out to the bars, she had to be twenty-one or have a fake ID, but she looked eighteen with tears about to fall and raw vulnerability on her face.

"I usually have an extra seat in case I bring a friend or Logan's sister is in town. If no one is there, you and Murphy are welcome to sit next to me."

Roxy straightened. "I-I'd love that. Thanks."

"Hey, babe." Logan stepped into the room. He wore a designer suit, silk tie, and leather shoes—his team travel clothes. "Whatcha got there?"

Selena showed him a sleeping Murphy. "I made two new friends tonight."

"Hey, Rox." Logan smiled. "Be careful with the kid. My wife has a thing for babies."

"It's true." Selena handed the baby to Roxy. "Thanks for letting me hold Murphy."

"Anytime." Roxy's gaze bounced from Selena to Logan. "Do you have any kids?"

"No," Selena and Logan said at the same time.

Their eyes met.

"I…" The dark, hollow space where her uterus used to lie expanded. Selena took a breath. "I can't have kids."

Roxy blushed. "Oh, I'm sorry. Open mouth, insert foot."

Selena laughed. "It's not the first time someone did that."

"I hope it's the last." The sincerity in Roxy's voice tightened Selena's throat. "To make up for my faux pas, you can hold

Murphy whenever you want, and I won't make you change his diapers."

"Deal." Selena glanced at Logan, who toyed with the ends of her hair. "Ready to go?"

"You read my mind again." He held her hand. "See you around, Roxy."

"Bye, Roxy." Selena followed him into the hallway.

Logan pulled her against him and kissed her. His soap-and-water scent tickled her nose. She leaned into him, letting the sensations take her far away from the space on the lower floor of the arena.

"You were the MVP in the game." She ran her palm along his suit jacket. "And I'm also awarding you the MVP in kissing."

"I aim to please."

"You don't disappoint."

He placed his arm around her and led her outside to where the team's bus idled. "I'm going to miss you so much."

"Same." It was always this way, only something felt different this time. "The season began a couple of weeks ago, and I'm ready for it to be over with."

"Shhhh. You'll jinx us. I want to make the playoffs."

That would keep the season going longer. "You always do."

"We've got an excellent chance if Ramson keeps scoring the way he has. Even Grable has turned it up a notch. And we're on a winning streak."

"Which explains the beard you're growing."

"Like I said, don't jinx it."

"I won't." Hockey players and their superstitions could fill volumes of books. "I decided not to stay in Seattle while you're away."

"Work?"

"No, Berry Lake." The house was beautiful but so big and barren when Logan was away. The succulents didn't need her. "I'm driving there tomorrow."

"Did something come up with the lake house?"

"No."

He smiled. "You miss your friends."

Not as much as she would miss him. "There's a lot going on with them."

"There usually is."

She laughed. "You're right. It's been crazy since Elise died. But I want to be there to help them."

"You're such a good helper." He brushed his mouth over Selena's hair. "I don't mind sharing you with your Posse."

"Good, because I have to do what I can."

"You give one hundred and ten percent of yourself to those you love."

"Hey, I give you one hundred and fifty percent."

He pulled her against him once again. "You do, and I wouldn't want any less of you."

When will you give me the same?

The question wanted to burst out, but she wouldn't say it. Marriage wasn't a quid pro quo. Couples keeping a list of who did what was a sure ticket to trouble. And she'd known a marriage with Logan meant hockey came first. During the season, he was on the road a lot. But Selena wanted to say goodbye to hockey forever, not only during the off-season when the specter of what was to come lingered over them.

That decision, however, was Logan's to make. She wouldn't push. That wouldn't be fair. Even if it meant putting their dreams on hold for yet another season. She would have to wait for his timing to align with hers. Even if the reality of that sucked, which it did.

He kissed her again. His warmth and earthy sensual taste made her want more.

Logan ran the side of his finger along her jawline. "Did I tell you I'm gonna miss you?"

"Yes, but I don't mind hearing it again." She kissed him.

"Get a room, Tremblay!" one of his teammates yelled.

"Gotta teach you single guys the secret to a lasting relationship," Logan chirped back, and then he gazed into her eyes. "I have to get on the bus."

A lump formed in her throat. Something that hadn't happened in… Selena couldn't remember the last time. She nodded.

"I'll text you when we arrive. It'll be late."

Another nod.

Her chest hurt, but she had no idea why. Selena had done this so many times. Too many times.

It was getting old. And the house would be silent when she arrived home.

He brushed his lips over hers. "I love you."

"Love you." She did. But talking to Roxy tonight brought home something Selena had known but hadn't wanted to admit. She was out of alignment with her values and who she was. It was against everything she taught her clients, students, and listeners. Yet, the truth was as clear as the players stepping into the bus or holding little Murphy the way she had a few minutes ago.

As Logan joined his teammates, he glanced over his shoulder and waved.

Selena waved back and turned to walk toward her car because she wasn't smiling.

Like Roxy, Selena was lonely.

Oh, she'd known that was the case, but until tonight, she hadn't admitted to herself how lonely she truly felt. How being in their big house alone filled her with dread and made saying goodbye to Logan that much harder.

And her feelings made a mockery of her mission, of Selena T.

If Selena took her own advice—the same she gave to thousands of listeners each week—she would do something to stop the feelings of loneliness. Going to Berry Lake would help. She'd visited her hometown multiple times since September. That should have clued her in to something being wrong.

Running away, however, wasn't the answer. Oh, Selena would still head east tomorrow. But she needed to face what was causing her to feel that way first. She had to accept that this was how life would be for the near-term, or change it.

The only question—what did that mean for the future?

Selena wasn't sure she wanted to know the answer.

🧁 chapter ten 🧁

ON WEDNESDAY NIGHT, Missy sat at her kitchen
table with Bria, Juliet, Nell, and Selena. Containers
of Italian food from Lago Bacca, a bottle of Chianti,
and two bottles of sparkling water filled the space between
their plates.

"We've hardly put a dent into the food," Missy said.

Selena, who'd ordered the meal, shrugged. "Leftovers are
always good."

Missy had a feeling Selena had intentionally ordered more
than necessary. Not that Missy was complaining. She'd been
living off frozen entrees and bagged salads for so long. Something
different would be nice. "Thanks for bringing dinner and coming
to me tonight."

"This is the future temporary home of the Berry Lake Cupcake
Shop, so it's the logical meeting place," Bria said, even though
she didn't sound as chipper as usual. But she smiled and put on
a good front.

Missy had hugged Bria extra-long when she arrived tonight. It was all Missy could do not to give her friend another hug now.

"And you have kittens," Juliet joked.

Selena nodded. "Once we heard you were fostering, no one wanted to go anywhere else."

"And they are so adorable." Nell practically purred. "I vote if kittens are in residence, we have all Posse gatherings here."

Bria, Juliet, and Selena raised their hands.

"It's unanimous," Nell announced.

Missy glanced at her friends. "Don't I get a vote?"

Selena winked. "Not when kittens are involved."

"Fine." Missy wasn't upset but relieved. She'd forgotten how much she enjoyed having company before Sam dropped by. Speaking of him... She'd left him a dozen cupcakes at the sheriff's department earlier. She hoped he enjoyed her putting a creative and personalized spin on his cupcakes. And yes, she might have gone overboard on the flavors, but she enjoyed being creative when she baked.

"What are you smiling about?" Nell asked.

"The kittens." Not a lie. The kittens and Sam were wrapped together in Missy's mind. She didn't think of one without the other. "They'll be here for several weeks, until they're ready to be adopted, and I can't wait to watch them grow."

"I'm just relieved everything worked out." Juliet raised her glass of Chianti. "I can't believe when Jenny called you were stuck in a recycle bin with the kittens."

"It all turned out well." But that was another experience Missy never wanted to relive. "My cuts are healing."

"And your foot?" Nell asked, always the nurse.

"Doing better. I see the doctor on Friday."

Missy had a feeling he wouldn't do much other than check her progress, but burns took time to heal, especially the ones on the sole of her foot.

"Anything else going on?" Selena asked.

Sam Cooper popped into Missy's mind, but there was nothing to tell. Her imagination had gotten carried away making up another reason he gave her a phone, which was weird because she hadn't daydreamed in forever. But he was only being kind to the Gold Star widow in town, and she didn't want them to read more into his actions.

Missy shook her head. "Just the kittens and checking my mail obsessively."

"Don't forget, the inspector said six weeks to hear back," Bria reminded.

"I searched, and a few have heard back sooner." Missy couldn't work until they had the permit, but getting paid wasn't her only concern. Having too much time on her hands wasn't healthy for her mental state. Even though she helped with Briley as much as she could, and the kittens would give Missy more to do now, she needed to bake.

Nell crossed her fingers. "I can't wait until we get the permit and for probate to close."

Selena raised her glass. "To the future owners of the Berry Lake Cupcake Shop."

The other women lifted their drinks.

"Cupcake Posse forever," Missy added.

They all drank.

"Who's next?" Missy asked.

"I'll go," Selena offered. "Not that there's much to tell. Logan's on another road trip, and I'm here."

"Is Logan considering retirement?" Nell asked.

"He hasn't mentioned it. I don't press, but during preseason, he was upset when some rookies called him old."

"Doesn't sound like he's ready," Bria said.

"He's playing well, so who knows?" Selena sounded resigned, not upset. Missy had never heard her that way. "But we're making plans for the Berry Lake house, and the five of us are together again, both of which I wouldn't have imagined happening two months ago, so I keep reminding myself whatever's meant to happen will, but in its own time, not mine."

That was the Selena T side of her coming out. It surprised Missy to be concerned about Selena. The woman always had everything under control, living her best life and helping others do the same.

"Must be hard to be apart so much," Juliet said.

Selena hesitated. "I'm not going to lie. That big house gets lonely at times. But Logan was a professional hockey player while we dated. I knew what I was getting into. And this is just a season in our lives. He won't play hockey forever."

Missy had a feeling Selena would be happy when that day came. Missy had hated being apart from Rob when he had training exercises or deployed, but his dream had been to join the Marines. She'd supported that, even if it meant he'd come home in a box that she and Jenny had met at Dover Air Force Base.

Nell grabbed a breadstick. "I expect no less of an answer from Selena T. I, however, might not be as gracious if I were in your shoes."

"That's why Selena makes the big bucks," Missy joked.

Selena laughed. "I might have to see if Logan would be open to adopting a kitten."

Missy straightened. That would be awesome. She hadn't met Logan—Selena had left Berry Lake and not looked back until Elise's death—but Selena would be a wonderful cat mom. "You would have the pick of the litter. But I recommend adopting two. They do better in pairs."

"My stepmother has trained you well," Nell teased.

"Sabine is the master when it comes to animal rescue," Missy admitted. "But if you run a search, you'll find she's not the only one who suggests that."

"Enough about me. Who wants to go next?" Selena asked.

Juliet raised her hand. "I will."

"How's the friendship with Roman?" Missy asked.

"I guess it's going." Juliet's uncertainty matched her cloudy gaze. "So far, all our friendship means is that Katie comes over more. Sunday night, he was at work, but Katie let it slip he had a date on Monday."

"Who with?" Nell asked.

"No idea. I…" Juliet blew out a breath. "I don't want to know. It's clear Roman wants to get married. I don't know whether he wants it or if he thinks Katie needs a mom figure in her life, but I'm glad things ended. A friendship with a guy is all I can handle right now."

"I'm so happy you recognize it." Selena refilled her wineglass. "It's best to wait a year from the official date of a divorce before getting involved seriously. That doesn't mean you can't fall in love. You should. With yourself. After you spend every day for an entire year loving yourself, you'll be ready to date. You don't want to find your missing half. It's stronger when two whole people get together."

"I feel like we should play Selena T's theme song," Nell said, sounding a bit gobsmacked. "That's excellent advice, as usual."

Selena started to speak and then stopped herself. "Thanks. I don't mean to lecture you, Juliet. Occupational habit."

"Feel free to lecture me anytime." Juliet gave her best princess smile, the kind that made small animals and rodents want to do housework, or theme-park guests ask for autographs and photos. "I've made so many mistakes with Ezra. I want to do better if I meet someone else and give love another try."

"You'll get another shot. Maybe more than one." Selena didn't miss a beat. "When you're ready. Being ready is the most important piece. You can't rush the process or skip the steps, or you'll find yourself back in the same place that didn't make you happy. Fall in love with the beautiful, talented creation you are, and the rest will work out."

Juliet rubbed her face. "Thanks. I want to have as much belief in myself as you have in me."

Selena reached out to touch Juliet's hand. "You will. You're doing great. You've made so much progress so far."

Missy's heart sighed. The others appeared to be as touched. Why wouldn't they be?

Selena spoke the truth. Juliet was rebuilding the confidence Ezra had torn down. It was exciting to watch, even if the short-lived episode with Roman had brought tears and heartache.

"Enough about Dr. Byrne," Juliet said. "The big news is... Lulu came home yesterday."

Nell took another slice of the sauteed chicken breast with cream sauce and capers. "How's she doing?"

Juliet reached for a piece of garlic bread. "Lulu is on meds and doing much better. The only problem is she hates resting. The poor dog looks miserable in her crate, but her health is more important than playing right now."

Spoken like a true dog mom. Missy grinned.

"Don't forget the whining," Bria said.

Juliet sighed. "The whining! Lulu whines whenever Butterscotch jumps onto the couch where she likes to sit. I almost think the cat does it on purpose to irritate Lulu."

"Sounds like Welles," Nell added.

"Oh, what did Paramedic Welles do now?" Selena teased. "Invite you to Paris for a weekend?"

"I might say yes to Paris, but not for a weekend. The jet lag would be horrible."

"It is," Selena agreed. "So, spill what's happening, Nell, before we go on to Bria."

Bria sipped her wine.

"It isn't so much what Welles did, but what he didn't do. I introduced him to Gage. I thought they'd be perfect weekend warrior bros, but they want me to go with them."

"Two handsome guys wanting to hang out with you?" Missy scratched her chin. "I don't see the problem."

"The problem is Gage thinks I'm this extreme outdoor adventurer."

Juliet choked on the bread. She coughed. "If by extreme, you mean walking to your mailbox in the snow."

"And the path to her mailbox is covered," Missy added.

Nell held up her hands. "I admit it. I had high hopes for a Gage-Welles bromance. I wanted the two of them to do all the stuff that'll stop my heart. Literally. That way I could spend time with Gage enjoying less strenuous activities such as eating cupcakes and watching a Hallmark movie marathon. He's gorgeous, but I want to get to know him without my pulse racing, adrenaline pounding through me, and a prayer on my lips."

"It can't be that bad."

"We climbed a mountain. Okay, there was a trail, but at one point, it narrowed." Nell put her hands about a foot apart. "If Welles hadn't held on to my hand, I'd probably still be up there."

"Wait." Missy leaned forward.

She was the closest to Nell since they were the two who'd been in Berry Lake the longest and Nell had stopped by the cupcake shop almost daily after work. Juliet had moved back last December, and even then, Missy hadn't seen much of her except for an occasional visit to the cupcake shop. Nell joked around, but she wasn't one to exaggerate unless it was about her mom.

"Where was Gage?" Missy asked.

"Way ahead on the trail." Nell shook her head. "He doesn't like to go slow, so I'm always lagging behind."

"Gage doesn't sound like good boyfriend material," Bria said.

Juliet nodded. "He should care about you and your safety. Trust me, how a man treats you will only go downhill after you're married."

"Whoa." Nell raised her hands. "We're a long way from that. We're not dating, just hanging out. Welles just happens to always be there. We're like the Pacific Northwest version of the three musketeers. Instead of carrying swords, we wear backpacks."

"Make googly eyes over Gage all you want, but it's a good thing Welles was there if you were scared, and he made sure you didn't fall." That gave Missy a brilliant idea. "You should go out with him."

Four pairs of eyes stared at her. Nell's, however, bugged out.

"What?" Missy asked.

Lines creased Nell's forehead. "You want me to go out with Welles Riggs?"

Missy nodded. "He's handsome, a hero, and cares more about your feelings than gotta-get-there-the-fastest Gage."

Nell burst out laughing. She ended up doubling over.

Bria bit her lip. "Nell?"

"Should we call nine-one-one?" Juliet asked.

Missy shrugged, not knowing what had gotten into her friend. "Maybe Welles is on duty."

"Sorry." Nell wiped her eyes. "It's just..." She laughed again. "Gotta-get-there-the-fastest describes Gage to a T. Oh, my goodness. That's perfect. Wait until I tell Welles."

"Game, set, match." Missy smiled smugly.

The others nodded.

Everyone except Nell. "We're neighbors. Friends."

Selena winked. "Keep telling yourself that, but you should consider what Missy's saying."

"I'm not wrong," Missy added. "You'll see."

Nell shook her head. "Love you, Miss, but Welles and I aren't... We're not... It would never work."

"What's that line about protesting too much?" Juliet asked.

Bria tilted her head. "From *Hamlet*."

"Yes, that one." Juliet popped a black olive into her mouth.

"Stop it, guys." Nell used her fork to push food around on her plate. "We all know Welles only asks me out as a joke. He'd die if I ever said yes and come up with a million excuses not to go through with the date."

"Try it and see," Missy urged.

She didn't know why she kept pressing, but Gage was wrong for Nell, and Welles would be perfect for her. All Nell needed to do was stop seeing the Welles she grew up with, the one who shadowed her and made puppy dog eyes when she looked at him.

"It would be a waste of my time. And his, if he even agrees to take me out." Nell's cadence picked up as if she were trying to convince them. Or herself. "Besides, you know my mom and his dad aren't the biggest fans of each other."

"True." Missy had to admit there was no love lost between Charlene Culpepper and Buddy Riggs. "But they wouldn't have to know about one date."

"Sorry," Juliet chimed in. "Charlene would know."

Bria nodded. "All gossip goes through Charlene."

"Sorry, Missy. But they're right." Nell smiled as if that would soften the words. "And part of Gage's appeal is that my mom thinks we're dating, so she's stopped trying to fix me up with every eligible man in town. And thank goodness because I couldn't stand the embarrassment."

Bummer. Missy leaned back in her chair. "Your choice, but be careful around Gage. He may be gorgeous but—I'm sorry if you like him—I'm worried he'll get you hurt."

"I'll be careful."

"And Welles will keep you safe," Missy added.

Selena eyed Missy slyly. "Do you have a crush on Welles?"

"What? No." She needed to breathe. "He saved me. Sounds like a hero would be a better guy for Nell. That's all."

"Just teasing you," Selena admitted. "But you championing Welles makes sense."

Even Nell nodded. "You should go out—"

"It's Bria's turn." Missy didn't need her friends to tell her to date. That wasn't happening. And her feelings for Welles were nothing but friendship since they'd grown up together and gratitude for saving her life. Not to mention, he would be perfect for Nell.

"You're looking at the new accountant for Brew and Steep," Bria announced. "They called me today, and I said yes."

"Woo-hoo!" Nell cheered. "You're on your way to having your own accounting firm."

"A baby step, but yes." Bria sounded relieved.

"It's wonderful," Selena said, and the others agreed.

"Have you heard anything more about your dad?" Missy asked.

Selena nodded. "Or your mom?"

Bria flushed. "I don't know much more than what I texted you on Sunday. I spoke with Marc Carpenter earlier. He thinks my dad will be released soon. Maybe tomorrow. He submitted a motion for dismissal. The judge scheduled a hearing."

"That would be great." Except that meant the arsonist was still out there. And Missy would become a suspect.

"If he's not released, Dalton and I will visit him tomorrow night," Bria added.

"I want your dad released, but I hope they still don't consider me a suspect," Missy said.

"They'll have to do a real arson investigation once Brian is out." Selena sounded confident. "Sounds like Reggie decided on a suspect and pressed charges without a lot of thought or evidence."

Unease slithered along Missy's back. She didn't want to go to jail for something she didn't do.

Juliet nodded. "It's weird to think the arsonist has been free all this time. They could be walking the streets of Berry Lake for all we know."

Missy shivered. "I hope not."

Juliet touched her shoulder. "I didn't mean to upset you."

"It's okay." Not really, but her friends didn't need to know just how afraid she was of being arrested. "I just don't want them to think I did it."

"They won't." Bria smiled softly at her. "I told Marc Carpenter to give Elias the heads-up about my dad in case it affects you."

Relief washed over Missy. She trusted Elias to do what was necessary. "Thank you. So did you learn more about your mom?"

"My dad signed the release, so I spoke to the assisted-living center yesterday." Bria stared into her wineglass. "They didn't know everything, but I learned she suffered a TBI as a result of a car accident more than thirty years ago."

"Oh, Bria." Nell's eyes gleamed. "I'm so sorry."

"Thanks." Bria smiled softly. "I suppose this explains why she vanished from my life."

"But not why your dad said she took off," Selene countered.

"I plan to ask him." Bria swirled the Chianti in her glass. "Her car was submerged in water. They aren't sure how long she was under. She also had a skull fracture, but without oxygen…"

"A double whammy to the brain," Nell said.

Bria nodded. "The TBI could have come from one or both. What memories she retains are scattered. She acts like a child, yet she thought Dalton was Paul. Early-onset Alzheimer's was mentioned as something they are looking into with a specialist."

Missy's parents had deserted her. She'd had that in common with Bria and her mother. But Missy couldn't imagine what it would be like to find out there was another reason—a tragic one—for not having a mom. She squeezed Bria's hand. "I don't know what to say, but I'm so sorry."

"Thanks." Bria rubbed her face. "I still don't know how to feel about it. The one thing I did learn is my dad has done everything he could over the years to help her. He got her enrolled in clinical trials and searched out new treatments. Her condition isn't for his lack of trying."

"At least you know why she never got in touch with you." Selena's tone was compassionate.

Bria nodded. "I hate knowing Molly's condition won't ever change, but I always wondered if she might be dead. So I guess this is better. I'm still in shock."

"You will be for a while," Juliet said.

"I need to understand the circumstances." Bria twisted her napkin. "The car accident, Dad's secrecy, why she remembered Paul's name."

"Do you think the letter in Elise's things has anything to do with it?" Juliet asked.

"I do." Bria took a breath. "I think Molly wrote it, and if she did, how did she end up with my dad? Charlene said Paul met her in college. It... It's all so confusing."

Bria's anguish ripped through Missy's heart. She knew what her friend needed. She got up and carried over the three-tiered tray of cupcakes. "This conversation is missing something. Cupcakes."

They each took one.

"There's no rush to find the answers." Selena peeled the liner off. "Yes, you want them, but they're not going anywhere. And once you can speak to your dad..."

"I'm trying not to anticipate what he'll say. Or what I want to hear." Bria stared at her cupcake. "Dalton says that might make things worse."

"Dalton's smart." Selena licked the frosting off hers. "But we knew that since he fell in love with you. Listen to him. My hunch is the truth will be more than you could have imagined. Mainly because it usually is."

Selena was so right. Missy wanted everything to work out for Bria.

For all of them.

Missy ate her vanilla cupcake. But in her case, she hoped her life continued to be exactly as she imagined—boring. As long as she didn't end up at the county jail like Brian Landon, Missy would settle for whatever else happened. She just hoped that would be boring, too, and not involve a certain hottie deputy.

Her heart couldn't stand much more excitement. At least not beyond what a litter of kittens brought.

chapter eleven

THE FOLLOWING DAY, Bria walked to the Carpenter Law Office on Main Street. The temperature was chilly and the air crisp, typical for October in Washington. A patch of blue poked through the clouds overhead, but her mood was downright overcast.

With each step, Bria's crossover bag bounced against her hip. The mysterious letter they'd found at Aunt Elise's sat inside the purse. Bria didn't know if she'd show the letter to her dad, but she wanted to bring it, just in case.

A text notification buzzed.

She stopped, pulled out her phone, and read the message.

> **DALTON:** *Thinking of you. Wish I could be there. Love you!*
> **BRIA:** *Almost there. You have an important meeting. I understand. Love you too!*

Bria tucked her phone into her purse and continued along the sidewalk. Dalton had planned to be there, but Tanner needed him at a meeting in Portland today. She would have loved for Dalton to be with her, but she could handle this on her own.

She entered the law office that had once been someone's home. The conversion to a commercial property hadn't lessened the house's charm. It was one thing she enjoyed whenever she visited. Something she'd done so many times since Aunt Elise's death. This time, however, she wanted to race into Marc's office.

That was a first.

And unlike her.

Practical Bria, who planned ten steps ahead and did nothing without analyzing the ways it could go. But now, she'd been thrown into an alternate universe where nothing made sense, and she could predict nothing with her family.

Nerves.

She forced herself to breathe.

Her nerves had gotten worse as the days passed. The need for answers had become an obsession that kept growing with what little she'd learned from Molly's care team.

Denise, the law firm's receptionist, sat behind a counter. Her dark hair was pulled off her face with an apple-print scarf that matched the apple pin on her sweater. She was in her mid-forties and had introduced herself at Aunt Elise's funeral. Bria hadn't remembered that until her first visit there when Denise reminded her that was where they met.

"Good morning, Bria." Denise greeted her with a big grin. "Help yourself to coffee and cookies. Elizabeth Carpenter baked them fresh this morning and just dropped them off."

Bria didn't remember cookies being out during her visits before, but she may have missed them, given her mind was on Aunt Elise's estate and the fate of the cupcake shop. But Bria knew Elizabeth Carpenter was Elias's grandmother and the senior partner's wife. Might as well try one.

Bria chose a molasses cookie. She hadn't been able to tell if the others were oatmeal or chocolate chip, and she didn't want to bite into one expecting chocolate and tasting a raisin. What had Selena T said in last week's podcast?

Set yourself up for success.

"Thank you." Bria took a bite. The sweet flavors melted in her mouth. Delicious.

"Go back to Marc's office when you're ready," Denise said.

Bria had been ready since Sunday night. She paced herself when her feet wanted to speed up. For all she knew, Marc wasn't even at the office yet. The way he hadn't been there when she came for the reading of Aunt Elise's will.

The office door was ajar. Bria squared her shoulders and pushed it open. The same dark wood and leather furniture and scent of books greeted her. Marc, in a suit and tie, sat behind his desk. Framed diplomas hung on the wall behind him, but that wasn't what caught her eye. Her dad was in the chair nearest her. Both men stood when she entered.

"You're out?" She cringed. Her question must sound stupid. *Of course, Dad is out of jail, or he wouldn't be here.* "I mean, the case was dismissed?"

"The district attorney dropped all charges," Marc announced. "Thanks for making the trip to Wishing Bay. I would have gone had Brian asked me, but I'm relieved he trusted you with the information. The Cliffside Manor provided videos, visitor logs, and witnesses to Brian's presence there the night of the fire."

Relief washed over Bria. Dad had aged so much since his arrest. His rumpled polo shirt and wrinkled khaki pants had seen better days. "You said you were innocent."

"And you proved it." Dad gave a closed-mouth smile. "Thank you, baby doll. You must have questions."

So many. The urge to ask all of them at once was strong, but Bria pressed her lips together and sat. "I do."

Marc walked around his desk. He patted Brian on the shoulder. "I'll leave you two alone. Let Denise know when you're ready for me to join you, so we can discuss what comes next."

The lawyer closed the door behind him. The click echoed through the office.

Her heart slammed against her rib cage.

Marc didn't lock the door. I'm not trapped.

But Bria wouldn't walk out that door until she had her answers. All she needed was Dad's cooperation.

And the truth.

She took a deep breath.

"Did you see her?" he asked before Bria could say anything.

"Yes."

Avoiding her gaze, he paced the length of the office. "I'm sorry."

"Why didn't you tell me?"

Dad faced her. He wrung his hands. "It's...complicated."

"Start uncomplicating it." She crossed her legs, but she couldn't get comfortable, so she uncrossed them. "Do you know what it was like to walk into room three thirteen and see Molly?"

It was easier for Bria to think of the woman as Molly, a woman-child.

"I'm sure that was difficult for you. I'd hoped you'd never find out about your mom." Dad brushed his fingers through his hair. He was usually so styled, dressed impeccably, with no hair out of place. That man was gone. "You were so precious, so innocent. I wanted you to remember your mother how she was before the car accident."

"Except I didn't remember her at all." Aunt Elise had been a surrogate mother, auntie, and best friend rolled into one, but even she couldn't change how Bria felt about herself growing up and even as an adult. That burned deep. "I thought Molly left us. Me. That I wasn't enough to deserve her love. That I'd made her take off. Because what mother leaves her two-year-old child?"

"Oh, honey." Brian reached out to her, but an inch from touching Bria, he dropped his hand to his side. "You were never at fault, far from it. Your mother loved you. She just…"

Bria leaned forward. "What?"

Dad's shoulders slumped. "…loved somebody else more."

"Paul Dwyer," Bria blurted.

Brian flinched. His face paled, and he hunched his shoulders. "H-How did you know?"

"I guessed." Bria hadn't meant to hurt Dad, but she had. "Molly called Dalton by his father's name."

"She remembered Paul?" A strange, almost disembodied laugh sounded. "Figures. I've tried to protect two families and…"

Protect them from what? "Molly didn't remember him the next day. She acted like she'd never seen Dalton or called him Paul the night before."

146

The corners of Dad's mouth tipped up slightly. He sat. "That shouldn't make me feel as good as it does."

Bria reached for her purse and placed the letter on the table. "My friends and I found this letter in Aunt Elise's closet."

"Read it to me please."

Bria unfolded the yellowed piece of paper. She took a breath. "My love. I wish with my whole heart that things could be different. I know you want to do the right thing, but I also see and hear how much you don't want to lose me. It's a tough spot to find yourself in. I know because I feel the same. And it sucks."

Dad sighed. "Keep going."

"I'll be honest. This whole 'be honorable' cloak you're wearing isn't helping heal my broken heart. Quite the opposite. But it proves the kind of man you are—caring and kind—and why I wanted to grow old with you at my side."

Dad inhaled sharply.

Bria glanced at him. She wished he hadn't asked her to read the letter. Not knowing what she knew now.

He motioned for her to keep going.

"But I can't smile and pretend to be happy with how things turned out. I'm not like you. I'm not that big of a person. And I hate myself because I know what this means for us. Well, what's left of us because that must end, too. From this day on, we must stop all contact. I don't want you to acknowledge me, not even with a wave. I can't go back to being just friends, and your new family deserves your full attention. There is no other way."

Dad rubbed his mouth.

"We find ourselves in an unexpected situation." Bria's voice cracked. The words were harder to read this time. "The future we planned is no longer possible, but the stakes are too high to ignore to put this off any longer. Doing this is the right decision. I feel that in my heart. And I also know in my heart it is one you would have made yourself eventually. So, I'm saving you the effort of having to decide this and saying goodbye now. It'll be easier for both of us."

Dad walked away from Bria so she couldn't see his face. "Don't stop."

"I stole my photo from your wallet. Don't be mad because it's not something you need any longer." Bria's voice trembled. She tried not to imagine how Molly must have felt writing these words. "Forget me. Don't look back at what might have been. Start fresh. Give your heart away with no regrets. You'll always have a piece of my heart, and I'll remember enough of what we shared for both of us. I love you. I will always love you."

Dad didn't turn around.

Bria folded the letter. She didn't want to look at it again, but this might be Molly's letter to Mr. Dwyer. Bria had to know for certain. "Did my… Molly write this?"

Dad faced her. He walked slowly to his chair, sat, and reached out to Bria.

She handed him the letter.

He unfolded it.

Bria dug the toes of her shoes into the carpet as far as they would go.

Dad rubbed his eyes. "Yes. This is her handwriting. And the situation… Your mother wrote this."

No relief came the way Bria thought it might. She'd connected the people in the letter with those from the past, but it wasn't enough. Bria didn't want to sit here and try to draw the story out of Dad. She couldn't.

Still unable to get comfortable, she stood and walked to the far wall with the framed diplomas. When she turned, Dad looked at the letter.

"Dad." Her voice was firm enough that he looked up. "You just got out of jail. Your head must be spinning. But so is mine. I assumed Molly was off living her life or dead, not lying in an assisted-living facility, child-like stuck in time. I feel like my entire childhood was a lie. You must have had your reasons for not telling me, but I need to know everything from the beginning. I need to know now."

Brian rubbed both palms on his thighs. "You deserve to know. It's just hard."

"Life is hard." She came toward him. "Sometimes you have to plow through to move on."

"Your friends are rubbing off on you."

She would take that as a compliment. "Yes, so…"

"First, I must tell you that Elise didn't know about the car accident and what happened to Molly. My sister believed as you did. That Molly left." He spoke fast, fast enough that Bria had to listen more carefully. He angled his shoulders toward her, but the lines around his mouth deepened. "Elise must have found the letter when I asked her to pack up what Molly left behind. Your aunt never mentioned the letter to me, but Molly told me she'd written Paul. This must have been a first draft because Paul told me he received a letter."

Aunt Elise not knowing, not lying to Bria, brought a wave of relief and love for the woman who'd raised her. "Thank you for telling me Aunt Elise didn't know."

"If your aunt had known, I doubt I could have kept Molly a secret for so long." Dad sighed. "Back to the beginning. Paul and I went to W-S-U. We pledged the same fraternity and met the most amazing woman at a mixer with a sorority."

"Molly."

Dad nodded. "She was beautiful, smart, and sassy. It was love at first sight for me. Unfortunately, it was also love at first sight for her and Paul. I became the tagalong friend, the third wheel."

"That must have been difficult."

"At least I got to keep her close. And honestly, Paul was the better match for her. Neither her family nor mine had money. Unlike the Dwyers. He could offer her things I couldn't."

"Except love."

"Paul loved her as much as I did." Dad scrubbed his face with his hand. "Paul and Molly broke up right before spring break our senior year. It was over something stupid, but Deena had had her sights on him for a while, and she used his heartbreak to make her move. But a couple of drunken nights with her over spring break was enough to get Paul to apologize to Molly. He proposed a month after that, and she said yes. They planned to get married after they graduated. Then Deena told him she was pregnant."

Some of the story was what Bria had imagined, but the extra details she couldn't have imagined.

This must be as hard on Dad as it is on me. Maybe harder.

Bria sat. "So the letter…"

"The letter shows you the woman Molly was. Kind, good-hearted." His affectionate tone told of his love for Molly. The sparkle in his eyes reflected the same thing. "She knew Paul would do the right thing, even if it meant marrying a woman he didn't love and leaving the one he did."

Something didn't make sense. Bria bit her lip. She wasn't that old. "Having kids when you're not married is more common now, but lots of people had them back then, too."

"True, but the Dwyers only cared about appearances. An illegitimate child might have been socially acceptable, but not to Paul's parents and grandparents." Dad massaged his temples as if trying to stave off a headache. "Paul's family forced the marriage, especially when Deena's parents brought up that this wasn't Paul and Deena's first time together. That happened when they were in high school. He was eighteen, and she was underage."

Oh, man. Bria didn't want Dalton to find out any of this, but he had a right to know. The same as her, which meant making sure she understood everything. "Mr. Dwyer was blackmailed into marrying Deena?"

Dad nodded. "It was all hush-hush."

"For the sake of appearances."

"Yes. Paul went home for the weekend and came back a married man. Deena stayed in Berry Lake with her folks. Molly was…heartbroken." Dad's voice cracked. "But she understood. We graduated. Deena ended up miscarrying."

Remy Dwyer popped into Bria's mind. Her hands balled. "Except she wasn't pregnant."

Dad's brows drew together. "What do you mean?"

"Remy Dwyer tried to do to Ezra Monroe what her mother had done to Paul Dwyer. Remy told him she was pregnant, so he asked Juliet for a divorce." Bria flexed her fingers, hoping to let go of the anger on her friend's behalf. "Then Remy was in a car accident. When they wanted to do an ultrasound on the baby at the hospital, she said she had miscarried. Nell was talking to her mom about it. Charlene said faking pregnancies ran in the family. HIPAA must not have been a thing or was new enough that when Deena claimed to be pregnant, someone from the doctor's office let it slip that Deena's pregnancy test was negative. She'd lied about being pregnant just like her daughter did."

Dad's face hadn't regained any color. His eyes turned dark, but she couldn't tell if that was regret or something else.

He took a breath and then another. "I never heard that, but it could be true. I do know Paul never loved Deena. Not the way he loved Molly."

A million things ran through Bria's mind. Mainly, how to protect Dalton. He would be hurting as much as her. She fought the urge to stand again. Instead, she bounced her knee. She had to do something to make sense of all this.

"Why didn't Paul divorce Deena after the miscarriage and marry Molly?" she asked.

"Paul felt so bad about breaking Molly's heart." Dad's gaze took in everything in the office, everything but Bria. "He also knew how much I cared about her."

Oh, wow. Bria leaned back in the chair. "That must have been awkward."

"No, because Paul was my friend. I would've never gone behind his back and acted upon my feelings. Not that Molly would have been receptive to them." Dad sounded adamant. "But Paul told me to take care of Molly."

"You did."

Dad nodded. "He gave us some money since we had none. As soon as we graduated, we left Washington. Paul's idea since he thought that would be easier on Molly. She didn't want to hear about the birth of his child or see Deena at all, so we headed south. When we hit Las Vegas, she was the one who proposed. I knew she was on the rebound, but…"

"You loved her."

"Body, heart, and soul." A dreamy smile spread across his face. "We got married in this little chapel and honeymooned on the strip. That's where we conceived you."

Bria's heart squeezed tight. "Unexpected."

"Yes, but not unwanted. It overwhelmed us with joy. Thrilled us."

"Really?" She hated how much hope filled that one word.

"One hundred percent, baby doll." The tension on Dad's face lessened, the lines around his mouth fading. "We were living in California when Paul called to tell us Deena miscarried. Molly told him she was pregnant, and he asked if she would get rid of the baby and marry him. She hung up the phone without saying another word."

"He didn't want—"

Dad's jaw jutted forward. "Paul wanted Molly all to himself. He was a great guy and a good friend, but he was selfish and didn't think beyond his needs, which is how he ended up with Deena. And why he didn't want Molly's baby."

Bria flinched. "You mean me."

"Yes, you. But you weren't born yet."

Bria tried to reconcile the man she'd known as Dalton's dad with the younger man Dad described. The two didn't mesh in her mind. "I'm glad Molly didn't get rid of me."

"She never would have. Nor would I have let her. We both loved and wanted you from the beginning, baby doll." A wistful expression formed on Dad's face. "And it turned out Deena had gotten pregnant again."

153

"Dalton."

Dad nodded. "Your mom and I had become close friends… best friends…in college. Paul used to joke he was jealous of our friendship. But in California, we were in love. It was romantic and wonderful and everything I'd dreamed about."

How Dad spoke about Molly was how Bria felt about Dalton. Love was present in every word and gave her all the feels. But that begged a question. "What changed?"

Because something must have, or the three of them would have lived happily ever after as a family.

"We had a few friends in California, but no family. Elise thought it would be better if we lived closer so she could help us with you."

Bria nearly laughed. "Sounds like Aunt Elise."

"And we thought it was the right move." Dad's eyes appeared more reflective. "That's where our Thursday date nights started. We had so much fun on those until…"

Bria had an idea of where this was going. She held her breath.

Dad held on to the chair arms. "Paul and Molly got back together again."

Bria sucked in a breath. "They cheated?"

"I…" Dad shifted in his chair. "I don't know for certain, but Molly couldn't stay away from Paul. Forbidden love is a powerful thing."

But still… Bria reached out to her father and touched his hand. "I'm sorry you had to go through that."

"Thanks." He sounded sincere, but he shook his head. "I knew she still loved Paul when we got married. And I wouldn't have you if we hadn't. No regrets. I promise."

"So what happened?" Bria asked.

"Molly came to me with her bags packed and in tears. She told me she and Paul belonged together and asked for a divorce." Dad stood once again. He shifted his weight from foot to foot. "I knew I was her second choice, but I never thought she would leave you. She finally admitted Paul wanted to be with her, but they needed to start fresh, so she asked me to keep you."

The words stabbed Bria in the heart. She closed her eyes as if that could erase the hurt and the past, but it did neither. She opened them. "So he didn't want me, again. Only this time, she didn't either."

"It wasn't only you. He didn't want Dalton, either." Dad took a step toward Bria. "Molly hoped to convince Paul that both of their kids needed them. She planned to come back for you. I was terrified. Because I didn't want to lose you." Dad reached out and touched Bria's shoulder. "I promise you, baby doll. She would have come back for you."

Bria's breath caught in her throat. Her chest tightened. She focused on her breathing but that didn't stop her eyes from heating up and her vision from blurring. She blinked. It didn't help.

Dad squeezed her shoulder. "This can't be easy for you to hear, but your mother loved you. That love remains in her heart."

"I don't remember her." Bria's words came out choked, uneven.

"You were too young. And a part of me is relieved you don't remember." Dad leaned against Marc's desk, but he hadn't let go of her shoulder. "Molly and Paul's love turned from something pure and beautiful to an obsession, with the ability to destroy two marriages—two families. Molly wanted him as badly as he wanted her. That blinded her to everything else, including you."

"How did she get into a car accident?"

"I wanted Molly to be happy. I'd gotten her by default, so I agreed to a divorce." Dad made it sound so simple, but his words couldn't hide the pain in his gaze. "Paul met her in Hayden Lake in Idaho. They planned to stay there while paperwork was filed, but then Molly found out Paul hadn't asked Deena for a divorce yet. They argued. She decided to return to Berry Lake. To us. But she never made it."

Bria covered Brian's hand with her own. "What happened?"

Dad rubbed the back of his neck. "The car ended up in the water. Paul was following her. An animal ran in front of the car. Molly swerved. The car crashed into the lake. That was before cell phones. He panicked when he realized Molly might die. It took a long time to free her. But at the hospital, finding out she would never be the same was worse than death for him. When he called me…"

Bria had a feeling she knew where this was going. She squeezed his hand. "You bailed him out again."

Dad shrugged, but he looked far from indifferent. "Deena had no idea that Paul was planning to leave her. Molly was still my wife. And I…"

"Loved her."

"I *love* her, always will, even if she's nothing like the woman I fell in love with."

Everyone made Paul Dwyer out to be such a paragon—a wonderful husband and father. But Brian Landon was the one who'd stepped up and cleaned up his friend's mistakes. The entire town had misjudged him. So had Bria.

She struggled to piece together the man she called Dad. For so long he'd been chasing the pot of gold at the end of the rainbow. His get-rich-quick schemes had embarrassed her. But now she understood his motivation—his love for his wife.

For Molly.

He'd sacrificed time with his daughter to earn money for Molly's car. Yet, he'd never told a soul what he was what doing. Only Paul had known, but he'd died more than fifteen years ago.

Bria's heart ached for him as much as for herself. *Love shouldn't hurt so much.*

"There'd been a big event happening in Hayden Lake, so the accident got little coverage." Dad held on to her hand. "No one in Berry Lake cared about what happened in a small town in Idaho. The story I told people wasn't a lie. I based it on the truth. Your mom left us. I just didn't tell anyone the rest."

"How did she end up in Wishing Bay?"

"We'd visited there, and your mother had loved it. She talked about living by the ocean someday. I discussed it with Paul, and we felt that was the best place for her. Four hours away from Berry Lake, so no one would recognize her there. Plus, the facility had the services she needed. I worked hard to make sure she had the best care."

Bria's mouth dropped open. "That's why you were always trying to find the pot of gold."

Dad nodded. "And why we traveled from job to job. I kept needing those bumps in salary. And no place had the right insurance to help your mom."

"Dad, I…"

"Don't apologize. I don't deserve it. Paul helped pay for her care whenever I hit a rough spot. He blamed himself for what happened. If he'd told her to bring you the first time or asked for a divorce like he said he would the second time…"

"That must have been hard to live with."

"When we found out about the brain damage, I had you to pull me through, but Paul was never the same. He came home to Deena and Dalton, acting as if nothing had happened on his 'fishing trip to Idaho.' They waited a few years before having Owen and Remy and then a few more to have Ian. But guilt ate away at Paul. He put everything into raising his kids as if that were his penance for Molly."

"And then he died of cancer."

Dad nodded. "When that happened, Molly's care fell all on me. Even though she planned to divorce me to marry Paul, we were still married. I vowed to love her in sickness and in health, and I intend to do that for as long as I'm alive."

The puzzle pieces clicked into place. "You wanted to sell the cupcake shop to pay her bills."

"I didn't want to do that. I needed to." Dad lowered his head and walked to the far side of the office. "I'd hoped there would be money set aside for Molly's care when Paul died, but I heard nothing."

Bria remembered what Dalton had told her. "Paul took out loans on his whole life insurance policy. There was little left for Deena and his kids to inherit."

"I never knew how he got the money to pay for Molly without Deena finding out about it. Loans would explain it. Paul must have thought he'd have time to pay it off."

Bria tried to take it all in. "I could have helped you with…her."

"I'd kept it a secret for so long, telling you didn't enter my head." He trudged to his chair like a man weighed down with a lifetime of baggage on his shoulders. "I'm sorry for that and your mother not being there for you. But she *couldn't* be there for you. And I never wanted you to feel obligated."

"If I'd known—"

His inquisitive gaze met hers. "Would it have made a difference?"

Bria picked lint off her sweater. "I-I don't know."

"Your mother's condition is getting worse. She used to remember more. Snippets. Occasional names. Now I'm some nice gentleman who brings her a gift and has dinner with her. She doesn't remember me from week to week."

Bria's heart tore in half. She wanted to help him. Not make him feel worse. "Dad—"

"I carry a lot of guilt, too. For agreeing to marry her when I knew she still loved Paul. For returning to Berry Lake, knowing Paul and Deena were here. For not trying to stop her from leaving us." Dad rubbed his eyes. "But deep down, baby doll, I wanted her to choose us. To choose me if only because of you. And she had. Paul told me she'd picked us over him, he wanted her to give him more time, but she was on her way back to Berry Lake when the accident happened. I often wonder if she would have come home to us for good or gone back to him eventually. Crazy, isn't it?"

The anguish in his voice cut deep. Bria swallowed. "Love isn't logical."

"You're right. It's the opposite."

"I've only been thinking about how this affects me," she admitted. "But none of this has been easy for you."

"Sometimes love makes even the hardest things seem like nothing." Dad stared at the wall, but he seemed to be looking farther. "Molly is still a part of my life. Even if she's not the same person I fell in love with, I'm grateful she's with me. Her memory lives in my heart and in you."

"You never considered divorcing her?"

"Not once." He didn't hesitate to answer. "If Elise had known what happened, she would have marched me to this law office and made me file for a divorce."

"Again, sounds like Aunt Elise."

"She told me to stay away from Molly. Told me I'd be the rebound guy. Told me if Paul ever wanted Molly back, she would leave me behind before I could blink twice. And that's exactly what happened."

Bria half laughed. "A good thing Aunt Elise didn't know, or she would have never let you live that down."

"No, but Elise was sorry when Molly left us. Especially for you." Dad's eyes were red. "I've made so many mistakes. But everything I've done has been out of love for your mom and you. Even if you might not think so."

"I know, Dad. But it's…a lot."

"You need time." The words shot out. "There's lots of blame to throw around, but none of it belongs on you. You were a child, a toddler when all this happened. Please know your mother loved you. She wasn't leaving you forever."

Bria swallowed around the lump in her throat. She forced air into her lungs. "Except she did."

chapter twelve

A FTER BRIA SPENT the morning with her dad, she called an emergency Posse gathering. As soon as Missy received the text, she drove to Elise's house, where Juliet had soup and sandwiches waiting for them. They'd eaten lunch while Bria told them what she'd learned about her dad, her mom, and Dalton's dad.

The mystery surrounding the letter went deeper than Missy could have imagined. It was a tragic love story made worse by bad decision-making. Her heart ached for all involved.

The atmosphere was heavy and quiet as what happened in the past sank in. But the Posse wasn't known for silence, so Selena mentioned the fresh air would be good for Bria. Nell wanted to tag along to stay in shape in case Gage nixed her staying-in idea. Juliet had to check on Lulu.

That left Missy to clean up. She didn't mind. She enjoyed doing things for those she loved.

As she loaded the dishwasher, Missy couldn't stop thinking about what had happened between Molly and Mr. Dwyer. If he hadn't tried to soothe his broken heart by rebounding with Deena, none of this might have happened. And if that were the case, Bria wouldn't have been born.

Missy shook that horrible thought from her mind. She stuck spoons into their slots on the bottom rack. She wanted to support Bria, but a gnawing in Missy's stomach made her want to drive home and check on the kittens. Mama Cat was good with them, but kittens were so fragile Missy hated leaving them unattended for too long. With the rest of the Posse at the house and Dalton arriving later, Bria was in good hands. No reason for Missy to stay.

Juliet entered the kitchen and turned on the electric teakettle. An orange light illuminated. "Lulu got her meds and is ready for a nap. Go home. I'll do the dishes later."

Missy rinsed off a soup bowl. "I'm almost finished."

Juliet removed a teacup from the cabinet and placed a tea bag into it. "Thanks for bringing the cupcakes and flowers. They were just what Bria needed."

"Least I could do." Missy put a bowl into the dishwasher and washed her hands. "All Bria wanted was the truth, but what she heard… It's a lot to take in."

"I'm still in shock." Juliet put away the salt and pepper. "I feel sorry for Mr. Landon. I never thought he was a good father, not that mine was anything to go by."

"You're not the only one. I remember my folks saying Brian dumped the chubby girl with Elise again. That was what some people called Bria. The chubby girl."

"It's awful. The whole situation is." Juliet shook her head. "I've been open about my feelings towards the Dwyer family.

Remy is the poster child, a mini-Deena, of what they're capable of doing, but the truth will hurt them, and no one deserves that, especially the kids. As for Deena…"

The light on the teakettle went off.

Juliet filled her cup with the hot water.

Missy pictured Deena DeMarco in her designer clothes and plastic-surgery-enhanced body, spreading ugly lies about her stepdaughter, Sheridan DeMarco, to justify her own daughter taking over Sheridan's job at her dad's gallery.

"I'm not a fan of hers, and she totally trapped Paul Dwyer, not that he should have slept with her if he still loved Molly," Missy said. "But she and her kids paid for what he did."

Juliet nodded. "When I found out Ezra cheated, my heart withered. I didn't know what to do. I wonder if Paul ever confessed the truth to Deena, or if this will blindside her? For him to spend his insurance to take care of another woman and leave his family with nothing… I don't have to like Deena to feel for her."

"She must have been desperate with four kids and little money."

A thoughtful expression crossed Juliet's face. "But to be honest, getting a job might have been a better option than marrying and divorcing rich men to support her family."

Missy nodded, closing the dishwasher. "When we first read the letter, it was an intriguing mystery. Now, I'm sad over how everything impacted the Dwyers, the Landons, and all those families who lost their money in Deena's many divorce proceedings."

"It also didn't have to turn out the way it did."

"Very true." Missy had learned no matter how much she wanted to change the past, the do-over she wanted wasn't possible. But that had led to another realization. "That's why you must grab onto love and not let go. Don't wait, because you never know how long it'll last."

"I suppose. But right now, I'm happy I'm on my way to being single again." Juliet gasped. Regret filled her eyes. "Sorry, Missy. You didn't have a choice. I hope I didn't offend you."

Sweet Juliet. Missy smiled at her. "None taken. You don't have to tiptoe around me. I didn't decide to be single, but that's the card life dealt. I hope you embrace your singlehood and find the life you've dreamed about."

"I plan to, but…"

Missy leaned against the counter to take the weight off her foot. "What?"

"Nothing is stopping *you* from dating."

Except for Rob.

Even before he'd returned in her coma dream, she hadn't wanted to love again. She'd been so fortunate to fall in love with an honorable man—well, a boy who grew into a man—a hero. No one would understand and love her the way he had. Rob had been her first and last. And she was his.

When a day was darker than usual, she found solace in knowing that. But her friends would do what they always did—say Rob wouldn't want her to be alone and talk about all the success stories of those who found love a second time. She didn't need to hear it again, especially when Rob said the same thing in that dream.

Missy shrugged, even if she wanted to scream no.

"Sabine came over while Bria was with her dad." Juliet dunked the tea bag in her mug before tossing the soppy packet into the garbage. "I think she wanted to make sure we had everything under control with Butterscotch and Lulu. I finally called Mrs. Vernon. She didn't answer, but I left a message."

The underlying concern in Juliet's voice made Missy want to reassure her. "Don't worry. Mrs. Vernon will understand. And she knows Sabine well."

Juliet shrugged. The uncertainty in her eyes needed to go away, and Missy knew what might do the trick.

She removed a cupcake from one box and handed it to Juliet. Sweets always helped, especially if they came with buttercream frosting.

"You two are doing great with Lulu and Butterscotch. Don't let Sabine worry you. It's just how she is," Missy said.

"Sabine can be a little intimidating."

That was true, but Missy had been volunteering for the rescue since high school, so she was used to Sabine. "Think of Sabine as Mother Nature personified. She's mom to three daughters, one stepdaughter, and every animal that's passed through her rescue's door, or that she's ever met. She loves all creatures big and small by taking them under her wing and making sure they thrive."

"Sounds like Elise."

A pang hit Missy's heart. She almost expected Elise to bounce into her kitchen with a new idea for a cupcake flavor. Only, the kitchen belonged to Bria and Juliet, who lived there now.

"Except Elise focused on people. Besides Butterscotch. She spoiled that cat." Missy didn't want to talk about her late boss. "What did Sabine say?"

"She gave us the thumbs up on caring for Lulu and Butterscotch, which was a relief."

Missy glanced around the kitchen to see if she'd missed cleaning anything. A lone saucepan was on a stove eye. She grabbed it. "Wouldn't expect any less from two of my best friends."

Gratitude shone in Juliet's eyes. "I need to stop worrying so much."

Missy rinsed the pot. "Remember what Selena T says."

"Worry is a waste of time and energy. It can't change anything."

Missy grinned. "You've been listening."

"I never imagined myself becoming Ezra's doormat during our marriage, but it happened, and I never want to do that again. I have so much to learn."

"You'll get there." Missy had no doubt. Juliet had grown so much over the past month since she'd gotten away from Ezra. He'd been the snuffer trying to douse Juliet's dazzling flame.

Juliet held her teacup in front of her mouth and then lowered it. "Oh, Sabine told me the kittens are thriving. You must be so happy."

Missy shimmied her shoulders. Thanks to the kittens, she was contributing again. She hated being useless. "They are doing well. But all the kudos go to Mama Cat. The entire litter is adorable."

"That's great." Juliet took a sip of tea. "Sabine also said Sam Cooper was the deputy who got you out of the recycle bin."

Missy's muscles bunched. She hadn't told Sabine or anyone about Sam. No one knew he'd come over the next day with her phone and a new one. He'd been gone by the time Sabine arrived with the kittens. And Jenny, on another deadline, and Dare, busy with Briley, hadn't noticed Sam's car in the driveway. It must have been the clinic's receptionist. Gossip traveled at lightspeed in Berry Lake.

"Missy?" Juliet asked.

"Yes. Sam was the deputy who came to my rescue." The words tumbled out of Missy's mouth. She nearly groaned.

Why did I say rescue?

Sam Cooper wasn't a knight in shining armor. At least not outside her dreams. Make that, one dream. One all-consuming-made-her-think-it-was-real-dream she'd been trying to forget ever since it happened. No would ever know it happened.

Not Jenny.

Missy hadn't even told Peach and Mario.

"Sam responded to my fender bender," Juliet said.

"I remember you mentioning him." Missy straightened the boxes of cupcakes, even though they were aligned perfectly. She needed something to do. "Nice guy."

"And attractive."

Wait, what? Missy's throat tightened so much that she struggled to breathe. She wasn't sure she wanted to know the answer because Juliet could play a theme park princess if she wanted to, but Missy had to ask. "Are you interested in Sam?"

"What? Me? No." Juliet shook her head as if for emphasis. "Even if I were, I prefer someone older than me. I always have."

"Change is good," Missy said.

She wondered why she was pushing this so hard, but even she could see Sam and Juliet would look stunning together. Both were gorgeous.

"It is," Juliet agreed.

"Sam's not that much younger than you." Missy might as well go all in. "He's come to your rescue and mine now. I didn't know him well in high school, but Rob did. He said Sam was a great guy. And Sam is. He offered to dry out my wet phone and brought me another one to use in the meantime. Who does that? A nice person who is also the tastiest-looking eye candy I've seen around Berry Lake in forever. So, reconsider dating him."

"Nope. Not interested since I'm not officially divorced." Juliet pointed at Missy's chest. "But you should be."

"Huh?"

Juliet winked. "You provided me with a list of why Sam would be perfect for you. Tasty eye candy? Someone sounds smitten, and it's not me. Sam even has Rob's approval."

Missy stepped backward and bumped into the counter. That might leave a bruise, but what was another one? "Sam wouldn't be interested in someone like me. You'd be a better match for him."

"Not true. I'm still married, and you heard what Selena recommended about waiting a year after a divorce before dating anyone."

"Sam just returned to town. He needs time to settle in. A year will fly by. And for all we know, he left a girlfriend in Seattle."

Juliet eyed her mischievously. "Sabine said Sam's very much single. He wants to buy a house, which suggests he's interested in having a family. Something you wanted."

"With Rob." Missy hadn't allowed herself to daydream without her husband being a part of the dream. She didn't dare.

"Rob wanted you to find love again."

Rob had mentioned that when he came to her in the hospital. "What kind of love? More cats? Friends?"

"I was thinking romantic love." Juliet sipped her tea. "Did you ask Jenny? She was Rob's older sister. She would know what he wanted for you."

To be honest, Missy knew. She wasn't living the life Rob would have wanted. But what Rob wanted for her and what *she* wanted were two different things. "That's private between them."

"You could try."

"Or not." Missy didn't want to get into an argument. "I'm doing better health-wise and emotionally. Managing the cupcake shop once it reopens will take most of my time."

"You've got it all figured out." Juliet's disbelieving tone didn't match her words or smile.

"I do. And I should get…"

The front door opened. Missy recognized three of the voices, but the fourth, a male, she didn't recognize.

"Come in," Bria encouraged. "This won't take long."

"We had plenty of leftovers from lunch," Selena added.

"Please have one," Nell said. "Otherwise, we'll eat them. Our stomachs will be happy. Our jeans, not so much."

Her three friends entered the kitchen, followed by…

"Sam?" Missy hadn't realized she said the word aloud. He looked way too handsome in his deputy uniform. Not that she noticed him. Not much anyway. "What are you doing here?"

"He's here for a cupcake." Selena came toward Missy with purposeful steps. "Sam also mentioned the personalized cupcakes you made for him after what happened at the market."

"Why didn't you tell us?" Bria asked.

"I…" Missy didn't know where to start. "The cupcakes were for fun."

Nell snickered. "Fun, huh?"

"Sounds fun to me," Bria agreed.

Selena's mouth tightened. "I didn't mean the cup—"

"They were delicious. And so creative." Once again, Sam came to her rescue. Missy hadn't needed to prompt him, either. "I'm partial to the Deputy's Doughnut Delight. Though the Bye Seattle one was the most creative."

Missy gulped. Okay, she may have gone slightly overboard. But she had a lot of free time on her hands right now.

Not knowing what to say, she smiled.

Her friends glanced between Missy and Sam as if they were watching a tennis match.

Missy fought the urge to cringe. She had no idea what they were thinking, but the mischievous smiles set her nerves on edge.

Sam took a step closer, making the kitchen seem smaller. "Did your phone dry out yet?"

"No." Missy tried for a lighthearted tone, but she wasn't sure if she succeeded. "But I'm not giving up hope yet."

Sam came even closer, her friends parting like the Red Sea to make it easier for him to reach her. *Traitors.*

"Does the Tracfone work?" he asked.

"Yes." No way did she trust herself to say more. If Bigfoot were chasing her, she doubted her pulse would race so hard.

Bria's eyebrows scrunched. "When did you get a Tracfone?"

Okay, the phone seemed to be a safe topic. Missy opened her mouth...

"I bought it for her," Sam said before she could speak. "Can't have Missy without a cell phone, especially with her foot healing. Plus, she has the kittens now. It wouldn't be safe for her not to have a phone."

"It wouldn't," Selena agreed, her eyes doing the tango. "Very thoughtful of you."

Bria nodded.

Nell pressed her lips together. Probably to keep from laughing.

"That was kind." Juliet grabbed the top cupcake box and opened it. "Help yourself. We've got an in with the baker."

Sam took a vanilla cupcake.

Missy's jaw dropped. *Are you kidding me?*

He'd taken her favorite kind. Rob had done the same thing during her first shift at the cupcake shop when she was fifteen.

Not a sign.

Coincidence.

That's all.

"Though these don't sound nearly as fun as the ones she made you," Juliet added.

Now it was Bria who tried not to laugh. "I wonder why that is?"

Selena shrugged and threw up her hands. "No idea."

"I'm clueless," Nell said.

He took a bite of the cupcake. A dab of white frosting stuck to his upper lip. He used his tongue to wipe it off, and Missy watched as he did it. She gulped.

Her friends *definitely* noticed.

Heat burned in Missy's cheeks. She would never live this down.

Please let Sam have missed me staring at him. Okay, leering in a borderline creepy way.

Ugh! "I need to go. The kittens. I'll check in via the chat later."

"I'm leaving, too." Sam ate the rest of the cupcake. "I finished a call a few houses down when I ran into your friends. I need to get back to work."

Why did Missy notice his every move? Based on her friends' amused expressions, they saw that, too.

Sam held the paper cupcake liner. "Where..."

Juliet stuck out her hand. "I'll take that."

"Thanks." He hadn't taken his gaze off Missy, which made her squirm. Usually, people noticed Selena or Juliet. Missy didn't enjoy being the center of attention.

Bria nudged Selena, who elbowed Nell.

Oh, man. Missy hoped Sam didn't see that either. Or Juliet's not-so-subtle thumbs up to Missy.

What had gotten into them? For some reason, they were channeling Charlene Culpepper.

It had to stop.

Before they completely embarrassed Missy in front of Sam Cooper. She didn't want to be rude, but she needed distance from Sam. That meant one thing.

Time to get out of there.

Where was Missy going?

Sam hurried out of the kitchen after her. Had he said something wrong? Not that he'd said much. But something had flashed on her face before she bolted. It had been there for an instant and then disappeared too fast to name.

Excellent observation skills, Cooper.

A knot in his gut tore at him.

Why would his observation skills would kick in now when they'd failed his partner? Strange, given Sam's brain went haywire around Missy Hanford.

Missy grabbed her purse and raced out the door as if an earthquake were hitting. She'd mentioned getting home to the kittens, but this was weird.

By the time he stepped outside, she was almost to her car. Not bad for someone with an injured foot.

Standing next to the driver's door, she removed her keys from her purse.

"Missy!" Sam called out. "Wait up."

She said nothing, but she lowered her right hand, holding the keys, to her side.

He came around the front of her car. Standing in the street wasn't the safest place, but midday meant slow traffic in Berry Lake, especially in the residential neighborhood.

"Hey." That was the first thing to come to mind.

She shifted her weight to her good foot. "Was there something you wanted?"

Yes. Sam wanted to spend time with her, even if that amounted to a minute because one more minute was more than he'd had before. He couldn't explain his infatuation other than remnants of his leftover crush.

"How are the kittens?" Fool that he was, Sam didn't know what to say next.

Missy's posture relaxed, suggesting he'd said the right thing. "They are so cute."

"Bet they're already growing."

"They are." She glanced at her car. "They still aren't mobile, but I don't like to leave them alone for too long."

He recognized the brush-off, though maybe she needed to go. "I'll let you get home to them."

Ask her out.

Yeah, right. The voice in his head came from either his subconscious mind or teenage dreams. Whichever, he wanted to shut it up.

He forced his feet to move. Otherwise, he might stay there. Talk about borderline stalker behavior.

Sam had been there before. In high school, he'd memorized her schedule and, more than once, found himself in her path. Yes, he'd been late to several of his classes when he did that. Sam had also seen far more kisses between her and Rob than was healthy for Sam's heart. But when she was alone and said hi to Sam, that had been enough to make the other stuff worth it.

Yep, he'd been a lovesick idiot.

Something he shouldn't want to be again, yet there he was.

His patrol car was down the block. Funny, he hadn't even noticed Missy's car. He'd been too focused on seeing her when he'd bumped into the three women, and Bria had mentioned Missy and Juliet were at the house.

Pathetic.

He forced himself not to watch Missy get into her car, but he heard the door slamming.

Keep walking, Cooper.

And he did.

Except…

His pace slowed.

Missy's car hadn't started.

He slowed more.

What was he waiting for? He wasn't a kid anymore. Keeping everyone in Berry Lake safe, including Missy, was part of his job. Sam turned and returned to her car.

Missy's head rested against the steering wheel.

His heart slammed against his chest. He hurried to the driver's side and knocked on the window.

She straightened before opening the door. "I think my battery's dead. The car was hard to start when I came here, but I thought the drive over would help recharge it. The battery is old, but I thought I had a little more time left before replacing it."

Sunday, she'd left her lights on at the market. That might explain it. "We're not allowed to jump cars."

"I have roadside service coverage, but I don't have time to wait."

"The kittens."

She pulled out her cell phone. "I'll call Jenny. She can send Dare."

"I can drive you home." The offer burst from Sam's lips like water from a fire hose. He wasn't sure if the emotion flowing through him was relief or regret.

Missy lowered her phone. "What?"

"I'll drive you so you can get to the kittens sooner. You and Dare can jump your car later." That sounded like a viable plan. Not bad for putting zero thought into it.

She tilted her head as if considering his offer.

Sam pressed his lips together to keep himself from saying more.

"That'll work." The relief in her voice matched how he felt. "I won't need to drive again today, so there's no rush. I'll text Bria and Juliet to tell them why the car is still here. Thanks."

"Not a problem." Except for the sweat dripping down his neck, giving her a ride wasn't any trouble. And he would get more than one minute with her because Jenny lived on the outskirts of town. "Do you need anything out of the car?"

"My keys and purse." Missy grabbed her things, shut the door, and locked the car with the key fob. "Were you on a call?"

"Down the street. Someone called in a stolen bicycle. It turns out they forgot they biked to the library and walked home."

"Sounds like someone has too much going on."

"Could be. I bumped into Bria, Nell, and Selena on my way to my car." He opened the patrol car's passenger door. "Here you go."

"Oh, I get to ride in the front seat this time," Missy joked.

"You were only in the back because of the kittens."

"Made sense on Sunday night, but I prefer the front. Not that I ride in police cars often. This is my second time. I should just be quiet now."

"You can ride in mine anytime you want." Sam closed the door, headed around the vehicle's trunk, and got into the driver's seat. He grabbed his radio. "This is unit three. Taking a code seven."

"Ten-four," the dispatcher replied.

Missy buckled her seatbelt. "What's a code seven?"

"Lunch break."

"But if you drive me home, when will you eat?"

He started the car and pulled away from the curve. "Between calls, if I can."

"If you can? You need to eat."

"I will."

"Promise?"

Her adamant tone brought a smile to his face, even though she likely acted the same with kittens, cats, and friends. "I promise."

She typed a text.

A notification sounded.

Missy blew out a breath.

Sam couldn't tell if her sigh was good or bad. He tightened his hands on the steering wheel. "Everything okay?"

"Jenny and Dare are going to Brew and Steep. They'll take care of the car for me, and I can stay home. I'm so lucky to have them."

Missy's parents had disowned her for wanting to marry Rob. The drama had played out in public. First inside the cupcake shop and then outside on Main Street. Thankfully, the Hanfords had taken Missy in. She and Rob had been together for years, so she was an honorary member of the family.

"Family is important," Sam said.

She angled toward him in the car. "Yours must be happy to have you home."

"Ecstatic."

"You don't sound as enthused."

He laughed. "Never expected to move back in with my parents."

"You haven't been here long."

"True, but I hope to find a place soon."

"Do you want to rent or buy?"

Sam considered the question. "I rented an apartment in Seattle. Housing was expensive there, but I would consider buying if the right house was available."

"You plan on staying in Berry Lake."

"I do."

He didn't need to tell her about the low turnover rate in the sheriff's department or how he wanted Josh and Hope to have lots of kids.

Sam also knew how fast life could change or how quickly it could end. His parents weren't old, but he wanted to spend more time with Mom and Dad even if he didn't enjoy living with them.

"Do you remember Mrs. Vernon?" Missy asked.

"I did yard work for her one summer."

Missy laughed. "Every teenage boy in Berry Lake has done something for her."

"At least she hired locally."

"True."

"What about Mrs. V?" he asked.

"Her house will go on the market soon. I was thinking of making an offer, but I'm going to use the money I saved for a house to buy into the cupcake shop with the rest of the Posse."

He laughed. "The Cupcake Posse. I haven't heard that name in a long time."

"Over fifteen years, probably."

"Doesn't seem that long ago."

"No." Her voice was hoarse. She cleared her throat. "Anyway, the house is solid, with a fenced yard and garage. It needs some work, but you can build equity fast with only a few projects. You should check it out."

The longing in her voice was impossible to ignore. "Are you sure you don't want it?"

"Oh, I want it, but I want to own the cupcake shop with my friends more. Someone else is going to buy Mrs. V's house. Might as well be you."

"Thanks. I'll check it out." He flipped his blinker to turn into Jenny and Dare's driveway.

Sam parked in the space next to a top-of-the-line SUV. He didn't want to drop Missy and go. Plus, he still had time on his lunch break. He went around to her side, but she'd already gotten out of the car.

Jenny hopped out of the SUV's passenger door. Her wide-eyed gaze traveled from Missy to Sam. "Um, hi."

Missy appeared startled. "Oh, I didn't realize you were leaving right away."

Jenny glanced at Sam again. "Dare doesn't want to wait in case he needs to replace your battery. We realized we no longer have a set of keys to your car."

A shadow fell across Missy's face. "I forgot, too."

Not a literal shadow, but something caused the light to dim from her face. Sam wanted to know what. "Did you lose your keys?"

"The fire," Missy and Jenny said in unison.

Oh, right. He hadn't been in town then, though he'd been following along with what his family told him, trying not to ask too many questions about Missy. He'd done internet searches for that.

"That reminds me." Missy gave him a closed-mouth smile. "Sam, not sure if you remember Jenny or vice versa, but you've been reintroduced now."

Jenny outstretched her arm and shook his hand. "Thanks for driving Missy home."

"Happy to help."

"Let me guess." Jenny grinned. "You have an ulterior motive."

Heat rushed up Sam's neck. Had Jenny known about his crush on Missy when they were kids? He swallowed around the lump in his throat and tried to play it cool. "What might that be?"

"The kittens. You want to see them?"

Don't react. He let a slow, lazy smile spread. "Who wouldn't want to see them?"

Missy handed Jenny the car keys. "Thanks again."

"Happy to help." Jenny's gaze bounced between Sam and Missy once again. "And hope to see you around."

Missy's cheeks reddened. *Too cute.*

Sam tried not to stare. "Same."

And it was true. He hoped to return. And not only because of the kittens. All he needed was a sign Missy was open to more. A friendship or a date. He wouldn't push, even if he wanted to.

For now, seeing the kittens would be enough.

His radio sprang to life. "Unit three..."

His stomach sank. Duty called, which meant the kittens and Missy would have to wait.

chapter thirteen

D ALTON CUT OUT of work early to avoid the rush hour traffic in Portland, but he didn't arrive in Berry Lake until six. Bria greeted him with red-rimmed, puffy eyes and a hug. He kissed her forehead. "Did you eat?"

"Selena and Juliet fixed dinner before they went to a movie to give us time alone."

That was nice of them. "Want to talk now?"

She nodded. "Please. I need to get it out so I can move on."

"Sure." Dalton sat next to Bria on her couch. He remembered sitting there in September, telling her he wanted to keep seeing her long distance. They'd kissed, and he'd driven her to the airport. Talk about a difficult goodbye, but the strain on her face tore at his heart now.

Should've left work as soon as she called.

He placed his arm around her. "I'm here. I'm not going anywhere."

Bria nodded.

"What did your dad say?" Dalton asked.

She took a deep breath and then another. "Molly and your dad loved each other."

With each word Bria said, Dalton's muscles tensed. He'd eaten dinner on the drive, but he wished he hadn't. His stomach churned. He might be sick.

Still, he didn't interrupt Bria, even though he'd wanted to from the first minute of her repeating what Brian had told her.

The worst part?

She believed Brian's lies about Dad.

Dalton's hands balled.

Couldn't she see this was one more of her father's schemes? "I'm sorry about Molly's car accident, but there's no way it happened the way your dad said."

"Y-You don't believe him?"

Dalton needed to tread carefully. He didn't want their families to come between them again. "I don't. My dad had nothing to do with this."

"My father has no reason to lie."

Dalton nearly laughed, which wouldn't have gone over well. "What your dad said isn't true. My dad loved my mom, all of us, more than life itself. He would've never been unfaithful. Never. Dad might have owed your dad a favor, but it wasn't for Molly."

"She thought you were your dad."

"Paul is a common name. She has a TBI. Her memory isn't good. We saw that firsthand on Monday morning."

"And the insurance loan?"

"My dad probably invested in one of your dad's projects."

Bria bit her lip but said nothing.

Dalton would give Brian Landon points for creativity. "It's a tragic story. Your dad must've watched a movie or read a book with that plotline. It isn't what happened."

Her dark gaze met Dalton's. "And you know this how?"

"My dad was the most honest, self-integral, responsible man I've ever known. Everyone in Berry Lake says the same thing about him. Paul Dwyer would never do any of the things your dad claims he did."

Bria inhaled deeply and then exhaled. She grabbed a piece of paper lying face down on the coffee table. "I found a letter in my aunt's things. Molly wrote this to your dad. It's the only thing I have of hers, so I made a copy for you."

As he read the letter, Dalton's hands trembled. The words matched Bria's story, but this wasn't about his dad. It couldn't be. "Did Brian know about this letter?"

"Not until I showed it to him this morning. He looked as if he might pass out, but he said Molly told him about giving a letter to Paul."

Dalton waved the paper that fluttered like a surrender flag. "What's this one then?"

"A rough draft, maybe." Bria touched his knee. "It fits with everything my dad said."

"I'm the oldest. This doesn't fit with—"

"Deena told Paul she miscarried the first time she was pregnant, but Charlene heard Deena was never pregnant."

"No." The word catapulted out of Dalton's mouth, even though Remy had done the same to Ezra Monroe. "I mean, my mom would do anything to get what she wanted, but my dad wasn't like that. He was a good man."

"Your dad did the honorable thing and married your mom, but he wasn't perfect."

Heat flushed through his body. He ground his teeth. "I never said my dad was perfect, but he's not here to defend himself against these ridiculous claims. And let's be real. Your father might not be an arsonist, but he's a con artist."

Bria stiffened. She pulled her arm away. "My dad may have gone about things wrong, but what he did, he did out of love. And he bailed out your father more than once. My father is the responsible, selfless one."

"He's playing you. Again."

"What if he's not?" Her question cut through the tension like a machete. "What if everything my dad said is true?"

No way. Dalton shook his head. He'd looked up to Dad. *Dad was everything, the glue. My family fell apart when Dad died, and we still weren't back together.* "It isn't."

Bria didn't scoot away from him, but the distance between them increased as if someone built a border between them, and they'd each chosen different sides.

He hated it.

"Bria—"

"Prove it."

"What?"

"Prove my father wrong. I believe him." She pointed at the letter. "That corroborates his story. It all fits together. I need more than your *opinion* of your dad to change my mind."

Dalton's body was so heavy. The tightness in his chest was painful. "Even if what you say is true, my dad would never ask a woman to leave her child. And he wouldn't leave me. He wouldn't do that."

"You didn't know him when he was younger. And after listening to my dad this morning, I discovered I don't know my father at all."

Her earnest tone suggested nothing Dalton said would change Bria's mind. And that imaginary line between them had the power to separate them. He couldn't allow that to happen. She meant too much to him.

"I'll prove it." Dalton didn't want to wait. He folded the copy of the letter. "Are you okay if I leave you alone?"

She nodded. "Go do what you need to do."

He stood. This wasn't the time for kisses and long goodbyes. Not when he was a man on a mission.

Dalton walked out of the house without saying a word. One person likely knew the truth. He only hoped Mom would be honest with him. If what Brian Landon said was true, then Paul Dwyer wasn't the father that Dalton had known and loved. The man that he'd wanted to emulate and be. It just couldn't be true.

Or his entire life had been based on a lie.

Twenty minutes later, Dalton opened the door to the house where he'd grown up. He hadn't been there in years. He couldn't keep watching Mom marry and divorce husbands—some nice men who tried to be father figures to him—for money. It was easier to stay away.

Dalton stepped inside.

Marble floors and gilded accents greeted him. Sal DeMarco married Mom in October—Dalton had skipped the wedding—so these additions must have come from a previous ex-husband.

Mom swore she would never sell the house Dad built for her, and she hadn't.

He closed the door behind him. "Mom?"

"The prodigal son returns." Mom stood in the arched opening that led to the kitchen and family room. She wore designer clothes and salon-styled hair as if she were the star of *Housewives of Berry Lake*. Plastic surgery and expertly applied makeup kept her looking a decade younger. "Everything okay?"

The concern in her voice sounded genuine. Mom loved him and his siblings in her own way, but she was so into appearances Dalton had a hard time knowing what was real and what was for show.

"I'm not sure," he admitted. "I have some questions about Dad."

She sighed with a resigned expression. "Let me guess. That chubby Landon girl—"

"Bria is my girlfriend." The words came out harsher than Dalton intended. He took a breath. Irritating Mom wouldn't get him the answers he needed. "Please don't talk about her that way."

Mom rolled her eyes. The signature gesture was as much her personality as her Louis Vuitton purses. "Fine."

He followed her into the kitchen-family room area—the entire backside of the house courtesy of ex-husband number two.

As football highlights played on the large TV, Owen and Ian sprawled on the couch. Sal DeMarco sat in a leather chair.

As soon as Sal noticed Dalton, he stood. His tan sweater and black trousers screamed top-of-the-line. His tight smile and unlined face had Botox written all over it.

Maybe this time, Mom found a husband as into labels and looks as her.

"Nice to see you." Sal extended his hand.

Dalton wanted to ask about Sheridan, Sal's daughter. He'd fired and evicted her from the apartment above the art gallery and given Remy the job and a place to live.

Once again, Dalton had to keep the peace if he wanted answers, so he shook his stepfather's hand.

"We're catching up on football." Sal motioned to an empty chair. "Join us. Your mom's about to bring in a charcuterie board."

"Thanks." Dalton glanced at his brothers. As usual, Ian stared, mesmerized by the sports show. Not surprising since football and his position as quarterback were his life. "Any more recruiting trips, Ian?"

Ian didn't glance away from the screen. "Yeah, but I'm hoping I get an offer in-state. My friends are applying to W-S-U and U-dub."

Owen snorted. "You mean the geeky cupcake guy who's come over?"

"Bentley works at Brew and Steep now." Ian's jaw jutted forward. "He's tutoring me so I keep my grades up. I'll need a tutor in college to do the same."

"You don't have to attend college where your friends go." Sal returned to his chair and sat. "Both are excellent schools, but you already have offers. And universities make sure their players have academic support."

Ian's eye roll mimicked Mom's. "Who wants to live in the desert and play in that heat?"

Owen snickered. His bloodshot eyes suggested his half-full wineglass wasn't his first that night. "Mom will make you if they give you a full ride."

Sal side-eyed Owen. "Ian will play football at the best school for him."

Mom carried in the tray, which must've been catered because she had never been an impressive cook. She set the platter next to plates and napkins on the coffee table.

She looked at Dalton. "Let's go into the kitchen and talk."

Dalton followed her. He sat—the fancy stool as uncomfortable as it looked. A plate of goodies sat on the counter. "Is Remy still living in the apartment above the gallery?"

"Yes, but she and Ezra are working things out after a slight misunderstanding."

Misunderstanding? Or Remy's lie about being pregnant and causing the breakup of Ezra's marriage to Juliet? That reminded him of the letter in Dalton's pocket.

Deena sat next to him. "She might move out of the apartment soon. If that happens, Owen will move in there, since he's taking on more management responsibilities at the gallery."

Dalton didn't feel like eating, but he picked up an almond since his mom put out the food. "What's Sal going to do?"

"Relax." His mom smiled. "He's worked so hard over the years. It's time he slowed down. And once Ian is off to college next fall, we plan to travel."

Mom might have finally met someone who would last more than a couple of years. "You've always wanted to do that."

"Sal loves traveling." She glanced over her shoulder at the family room. "You haven't approved of all my marriages, but this one is different. It feels...right."

"I'm happy for you, Mom."

Few people in town liked her, but she'd done her best with what Dad had left them. Dad hadn't made the best investments with his money, but he'd loved his family. He would never cheat or leave his wife and two-year-old son or use his insurance money on a mistress, injured or not. That defied everything Paul Dwyer stood for and had instilled in Dalton.

Mom popped a cube of cheese into her mouth. "What questions do you have about your dad?"

"Bria and I met Molly on Sunday. Earlier today, Brian filled in the gaps, but his story..." Dalton's throat tightened. "Brian said stuff about Dad. And I need to know—"

"If it's true?"

Not trusting his voice, Dalton nodded. He handed over the copy of Molly's letter.

Mom read it. Frowned. She placed the paper on the island's counter. "Molly wrote this to your dad before you were born. He was still in college."

Dalton struggled to breathe. "You're sure?"

Mom touched his shoulder. "I found a similar note after he died. His name was on it. Molly had signed the letter."

"You lied about being pregnant."

It wasn't a question.

Mom didn't cringe or flinch. She tilted her head. "Lie is such a harsh word. I went after what I wanted. I loved your father so much. From the time I was fourteen. Molly wasn't from here. She wouldn't have fit in. I was perfect for your dad."

"You pretended to be pregnant."

"I heard about Paul's engagement. I had to stop him from marrying someone else."

"And then you conveniently miscarried." Dalton made air quotes around the last word.

"I tried hard to get pregnant right after we married, but he returned to W-S-U to finish his degree. I waited as long as I could, and then I had to tell him the truth." Mom sighed. "I had no choice unless I wanted to lose him. I loved him so desperately. He was my world. And then I got pregnant with you. Better late than never."

Bitterness filled Dalton's mouth. He couldn't believe how she justified her actions. "Did you tell Remy to do the same thing with Ezra?"

"I may have put a bug in her ear, but that's what mothers do to make sure their children have the best lives."

Dalton rubbed his eyes. He wanted no part of Mom's justifications.

"What else did the loser tell his daughter?" Mom asked.

He cringed. "Mom, Brian is my girlfriend's father."

"Not my problem," Mom said flippantly. "What did your girlfriend's father say."

"That Molly and Paul got back together when she and Brian returned to Berry Lake. They were going to divorce you and Brian. Only she got into a car accident, and Molly ended up with a TBI."

No shock or surprise appeared in Mom's eyes. She sat as still as a statue.

Time seemed to stop. The noise from the TV faded. The beating of Dalton's heart was the only sound. "Is it true? Did Dad—"

"Your father was a good man, but he had one weakness. Molly." Mom stared at the plate of food. "When she and Brian moved back to Berry Lake, Molly threw herself at Paul. Her flirting was so embarrassing. Brian always struggled to hold down a job. Paul had money. He'd loved Molly once, and he was only human…"

Heat rushed up Dalton's neck. "Dad…cheated? On you?"

Mom nodded, not meeting his gaze. "But he told me what happened. Apologized. Begged for forgiveness."

Dalton tried to make sense of everything. But he couldn't. That wasn't the man Dalton grew up idolizing, the father he loved. "Was this before or after the car accident?"

"Before."

Relief washed over Dalton. His eyelids heated. "Dad wasn't leaving us for her?"

Mom hugged him, and Dalton clung to her like he hadn't in fifteen years, perhaps longer than that. "Your dad loved us. He would have never left us. Never."

The truth didn't erase what Dad had done, but the sting lessened. Dalton didn't know why Brian would lie to his daughter, but… "Then why was Dad at Hayden Lake with Molly?"

Mom let go of Dalton. She cupped his cheek. "Because your dad was a caring man. You and Ian take after him physically, but you're the best parts of him inside."

A lump burned in Dalton's throat.

"Molly asked Brian for a divorce and left Bria with him. She demanded your dad meet her at Hayden Lake. He went there to tell her the affair was over. They argued. She left. Your dad wanted to head home to us, so he drove behind her."

That made more sense to Dalton than Dad wanting to run away with another woman. He remembered what Bria had told him. "Molly swerved so she wouldn't hit an animal and crashed into the lake."

Mom shook her head. "I can see why Brian told her that."

"What really happened?"

"She drove into the lake on purpose."

Dalton inhaled sharply. "But—"

"Your dad was the only witness, honey. Molly didn't want him to break up with her. Perhaps Paul told Brian something other than his wife tried to kill herself. They'd been friends since high school."

"Molly can't tell them what happened."

"Paul said she was injured badly. Karma, if you ask me." Mom's flippant tone bristled. "It took your dad and me some time to get back to where we were, but our marriage got stronger. Then we had the twins and Ian."

"I was afraid my entire life was a lie."

"No, sweetheart. I'm sorry Brian and Bria made you feel that way."

"Bria only relayed what she heard."

Mom studied him, but her gaze was surprisingly loving, not judgmental. "You're so quick to defend her."

"I love her."

Mom flinched. "Already?"

"Not sure I ever stopped. Is that weird?"

"No. I felt the same about your father." Mom's eyes darkened. "Just…be careful. If she's anything like her mother…"

"Bria's her own person. Nothing like her father. And I have no idea about Molly beyond the letter." But Mom mentioning her reminded Dalton of another question. "Dad took out a loan on his life insurance policy. Did you ever find out what he used that money for?"

"I did, but…" Mom rubbed her lips together. "Are you sure you want to know?"

"Yes." Dalton didn't hesitate.

"Your dad invested the money with Brian Landon. Your dad thought he'd double or triple his money and repay the loan. But it turned out to be another one of Brian's get-rich-quick schemes. Did the loan come up in your talk with Bria?"

Dalton nodded. His mom had been honest with him, so he would be the same with her. "Bria said whenever Brian didn't have enough money, Dad took out loans to pay Molly's medical expenses."

Mom's mouth fell open as if all her facial muscles stopped working simultaneously. "That's… Don't listen to Brian Landon. I don't know what he's trying to do other than drive a wedge between you and Bria. He's nothing but a liar and an arsonist."

"A liar, yes," Dalton agreed. "Not an arsonist."

"He's in jail for setting the cupcake shop on fire."

"They dropped all charges against him this morning."

"What?" Mom's screech hurt his ears. "How?"

"Brian sent Bria to pay for Molly's room and get him an alibi. He was in Wishing Bay the night of the fire."

She adjusted her blouse. "I was so sure it was him."

"Everyone was."

Her gaze bounced around the kitchen, not remaining on anything, including Dalton, for long.

"Mom?" he asked.

She tugged at her collar. "I hope they catch the arsonist before another business on Main Street goes up in flames."

"It's been long enough. I don't think that will happen."

"Let's hope so." She motioned to the food. "Eat."

"Not hungry."

"Let me guess. Bria."

Dalton hung his head. "I didn't believe her. Not everything she'd said was true, but you confirmed some of it was."

More than *some*, if he were being honest.

"Give her time. Women need space. Then you can talk to her."

That sounded like good advice. There wasn't a rush. "Should I tell Bria the truth about the car accident?"

Mom touched the spot above his heart. "Listen to what your heart tells you to do."

That didn't sound like Mom at all. Strike that. It sounded like the mom he'd grown up with. Nurturing and always saying the right things. He hadn't seen this side of her in years. More than a decade and a half to be exact. It almost seemed too good to be true, but he didn't want it to stop.

"What if all I hear is crickets?" he asked.

She tilted her head. "Ask yourself what Bria will gain by knowing the information."

Her tone was a mix of compassion and practicality. Funny, but it reminded him of Bria.

"Withholding the truth isn't lying, but sometimes it's necessary to keep from hurting the ones you love," Mom added.

He didn't want to hurt Bria. "So, I shouldn't tell her?"

"Only you can decide that. But how will things change for her if you do? And how will it affect the two of you as a couple? That's what you need to ask yourself."

"I don't know."

"Then take your time and figure it out." Mom touched his face. "Whatever you decide, you must be willing to live with the consequences."

His days of being a kid and a teenager were far behind Dalton, but this caring woman giving him advice was the mom he remembered. The one who'd loved and raised him and his siblings. The one who believed Paul Dwyer was the best husband and father in the world. The one who never looked at another man let alone set her sights on anyone with a seven-figure or more net worth.

Dalton's kindhearted mom had disappeared with Dad's death, and a thrill shot through Dalton at seeing her old personality return.

"Thanks, Mom." Dalton hugged her, not wanting to let go. "I've missed you."

"I've missed you more than you know, my dearest son." Mom squeezed tightly and then let go of him. "But there's something else for you to consider."

"What's that?"

"Brian Landon's lies have the power to destroy your father's reputation. The name Paul Dwyer means something in Berry Lake. If Bria believes her dad, she could do the same thing."

"Bria wouldn't."

Mom smiled softly. "You're quick to defend her."

He imagined Bria's warm smile, and the way she made his life better. "She means everything to me. I want to make the most of our second chance."

"I see that. It's how I feel about Sal. Never thought I'd find that again after your father. I did what I did for you kids."

"I know. I'm glad you're happy now."

"I am. Sal isn't like your dad, but we fit. And I want to remind you the apple doesn't fall far from the tree. I see it with Sal's daughter, Sheridan, who takes after Sabine. And I worry about Bria. She has two parents who weren't the most, shall we say, stable."

Dalton stiffened. "Mom—"

"I'm sorry." She shook her head. "I shouldn't put this on you."

"Put what on me?"

Mom wiped her eyes. "It's just when I think of Brian Landon, I want to scream. He's the reason life was so difficult for us after your dad died. Brian might as well have robbed us in daylight and took away everything that mattered. It's because of him I had to do what I did."

Marry, divorce, repeat. Dalton hadn't considered that. "Bria isn't her father."

"I know, but I get sick to my stomach when I hear his name. And your father would hate Brian if he knew how much that man stole from us. But that's my cross to bear, not yours."

Except it was Dalton's now that she'd mentioned it. If he and Bria got married someday…

He didn't want to disappoint Dad or tarnish Dad's memory or make life harder for Mom.

She kissed his cheek. "I'm so happy you came over here tonight. You should come for Sunday dinner."

"It depends on my schedule for Monday, but I'll try to be here." Dalton didn't mention inviting Bria because what Mom said weighed heavily on him. He'd grown up wanting to make Dad proud, to be the kind of man Dad would point at and say, "*That's my son.*"

Whatever you decide, you must be willing to live with the consequences.

After everything Mom told had him, Dalton wasn't sure what to do next. Family was important. Bria was, too. But how could they be together when they believed completely different stories of the past? One that was a total fabrication. He didn't want to lose Bria, but would she be able to see the truth?

And if not, where did that leave them?

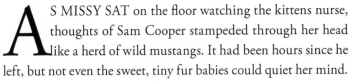
A
S MISSY SAT on the floor watching the kittens nurse, thoughts of Sam Cooper stampeded through her head like a herd of wild mustangs. It had been hours since he left, but not even the sweet, tiny fur babies could quiet her mind.

Ugh. What is wrong with me?

She hadn't seen Sam in nine or ten years. Perhaps longer since he'd gone away for college, and she'd spent some time in Oceanside with Rob before returning to Berry Lake.

Sam was tall and fit like his brother. But unlike Josh, Sam was more than athleticism and good looks. Besides the physical package, compassion shone in his eyes. His face radiated kindness. And his touch...

Nope.

Not analyzing that.

It was weird.

But not seeing someone shouldn't make her stomach all fluttery. She must not have eaten enough at lunch.

Oh, wait. She'd forgotten to eat dinner.

Low blood sugar might cause her to fixate on one thing.

One person.

One man.

Except that had only happened with Rob. He was always on her mind and in her dreams. The fact it was now Sam in her thoughts unsettled her.

Mama Cat meowed.

Warmth balled at the center of Missy's chest. "You're such a good mommy. I wanted to get home, but you had it all under control. I didn't have to worry about your babies at all. You've been feeding your kittens and keeping them nice and warm."

Mama Cat stretched as if to get more comfortable.

"I'm sure it can't be easy taking care of all of them. But you're doing a wonderful job and making my life easier." Some litters Missy fostered without a mama cat, which meant feedings and cleanings and keeping the wee ones warm. She didn't have to do much with this bunch. "Thank you, Mama."

A knock sounded on her front door.

Must be Jenny with the car keys. Missy stood.

A pain shot from her foot up her leg but not as bad as before, which meant she was healing. *About time.* "Don't worry, Mama Cat. I'll feed you, Mario, and Peach after I eat."

She couldn't take care of the cats if she didn't do the same for herself.

In the living room, Mario sat on his cat tree. Peach lounged on the couch.

"Hey sweeties." The two hadn't tried to get into the office. This wasn't their first litter of kittens. "You've been so good."

Missy made a mental note to get copies made of her car and house keys. Jenny and Dare kept a spare set in case they needed to move the car from the driveway. Missy would leave another set hidden in the cottage's window box.

She opened the front door. Jenny stood with…

Missy's heart dropped to her feet—*splat*.

Sam, who no longer wore his uniform, held a pizza box. "Hi."

She closed her gaping mouth. The ability to speak seemed to have vanished.

"Here are your keys." Jenny handed them to Missy. "We bumped into Sam at the pizza parlor. He worked the day shift, so he was ordering dinner. I thought it would be a perfect time for him to see the kittens, and knowing you, you probably forgot to eat tonight."

Jenny's chipper tone suggested she was up to something. But Jenny needed to stop treating Missy as if she couldn't care for herself. Until Dare, Missy was the one who made sure Jenny ate and survived her book deadlines without getting sick.

Missy raised her chin. "I was with the kittens and about to make dinner."

"Now, you don't have to." Jenny beamed brighter than a spotlight. "I told you, Sam."

Sam grinned sheepishly. "Jenny said you liked pepperoni with extra cheese."

"I do. Um, thanks."

"Invite him in," Jenny whispered.

Missy resisted the urge to roll her eyes like she was twelve. She didn't enjoy being told what to do, and since the fire, it had gotten worse. She forced a smile. "Come in."

Sam entered. "Where do you want this?"

"In the kitchen." She waited for Jenny, who remained on the welcome mat. "Aren't you coming in?"

"I need to get to the house."

"You can't leave me alone with…" Missy couldn't bring herself to say his name.

Amusement danced in Jenny's eyes. "Sorry, not sorry."

"You suck."

"You'll thank me later."

"Where are the plates?" Sam yelled.

Missy glanced over her shoulder. She didn't see Sam, so he must be in the kitchen.

"In the top cabinet to the right of the sink." She faced Jenny. Missy wanted to keep her voice low, so he wouldn't hear her. "What will I thank you for?"

"Pushing you out of your comfort zone."

"You sound like Selena."

A sheepish expression crossed Jenny's face.

Missy knew what that meant. "You spoke to Selena?"

Jenny nodded. "Juliet, Bria, and Nell, too. They said so many sparks were flying in Elise's kitchen earlier it surprised them the smoke detector didn't go off."

Okay, all of Missy's friends sucked, too. "I don't need—"

"Yes, you do." Jenny's gaze met Missy's. "You don't want to hear this, but you're why I moved forward with Dare and improved my life in ways I never imagined. Now I want to return the favor. It's time."

Missy's pulse sped up. She had a feeling where Jenny was going with this, but Missy still asked. "For what?"

"Your heart has been on hiatus for far too long. It's time for you to live again. It's what Rob would have wanted for you."

She forced herself not to remember what Rob told her during that dream in the hospital. "I'm living just fine."

"Fine isn't the adjective I would use. It's time for a change." Jenny leaned forward and lowered her voice and ticked off points on her fingers. "Sam's cute. Has excellent taste in pizza. Likes cats and cupcakes. And he crushed on you in high school."

Wait, what? No, that wasn't possible. Missy shook her head. "What are you talking about? He didn't. I would have noticed."

"You were so wrapped up in Rob you wouldn't have even noticed if Bigfoot stood next to you."

Jenny wasn't wrong. "But—"

"Rob knew. Told me Sam used to wait for you in the hall between classes with goo-goo eyes. Rob found it funny because you were oblivious. It made him love you more."

Missy glanced over her shoulder again. "High school was a long time ago. I'm not that same person."

"Neither is Sam. And Rob's no longer here. But he would approve of Sam. They were friends."

"I have friends, plus you and Dare. Briley."

Jenny touched Missy's shoulders. "I'm so happy the Posse is in your life again, but you need more."

Relief flooded Missy. Jenny was talking about... "Friends."

"Yes, and friends who turn into more."

Missy gulped. "I can't."

"You can but won't." Jenny lowered her arm. "I'm giving you a metaphorical push with the full support of the Posse and a thumbs up from Sabine."

Missy's jaw ached. "You *all* talked about me today?"

"Texted. Because we love you and want you to be happier."

As if it were that easy. Missy sighed.

"So go in there, enjoy the pizza, get to know Sam, introduce him to the kittens, and have fun."

Missy frowned. "You write thrillers, not romance novels."

"Who knows?" Jenny winked. "This might lead me to try a new genre. Love you."

"I love you. Even if I don't like you right now."

With a laugh, Jenny walked away.

Missy closed the door and headed to the kitchen. She glanced at Rob's photographs on the fireplace mantel.

Please help me, Rob. I'm not ready for this.

Nothing happened. Except… She did a double take. It almost looked like his smile widened in one photo.

I must be seeing things. Stress will do that to a person.

And right now, she wanted to jump out of her skin.

But Missy had survived worse, so she pushed back her shoulders, took a deep breath, and entered the kitchen. And…

She froze.

Sam had set the table with plates, paper towels, and glasses, which was so sweet of him. The packets of chili pepper flakes and parmesan cheese sat in the middle.

Funny, but that was where Rob used to put them on their pizza nights. He would stick the box in the oven because she didn't enjoy eating cold pizza. She'd forgotten that until now.

Missy forced herself not to glance at the mantel. She'd lived off her memories for so long it was hard to be in the present. But tonight, she would try for her friends, for Sam, and for herself. "You've been busy."

"I found the cups in the same cabinet as the plates. I didn't know where you kept the napkins."

Missy swallowed. "Paper towels are okay. That's what I use."

"Me too. Well, until I moved in with my folks." Sam moved to the stove. He used a dish towel to remove the box. "I didn't want the pizza to cool off, so I stuck the box in the oven. Much better hot, don't you think?"

The same way Rob used to do. What was going on?

Not trusting her voice, she nodded. But her insides reeled.

I asked for help, Rob. Not signs. Just stop it. Please.

The pizza was almost gone. Mario and Peach sat at Sam's feet, waiting for him to drop any food.

Traitors. Missy would deal with them later.

She refilled their glasses with water twice. So far, having dinner with Sam hadn't been awkward. They'd discussed their favorite TV shows, musicians, and sports teams. Some overlapped. Others didn't.

"Want to see the kittens now?" she asked.

Sam downed the rest of his water. "The dishes?"

"Your mom trained you well." She stood, headed into the kitchen, and washed her hands.

"My mom and Ava." Sam laughed. The rich sound wrapped around her like a thick blanket. He followed her to the sink. "Now that I'm home, Hope's joined in. It seems like married couples want everyone to pair up."

Curiosity got the best of Missy. She dried her hands. "Are you seeing anyone?"

"Well, I'm looking at you." Sam washed his hands. "But, no, I'm not dating anyone. I…I haven't for a while."

Something in his tone raised more questions. "Sounds like there's something to that."

He shrugged, drying his hands. "I dated someone for a few years, but she hated me working as a police officer. She considered it too dangerous a job."

"Isn't it?"

"Yes, but then, I would have said we're trained and understand the risks. That I could get hit crossing the street."

"What changed?"

"A domestic abuse call." Sam dried his hands, even though she thought he'd done that already. "Ritchie, my partner, and I had been to the house before, so had others, but the spouse never pressed charges. Only this time, she hadn't cowered. She fought back. He shot her and ambushed us before turning the gun on himself."

She touched his shoulder. "Were you…"

Sam moved her hand two inches. "A bullet hit right here."

"Oh, Sam." Missy made circles over the spot as if she could rub away his pain. "What about Ritchie?"

Sam took a breath and another. "He was…killed."

As her hand stilled, the rest of her froze. His grief-filled tone was all too familiar. She'd sounded that way herself. Sometimes she still did. "I…"

"There are no words, which I'm sure you, of all people, understand."

Of course, she did. "I do."

"Don't know why I'm telling you this." Sam shook his head. "I'm sorry."

"No need to apologize." Missy knew something that might help. At least temporarily. She held his hand, pretending the two didn't fit so well together or feel so right. "Come with me."

She led him into the office and let go of his hand. "Mama Cat and kitties, meet the man who saved you."

He half smiled. "*You* did that. I was just the driver."

"How about we share the credit?"

"I'm up for sharing." He peered closer. "Their eyes are still closed."

"They should open on Sunday. If not then, for sure a couple of days after that." She sat on the carpet with her back against the wall. "Their ears should unfold soon, too."

Sam sat next to her. "They're cute."

The cats wiggled and made quiet noises, more mewls than meows.

"Really cute. Is the mom protective?"

"Like a queen. She'll want us to keep our distance for another week."

"It's warm in here."

She motioned to the thermostat. "I keep this room warm. The kittens can't regulate their temperature yet."

"Worth sweating then."

"If you're warm, take off your hoodie." As soon as the words left her mouth, she hoped he wore something underneath. If not…

Her temperature shot up.

Sam pulled the sweatshirt over his head and tossed it near the door. His green T-shirt showed his broad shoulders and nicely muscled arms.

He stared at the kittens. "I see why you foster."

She forced her attention onto the cats. "I can watch them for hours. Who am I kidding?" She threw up her hands. "I do."

"There are worse hobbies you can have."

"Glad I'm a crazy cat lady and not a horse lover. Those show jumpers are so expensive." Missy sensed him looking at her. She glanced his way and saw she was correct. "What?"

"Did you ever worry about Rob after he enlisted?"

She nearly laughed. "I never got a full night's sleep after that. I hated when he joined the Marines."

Sam's lips parted. Surprise filled his eyes. "But that was his dream."

"And why I supported him."

"My ex-girlfriend wanted me to quit." His gaze returned to the kittens. "She was always texting me stats of shootings and officers killed in the line of duty."

Missy had kept her thoughts to herself, but… "Yikes. Is that why you broke up?"

"After I got shot, she gave me an ultimatum. Her or my job."

Missy pictured Rob in his dress blues. So handsome. He'd loved being a Marine. "Do you regret choosing the badge?"

"No." Sam didn't hesitate to answer. "I wouldn't be here if I hadn't."

"But you returned to Berry Lake."

"I didn't want to stay in Seattle. Too many memories. Good ones, but the bad ones took over."

"Must've been hard."

He nodded. "Was it with Rob?"

"Yes. I was so scared something might happen to him."

"Did you tell him how you felt?"

"Not beyond a loved one's normal worry."

Sam scooted closer. His eyes were on her so intently. "Why didn't you tell him?"

Her heart pounded in her chest so loudly she was sure Sam could hear each beat. "I was afraid Rob would choose the Marines over me."

"Never."

If she'd been brave enough to face the consequences, she should have asked, and he would still be with her. "I'll never know, and I lost him anyway..."

"Rob would have chosen you." Sam's tone was firmer than she'd expected. "If not, he was..."

"What?"

"A fool."

Her heart thudded. She needed to hear that. "Thank you."

Maybe Jenny and her friends were right. Oh, not about dating, but Missy enjoyed being with Sam in a way she hadn't expected.

But not even a herd of cats with claws extended and fangs showing would make her admit that to anyone.

Sam hadn't expected to have dinner with Missy, but there was nowhere he'd rather be. Even though she'd fallen asleep, still sitting on the floor, fifteen minutes ago.

Her head rested against his shoulder, and the left side of her body touched his. Nothing could pry him from this spot.

But Mama Cat kept looking at him, and the other two cats outside scratched at the door.

He fished his cell phone out of his pocket. Mom and Ava knew about his teenage crush on Missy. Josh, too, but he was traveling to announce a football game. *Forget Dad.* That left...

Sam hit Hope's name in his contacts.

One ring, two rings…

"Hey, Sam." Hope sounded a little out of it, which suggested she was painting. "Everything okay?"

"I'm fine. In your studio?"

"Yes. Inspiration struck."

"I'll make it quick." Missy's breaths remained even. He lowered his voice. "What does it mean when cats are scratching at the door or side-eyeing you?"

"They want something. Food or attention."

Missy hadn't fed them. At least not while he'd been there. Trust him. He'd been watching her so closely he would have noticed.

"Must be food."

"Did your parents get a cat?"

"No, I'm not at home. Thanks."

"Wait. Where are you?"

Busted. Sam hadn't gotten off the phone fast enough. Only the truth would do in a town this size. "Missy Hanford's."

"Get out of town!" The words rushed out. "Isn't she the love of your life? Well, the unrequited one?"

His face heated. This time, it had nothing to do with the temperature in the room. "I see my mom and sister have been talking to you."

"It was Josh, actually. So, is something happening with Missy?"

Only in my dreams. The position of her head on his shoulder gave him a view of her serene expression and closed eyes.

Just beautiful.

He raised his hand to push the hair off her face, but he pulled back his arm. Touching her while she slept would be creepy.

"No, she fell asleep while we were watching the kittens. But now the cats are acting funny, and I feel like I should do something."

Hope laughed.

Huh? Sam gripped the phone. "What's so funny?"

"All you have to do is wake Missy up."

"She's tired." He wasn't holding her like on Sunday night when he carried her to his patrol car, but this was a close second. And he wanted to enjoy it.

"Her other cats will be fine, but the mom cat might need to eat, so unless Missy showed you where she keeps the food..."

"She didn't."

"Then wake her up." Hope was too sweet to snicker, but the sound she made could have doubled for one. "Have fun."

Sam disconnected from the call. "Missy."

She didn't stir.

"Hey." He jostled her shoulder. "The cats might need to eat."

Her half-moon of eyelashes fluttered open. Her gaze was sleepy, and her lips remained closed.

"Sam?" Her head remained on his shoulder. "You're here?"

He never wanted to leave. If he lowered his mouth a little, he could kiss her. In an alternate universe where he saw her before Rob Hanford. Or if she'd only ask.

Focus, Cooper.

"Something's up with the cats," he said. "The big ones, not the kittens."

Her eyelids flew open. Her face reddened. She straightened. His shirt had left lines on her face. "I fell asleep. I'm so sorry."

"Don't apologize, but the cats might be hungry."

She pushed to her feet, favoring one. "They're used to eating on a schedule. I can't believe I forgot to feed them."

He stood and picked up his sweatshirt. "The kittens distracted you."

"Not only the kittens." Missy's gaze met his.

Something passed between them—a connection.

It wasn't his imagination. This was real.

Sam had no idea what it meant, but he intended to find out.

chapter fifteen

THURSDAY MORNING, NELL exited exam room three. The moon hadn't been full last night, but the nurse's station board was full of patients, which meant a busy day ahead. She didn't mind because her reward was watching a movie with Gage tonight. The busier she was, the faster her shift went.

She glanced around, looking for the orderly who would transport her patient to imaging. No one was there, only an empty wheelchair. This patient would be taken on the gurney.

Nell poked her head into the room. The man had fallen and appeared to have broken several ribs, but the doctor wanted to confirm that. "Imaging appears to be backed up. Someone will be here to take you for an X-ray soon. If you need me before that, press the call button."

The man in his forties groaned. "Okay."

She fought a grimace. The poor guy was in so much pain. "I'll be back to check on you."

Nell made her way to the nurse's station. Cami Marks, friend and coworker, sat behind the counter at the computer.

The cup of coffee Nell poured when she arrived had been sitting for nearly an hour. It must be lukewarm by now. "I need a refill. Want anything?"

"An IV of caffeine." Cami swiveled in the chair. Strands of hair had fallen out of her ponytail. Another sign this would be a long day. "The sun's barely been up, and this place is a madhouse. Is it too late to call in sick?"

"You used up your sick days when that stomach bug hit the twins."

Cami groaned. "Don't remind me. Hunter and Harper threw up for days. I've never done so much laundry in my life. Oh, I take that back."

"The lice incident," they said in unison and then laughed.

Life as a single mom wasn't easy, but Nell respected how Cami balanced her job as an RN with raising kids. Her ex-husband took them twice a month on weekends, but even that wasn't without difficulties.

Nell wanted kids, but after watching Cami struggle, Nell thought twice about having a baby on her own. She clapped. "That's for you always handling everything so well."

"It helped to have you bringing me dinners and detergent and whatever that little comb thingy was."

"That's what friends are for." Nell would continue to help Cami and be the best surrogate auntie and godmother when any of the Posse had babies.

An orderly approached her. "Taking three to imaging."

About time. Still, Nell smiled. She didn't want to upset the department, who transported the patients. "He's ready for you. Oh, there's a wheelchair sitting—"

He held up his hands. "I'm just here to transport the patient to imaging."

With that, the orderly headed toward the exam room at a leisurely pace.

Nell glanced at Cami, who typed on the keyboard. "Guess I'll take care of the wheelchair myself."

"Take care of what, Nurse Nell?" Welles sauntered to the counter. A clean-shaven face and cheeky grin replaced Sunday's dirt and stubble. His delicious, woodsy male scent hung in the air. "Anything I can do for you?"

The guy smelled good and had stealth moves down. She hadn't heard him, which was unusual for her and Cami. Their Welles radar was usually on point. They needed time to brace themselves for his incoming banter. But since he was here and offering, and Nell needed coffee… "Can you please get the empty wheelchair out of the way, Paramedic Welles?"

"At your service." He bowed before strutting away.

Nell went into the break area and refilled her cup. She took two sips and instantly felt re-energized. As she returned to the station, she noticed the wheelchair was in the same exact spot.

At least she got her coffee.

Cami tsked. "This is an interesting turn of events."

Nell checked the board of patients to see where she needed to be next. "What do you mean?"

"Welles doing you a favor means you'll owe him. My guess is he'll want repayment in the form of that date he keeps asking you out on."

"He's just being Welles." She glanced at the wheelchair again and saw Welles talking to the new lab tech. "See."

Nell motioned to him. The tech, who looked like she was in her early twenties, laughed.

Cami rolled her eyes. "Part of the firefighting academy must be training them how to flirt. Even his partner, Jordan, has all the moves down, and he's married."

"Happily, too. But yeah. Must be some special class they take." Nell tilted her head. "Though Welles didn't ask me out when he came up. That's usually the first thing he says to me."

"Perhaps Paramedic Welles is trying out a new plan of attack." Cami shot Nell a sideways glance that screamed *watch yourself.* "And it seems to be working, given how you keep watching him."

"Nope. I find him…amusing. Never fear. He won't beat me down."

"Hope not, since you have Gage."

Except Nell didn't have him. Not in the way Cami implied. Sure, he'd called Nell babe on Sunday night, but the word hadn't passed over his lips since then. He also hadn't kissed her when he left, but Welles had been there again. *Maybe tonight?*

"Wait." Cami's eyes grew wider. "You are still seeing gorgeous Gage, right?"

Nell shimmied her shoulders. She'd been trying to be lowkey since Bria didn't hear from Dalton last night, but Nell's excitement kept building. "We have a date tonight."

Nell wasn't sure Gage would call it that, but he'd agreed to come over and watch movies, so she defined that as a date. Not that it would be a date with flowers. That didn't seem like his style. Besides, if it weren't raining, he would insist on climbing or hiking or bungee jumping off a bridge. However, she doubted that the last one could be accomplished spontaneously. But Nell would happily take the assist from Mother Nature, so they'd stay inside where it was warm and dry and—she crossed her fingers—cozy.

"That must thrill your mom."

"She's ecstatic. Though, I wish she'd stop telling me how long it'll take her to plan our wedding."

"Events by Charlene," Cami joked.

"Don't remind me." But no matter Nell's label, hanging out with Gage, even if only hiking or climbing or watching a crazy skiing movie, had stopped her mom from meddling and matchmaking. "I texted her to make sure she didn't drop by unexpectedly tonight."

"Smart."

"Experienced." Control issues and overwhelming love for her three daughters fueled Mom's surprise visits, but at least she cared enough to stick her nose where it didn't belong. Missy didn't even know where her mom was. Juliet's had been killed traveling in some faraway land. And Bria's... Nell shook her head. At least Selena still got along with her mother. "But my mom's so keen on Gage, she's been keeping her distance."

"Talk about a win-win."

It was. Nell pictured Gage's green eyes, strong jawline, plump lips, high cheekbones, and ridiculously long eyelashes. Add in the blond hair and swimmer's build... She sighed. "If Gage weren't such an adrenaline junkie, he'd be the perfect man."

"Talking about me again, Nurse Nell?" Welles shot her a lopsided grin.

"The other perfect man in her life," Cami answered before Nell. "Gage."

"Oh, him." Welles didn't sound thrilled. The curve of his lips turned mischievous, matching the gleam in his eyes. "Never realized you loved outdoor adventures so much, Nell."

Nell glared at him. She hoped he saw each of the scalpels she imagined hitting him with. Of course, Welles knew the truth about her and "nature," but he egged her on whenever he got the chance. Even as a younger kid, he always tried to impress her. Only their ages had changed now.

Cami scoffed. She tossed her head so her ponytail went flying. "You act like you're an expert on Nell, but you don't know her at all."

Her friend was trying to help, even if she'd taken what Nell said out of context. Still, if Welles stopped...

"Nurse Nell can speak for herself." Laughter danced in his eyes. "Isn't that right, babe?"

That man. She clenched her jaw.

He winked. "Sounds better coming from me than Mister Perfect."

Nell blew out a breath. "You're—"

"Hot."

"Insufferable."

He gave a sexy smirk. "That's a big word when so many shorter ones would do. Sexy. Awesome. The one. Though, that's two words, still not as many letters."

"I have work to do." Nell picked up a file to emphasize her point. "Shouldn't you and Jordan be off to the station or on another call?"

"Jordan's making a report. And I had to see if my favorite nurse wanted to go out with me on Saturday night since it's still raining, and we won't be climbing. I promise we'll be inside and sitting. Oh, and the date will involve food."

Food always got Nell's attention. "Tempting…"

He waggled his eyebrows, almost making her laugh. But he kept staring. Nell wouldn't call it a connection, but something passed between them, and she jerked her gaze away.

Cami's gaze darted between Nell and Welles like a metronome. "Um."

That shook Nell out of whatever trance she'd been in. "Selena's leaving town on Sunday, so my weekend's booked with the Posse," Nell finished.

He shrugged with one shoulder, which only said how little he cared about going out with her. *But knowing Welles, in 3, 2, 1…*

"One of these days, you'll say yes, Nurse Nell. And then all your dreams will come true. With me."

"Not with Gage around," Cami mumbled under her breath.

Nell swallowed a laugh. She liked Welles as a friend and to have him along with the Gage adventures, but Welles was such a flirt. She'd been joking about the fire academy because with Welles, flirting came to him as naturally as breathing. He could break her heart without even realizing it. And she wouldn't put herself at risk so that could happen again.

"I've said this before." Staring down her nose at him, she used her serious-nurse voice. "If I ever agree to go out with you, you'd back out faster than the doughnuts disappear in the break room, Paramedic Welles."

His forehead creased. "Thought you preferred cupcakes?"

Cami snorted. "She does."

Welles beamed brighter than the red lights on his rig. He sidled up to her with so much confidence he could have been a cowboy or a fighter pilot if he hadn't become a paramedic.

"Have fun with Gage." Welles's gaze seemed to pierce into her deepest thoughts and desires, making her gulp. "It's only a matter of time before you realize you're better off with me."

Welles sauntered off before Nell answered.

Whoa. She needed a moment. Or ten.

Cami pushed away from the counter. "What was that?"

Not trusting her voice, Nell swallowed. "I'm not sure."

But at least with Welles on duty tonight, he wouldn't be dropping in on her and Gage. That was a good thing, right?

The weather forecast called for another dreary, wet, overcast day. Rain hit Elise's roof, more of a pitter-patter than a downpour, but the clouds didn't keep light from peeking through the curtain's edges in the guest room.

Selena rolled over, changed positions once more, and returned to the spot where she'd started.

Why can't I get comfortable?

She loved lazy mornings when Logan was with her. He was on a five-day road trip—six if she counted the Tuesday night he'd left. This wasn't the longest he'd be away during the season. And once he was home late Sunday night, they would sleep in and celebrate with breakfast in bed. Staying in bed today would only make her want something she couldn't have.

Selena glanced at the time on her phone.

Nearly eight. Far from early. Her clients on the East Coast and across the pond had probably sent her messages already. Hanna would contact Selena if anything were urgent. Her assistant always had everything under control.

But first…

Selena sat and closed her eyes.

A few minutes of meditation would clear her mind. Except Bria appeared in Selena's mind. Then the letter from Molly popped up. Missy and Sam, who hadn't been able to stop looking at each other yesterday, came next. Then sweet Lulu, who wanted to run free. And finally, Logan with his sexy smile and love-filled eyes.

The images and thoughts continued like a slide show.

That wouldn't do.

She focused on her breathing.

In-out, in-out.F

Slowly, the images and thoughts faded.

Selena relished the stillness.

The phone rang, breaking the silence and the quietness in her mind. The ringtone belonged to Logan.

Her eyelids flew open. She grabbed the phone so it wouldn't wake anyone.

Bria should be asleep. Dalton hadn't called or texted after talking to his mom last night. A jerk move in Selena's opinion, but Brian had rocked two families yesterday, and they might feel more fallout today. She hoped Dalton only needed time. The guy would never find a better match for himself than Bria. But good or bad, the Posse would be there for her.

Selena accepted the call. "Hey, handsome. This is the best way to start my day."

"Good morning, gorgeous." His warm voice washed over Selena like a hot shower, loosening the tension from her body. "I know a better way, if we were together."

Even on the phone, the innuendo in his voice practically caressed her cheek. Logan Tremblay wasn't known for being subtle—in the bedroom or on the ice.

"I'm sure you do." Selena slipped out of bed and went into the kitchen with the cell phone. No sign of her friends or their pets. The coffee pot was off. That needed to be fixed.

"What are you doing?" he asked.

"Sorry." She added water and ground beans and hit the *on* button. "Making coffee."

"You can't survive without a cup first thing."

She grabbed a mug from the cupboard. "One hundred percent."

"I just wanted to hear your voice. I miss you so much."

She gripped the phone. "Miss you, too. Last night's game was close. Looked rough."

You okay was implied but not spoken.

"Tough team. Refs missed some calls, but we pulled out the win at the last minute, thanks to Ransom's hot stick. The guy's on fire. But I'm feeling it hard today."

Meaning his body hurt.

Hope fluttered in her heart. Not over him feeling any pain, but Logan never used to talk about being sore the day after. Not even when his nasty bruises had to be killing him.

Maybe he'd moved beyond proving himself to the rookies who made fun of his age. If so, this could be his last season. She visualized their life post-hockey. It would be so good.

Except she couldn't get ahead of herself. Living in the now, being who she needed to be to have her ideal future, was how she would achieve everything she wanted. "Make sure the trainers take care of you. Tell them what hurts."

"They did last night and will again today." Logan exhaled loudly. "Just wish it was you taking care of me. I…"

Something in his voice caused her breath to catch. "What?"

"Any chance you want to join me on this road trip?"

The hope in his voice sent her heart stumbling. She needed to keep the excitement out of her voice. "The first month of the new season, and you're asking that?"

"I know." Logan half laughed. "But I miss you already."

The miles and time zones separating them faded. His words gave her all the feels. So much love. She hugged herself with one arm.

Despite the way *she* resented hockey, Logan loved her. She had no doubts about that. "Same."

"Since you didn't say yes, you must need to stay in Berry Lake."

"For now." She gave him a rundown of what they'd learned yesterday from Bria. "So that's why I have to stay."

"I understand. But man, it sucks for Bria and Dawson, no *Dalton*." Logan hadn't been to Berry Lake, so he had no reason to remember anyone, but she appreciated him trying. "Glad you're there to support them."

She inhaled the aroma of brewing coffee filling the air. A cup would be hers soon. Part of her wanted to fill a second cup for Logan, even though he wasn't with her.

"But I still wish you were here," he added.

"Me, too." Selena traveled to a few games each season, but the hotels and arenas got to her after a few days. She hadn't minded in the beginning, but that was when they were in their mid-to-late twenties. At thirty-seven, that wasn't her scene any longer. "I'll be home when you arrive."

"I'm counting on it. Any plans for today?"

"Dog sitting Lulu for Juliet while she works. I have a couple of one-on-one calls with clients. Oh, and an interview."

"Jealous you can work anywhere."

Is this an opening... "Someday, you'll have the same option."

"I will."

She waited for him to say more.

"Hey, I've gotta run." He sounded contrite. "I'll call you after the game."

"Can't wait." Even if Selena's marriage might not be exactly how she wanted it to be now, they would work things out.

"I hope things go well with your friends." He smacked his lips together in a kiss against the phone. "Love you."

"Thanks, and I love you. So much."

He disconnected the call, and she lowered the phone.

The conversation hadn't erased her growing discontentment. It wasn't until talking to Roxy that Selena had homed in on the problem. She wanted more time with Logan. She wanted to say goodbye to being a WAG. She wanted the dream life they'd planned for years.

Logan wasn't the problem. She was the one who'd changed. *Patience.*

She needed to remain patient for the rest to fall into place.

The only problem?

Her gut told her this would be the longest season yet.

When Nell arrived home, she put away the groceries she'd picked up on the way, showered, and tidied up the living room. Gage had been there for the late dinner on Sunday, but she wanted him to be comfortable when it was just the two of them.

She'd been thinking about Welles this afternoon. He provided a good buffer and made things with Gage easier. She hoped she wouldn't miss Welles tonight.

But someone else would be there. Not a buffer but an antagonist.

Nell headed to her foster cat, aka Mr. Teddy, and rubbed his fluffy fur. "Gage is coming over tonight. Please be nice to him."

Mr. Teddy ignored her. Typical. Her foster cat reminded Nell of a little old man in a fur coat with selective hearing.

The cat wouldn't deter her. "Gage is keeping Mom off my back. It's nice not to be called a spinster every time she talks to me. No one uses the word except for Mom. I'm not sure where things stand with Gage. Our coffee date was great. Hiking was bearable, but he acted weird during that skiing movie, more like a buddy than a date. Then, Welles joined in on our adventures, and things relaxed again. I'd like to see where things go with Gage. Though, not in a way to get physically fit and do cardio training while staring at his killer body. So, please be good?"

Mr. Teddy turned, so she had a perfect view of his butt.

She groaned. "I can return you to the rescue."

An empty threat because Nell enjoyed coming home to someone, even if that someone was a grumpy cat.

"Suit yourself, but you'll have to earn your nighttime treat. I won't just give it to you. No matter how much you stare and pout."

Nell plumped the pillows, arranged the throw on the couch, and ran through the beverage options in the fridge. They hadn't discussed dinner, so she hoped munchies were okay. Snacks were part of a necessary food group, and she'd replenished her stock at the store today.

The doorbell rang.

Nell wagged her finger at the cat. "Be good."

She opened the door and found Gage holding a bag in one hand and flowers in the other.

Oh, wow. Her pulse accelerated like the pole car on the first lap of the Indy 500.

His faded jeans and a tight T-shirt showed off his muscles. "I come bearing gifts. Dinner and flowers."

The exquisite bouquet contained her favorite flowers. Nell felt special in a way she hadn't since…she'd met Gage.

She smoothed her hair. "Thanks."

A part of her felt terrible. She'd been using him to keep Mom away. And maybe Nell had been guilty of keeping her distance because he was so out of her league. That would save her from disappointment when he no longer wanted to be with her. Because if her long-time boyfriend threw away years of dating her after knowing someone else for two weeks, any man could do the same.

And Selena T would tell Nell to get over that kind of thinking. "Come in."

Gage stepped inside. "It's good to see you. I brought Thai food."

She closed the door behind him. "One of my favorites."

"I know. I asked."

"Welles?"

Gage handed her the flowers. "Your mother."

"Oh." Nell's heart sank.

"I wanted to get this right."

"That's thoughtful." She brushed off her disappointment, since the guy had wanted to please Nell. Gage asking Mom would only have positive benefits.

She sniffed the blossoms. The light fragrance reminded her of the wildflower fields on the outskirts of town. "I'll put them in water."

Nell went into the kitchen, pulled out a vase, and filled it with water. She stuck the flowers into the vase and arranged the ones out of place. "These flowers are so gorgeous. They brighten the whole place."

"So does your smile."

Okay, this has to be a date. Exactly what she wanted. Nell wiggled her toes.

Gage removed the food containers from the bag. "I have chicken satay, yellow curry, shrimp Pad Thai, and rice."

Nell's favorites. Warmth spread through her. "I love all of them."

"Do you want to eat in front of the TV?"

"Sure." She opened the fridge. "I have beer, pop, iced tea, lemonade, water."

"A beer sounds good."

It did. "Do you want a glass?"

"Please."

They worked side by side in the kitchen until they carried the plates, silverware, napkins, food, and drinks to the coffee table. This was better teamwork than when he hiked ahead of her. That had to be a good sign. Especially since she hadn't expected him to be as easy to be around indoors.

Mr. Teddy curled into a ball at the opposite end of the couch. *Please be nice. Or stay asleep.*

That might be the better option.

As if on cue, the cat raised his head. Mr. Teddy looked at Nell and then Gage.

The cat hissed.

She cringed. "Sorry."

"No problem. I intend to win him over." Gage reached into his pocket and pulled out a…

A feather? Nell took a closer look. A stuffed mouse with a feather tail.

He wiggled the mouse in front of Mr. Teddy.

The cat pawed at the toy like a kitten.

Gage set the mouse in front of Mr. Teddy. "Have fun with it."

Mr. Teddy attacked it like he was a wild jungle cat.

Nell's heart melted. "Thank you."

He sat on the opposite end of the couch from the cat so she would be between them. "Mr. Teddy might prefer some distance from me."

"Looks like you just gave him his new favorite thing."

"You're my new favorite thing." Gage patted the cushion next to him. "What are we watching?"

She sat next to him. He was strong and warm, and this was really happening. "I was thinking old-school rom-com."

"A black-and-white film?"

"Not that old school." This morning, she'd set up the movie, so when she turned on the TV, the streaming service took her right there. "It's called *You've Got Mail*, and it's one of my favorites."

"Tonight's about your favorites." Gage handed her a plate. "My hope is by the end of tonight, I'll get added to the list."

Nell's heart skipped a beat. She grabbed a satay stick. "Well, no spoilers, but it's looking pretty good right now."

"Let's hope I can keep on track."

Anticipation surged. Nell crossed her fingers under the plate she held. She wanted to tell Cami and Welles, especially Paramedic Welles, Gage was the perfect guy; he was her new boyfriend, and he promised not to break her heart.

That wasn't too much to ask, was it?

chapter sixteen

S ATURDAY AT BREW and Steep, Bria sat with Juliet while Selena picked up their order. Customers packed the coffee shop, but thankfully, they'd gotten the last empty table and brought over two chairs in case Nell or Missy joined them.

That was something to be happy about, right? A morning with her friends and a table. Bria forced the corners of her lips upward. Too bad Dalton remained on her mind.

The bell on the door jingled.

Juliet inhaled sharply.

Bria couldn't see who'd entered, so she glanced over her shoulder. Ezra Monroe and Penelope Jones power-walked to the counter. If they'd noticed Juliet, they made sure not to look her way.

"You okay?" Bria touched her friend's hand.

Juliet squared her shoulder. "I still can't believe my grandmother sided with my soon-to-be ex-husband."

"Cheating ex-husband."

"They saw me. At least Grandma did, but they're acting as if I'm invisible." Juliet tucked her blond hair behind her ears. "For the best, given we're in such a crowded place. I did nothing wrong, so I don't care what people think, but appearances matter to both of them. Probably why they're thick as thieves now."

"You don't need them."

Juliet raised her chin. "I don't. I'd rather not talk to Ezra again, but my grandmother is the only family I have."

"You have a family." Bria squeezed her hand. "Us."

"Cupcake Posse forever."

"Forever." Bria let go of Juliet's hand.

Selena approached, balancing the three drinks. "Ignore the wicked witch and the minion following her."

Juliet laughed. "Don't you mean a flying monkey?"

"Monkeys, even evil flying ones, don't deserve to be lumped in with Ezra Monroe." Selena set the drinks on the table. "A berry tea for Juliet. And an Americano for me."

"Thanks."

Bria held her pumpkin spice latte. A barista had made a heart in the foam. A sweet touch, but she wished they hadn't bothered.

Selena sat. "Bentley made our drinks. He enjoys working here but asked when the cupcake shop would reopen. He misses the place."

"I'm still waiting on the insurance company." Bria hated that it was taking so long. "And there's probate too. We've passed the first month of the death notice. We've got three more to go."

Juliet stared into her teacup. "Doesn't seem that long."

Bria still couldn't believe Aunt Elise was gone. A month was nothing, but it felt longer.

The grief was never constant like it had been those first few days, but it still hit unexpectedly. Bria missed her so much. She always would. She sometimes felt as if she wandered around in a fog, doing things by rote. Other times, she was her old self, functioning as usual, until she saw something or listened to a song or smelled a familiar scent.

Then the fog descended, and her heart split open again.

Dalton had eased some of the grief. Not that she'd pretended Aunt Elise hadn't died, but he brought the light back into Bria's life. Her aunt would have supported Bria falling in love. But now that they hadn't talked…

"What about the cottage food permit?" Juliet asked. "Missy might need help once she's cooking in her kitchen."

"We're only two weeks into a six-week wait." Bria sipped her drink. That would be better than sighing.

"I told Bentley we'd keep him posted, but it sounds as if he's better off staying here." Selena sipped her coffee. "This place is busier than I expected."

Juliet blew on her tea. "Halloween's only a week from today. Don't people have pumpkins to carve or candy to buy?"

"Hey, more customers mean bigger profits for my client, so let's not jinx it." Brew and Steep had been Bria's first client. She'd added the Carpenter Law Office to her list on Friday. At least work would keep Bria busy. However, she would have enjoyed celebrating the clients with Dalton.

Get him off your mind.

Bria sipped her pumpkin spice latte and refocused on her friends. "Is Nell joining us today?"

"You read her messages to the group chat last night." Selena shook her head. "She's probably dreaming about her date with Gage."

"I'm happy last night went well for her. Nell's always dreamed about being a wife and mother." Juliet glanced around. "I hate to say this, but something's off about Gage and how he drags Nell off to hike or climb. That's so not her."

Selena set her coffee cup on the table. "Nell's smart, but she let Gage believe she's more outdoorsy than she is."

"Missy mentioned how Nell holds herself back to keep from getting hurt. Plus, seeing Gage as a friend or more accomplishes the same thing."

"Keeps Charlene from meddling," they said at the same time.

"Ever since that idiot doctor who-shall-not-be-named dumped her, Nell's been afraid to fall in love." Selena had a thoughtful gleam in her eyes. "But if she likes Gage enough, she'll open herself up and take a risk."

"One date doesn't make a relationship," Juliet added. "Even if it sounds like she got the romantic, stay-at-home, cuddle kind of night she wanted."

A text notification on Bria's cell phone buzzed. *Please let it be Dalton*. She scrambled to pull her phone from her purse.

Dad lit up the screen. Bria's shoulders sagged.

"Not Dalton?" Juliet asked.

"Nope. It's my dad." Bria read the message to make sure it wasn't anything urgent. "He's in Wishing Bay with Molly."

Selena stared over the lip of her cup. "Have you heard from Dalton?"

"Not a word since he left the house on Wednesday night. He hasn't answered my texts. I left a voice mail."

Selena took a sip. "He might need time to process what you told him."

"I know. But I would've appreciated him telling me that. Unless…" Bria's frustration sounded in her voice. Her chest tightened. She sucked in a breath. It didn't loosen the tension. "He's ghosting me."

"No." Juliet shook her head. "You guys are so good together. He loves you."

"And I love him." But Bria didn't know what to think now.

"He was going to talk to his mom, right?"

Bria nodded. "He didn't believe what I told him. Called my dad a con man."

"Who knows what Deena told him?" Juliet's princess voice turned evil stepmother. "She and Remy are so twisted. They're only out for themselves. I hope they didn't lie to Dalton."

Bria didn't trust Deena, but she was Dalton's mom. He would have to decide what and who to trust. "I only want the chance to talk to him."

"You'll get it." As usual, Selena brimmed with confidence. "I hate to say it, but patience is key here."

Bria nodded. "I had a feeling you'd say something like that."

Juliet made a face. "Patience is not my favorite word."

"I understand," Selena admitted. "I'm dealing with that myself."

Dumbfounded, Bria stared at Selena, who was the definition of success with her business and marriage. "Over what?"

Selena shrugged, which wasn't something Bria had seen her do before, and then she smiled. "I'm ready for Logan to retire so we can move to Berry Lake. But he loves to play hockey."

"Well, it's good to find out Selena T is human, too," Juliet said, sounding somewhat surprised.

"Oh-so-human," Selena agreed. "I have to be patient and let Logan decide when he's ready to leave the game."

The words struck at Bria's heart. "Is this your way of telling me to stop worrying and let Dalton figure out his stuff?"

Selena nodded. "Worrying won't change anything except making the situation seem worse, which it may or may not be. That's why it's a total waste of time."

Easier said than done, but… "I'll keep that in mind."

"Hey." Missy hobbled up to the table. She wore a hoodie, leggings, one slipper, and one suede boot that looked as if it had doubled as her cats' scratching post. "Sorry I'm late."

"Get distracted by the kittens?" Bria asked.

Selena smirked. "Or a sheriff's deputy?"

As Missy's face flushed, she sat. "The kittens."

"What do you want to drink?" Bria asked.

"Nothing right now. I don't have long. I have to get back to the—"

"Kittens," they finished for her.

Missy's lower lip stuck out. "They need me."

"What about Sam?" Juliet's princess sing-song voice had returned.

Missy sighed. "I told you guys all about Sam and our pizza dinner. There's nothing more to say. He's nice."

"Nice, yes," Selena said. "But also hot."

Bria nodded. "I agree."

"Me too." Juliet touched Missy's arm. "We're not trying to push you."

"Yes, you are." Missy pinned each one with a hard stare. "I get it, but I don't need a boyfriend."

Bria exchanged glances with Juliet and Selena. They'd wanted Missy to go on a date, but she'd jumped to saying she didn't need a boyfriend. That felt like progress. Nell, who knew Missy the best next to Jenny, might know if that was the case.

"No one needs a boyfriend or a spouse or any other label people put on others." Selena transformed into Selena T in an instant. "But everyone needs friends and companionship. If that comes in lovely packaging, such as the case with Deputy Cooper, why not spend time with him?"

"Rob…"

"Is dead." Selena's matter-of-fact tone was borderline blunt.

Missy flinched as if not expecting that.

"You're alive. But you buried your heart with him," Selena continued. "I only saw Rob with you that summer we worked together at the cupcake shop. He adored you. And I wonder if you'd been the one killed nine years ago if he'd still be single."

"He wouldn't be. Single, that is." Missy's voice was confident and strong. "When he told me if something happened to him, he wanted me to love again, I said I wanted the same thing for him. Rob had so much love to give. He wouldn't have been…"

Missy inhaled sharply.

Selena leaned forward. "He wouldn't have been what?"

Bria held her breath.

Underneath the round table, Juliet grabbed Bria's hand.

Missy looked at the table. "He wouldn't have been happy alone."

"Are you happy alone?" Selena asked, her voice gentler.

Missy shrugged.

"Could you be happier?"

"I don't know. Maybe?" Missy's lower lip quivered. "But Rob was my everything. The only man I've loved. How will I find someone like him?"

Bria exhaled. She'd forgotten Rob was Missy's first and only boyfriend. They'd been a perfect fit, and the idea of starting over with someone new must be intimidating. Not knowing where Bria stood with Dalton was frightening, and they hadn't been together that long.

Juliet glanced at Selena. "Can I take this one?"

Selena nodded.

"You won't find someone like him." Juliet held Missy's hand. "There was only one Rob Hanford. But other people will fit with you, only differently."

Missy laughed.

That was unexpected.

"I pulled a Nell on Sam," Missy admitted.

"Wait." Juliet let go of Missy's hand. "You fell asleep when Sam was over on Thursday?"

Missy nodded. "I used his shoulder as a pillow. He woke me up to feed the cats."

Selena arched a brow. "I like this deputy."

"We're friends." The words shot out of Missy's mouth. "Potential friends."

"That works," the three of them said at the same time again.

"Are you sure you don't want something to drink?" Bria asked.

"Positive." Missy's grin slid into place. "I have to get home and get ready for our Posse dinner tonight. But I wanted to stop by for a few minutes."

The bell on the shop's door jingled.

Juliet's eyes widened, and she stared into her cup as if the tea leaves held the secret to divorcing her husband faster.

"What?" Bria asked.

Juliet and Selena exchanged a look. Missy shifted in her seat.

Bria glanced around until her gaze collided with Dalton. He looked away and continued to the line of customers. His brother Ian was with him.

As she lifted her drink, her hands trembled. "I wasn't expecting to see him here. I assumed he was in Portland. But if he's been in town, I don't understand why he's ignored my calls and messages."

Spots appeared before Bria's eyes. She clutched the table.

"Take a deep breath," Selena said. "Fill your lungs all the way. Hold it for a count of five. Now exhale."

Bria did it. She didn't know how the breathing would help. Her other option had been to bolt, but that wouldn't be an appealing image to her client's customers.

"Good," Selena said. "Now try it again."

This time, Bria inhaled bigger. That helped. "Thanks. I was afraid I would lose it."

Selena smiled like a proud mama. "You held it together."

"Um, guys." Missy's face paled. "Dalton's coming this way."

That adage *be careful what you wish for* had never been more accurate than at that moment. All Bria wanted was for Dalton to reach out to her, but not like this in a crowded coffee shop and with his youngest brother right there.

"Keep breathing," Selena whispered.

Bria inhaled again, repeating the same exercise.

Dalton wove his way through the crowded tables until he stood next to Bria. He ignored her friends at the table. "Hey."

Her heart pounded so loudly she feared it might explode. "Hi."

Dalton shifted his weight between his feet and shoved the tips of his fingers into his pockets. His expression was serious. Too serious. "Can we talk?"

chapter seventeen

THE WALK TO the park in silence unnerved Bria. She focused on putting one foot in front of the other, mindful of the cracks in the sidewalk. Tripping and spraining an ankle wouldn't help. Her insides twisted enough.

The chill in the autumn air was nothing compared to the one between them. With each step she took, the sky darkened as more clouds moved in. The overcast sky matched her mood. However, if she were honest, a thunderstorm would be a better fit.

They waited at the curb for the street to clear.

Still, Dalton said nothing.

A truck stopped, and the driver waved for them to go.

As they crossed the street to enter the park, she sent him a sideward glance, willing him to say something—anything.

Dalton continued forward as if on a stroll by himself, and he hadn't invited her along.

It reminded Bria of when he'd broken up with her in high school. She'd become invisible. That had cut deep then, sent her poor eating habits into a full-blown disorder, and given her yet another data point proving she'd been unworthy of love.

Bria was past those things now, but the way Dalton acted hurt her. These past weeks with him—the laughs and the kisses and the declarations of love—had been everything to her.

But Molly and Dad had changed that.

Bria needed to know what Dalton was thinking.

The uncertainty was killing her. Not literally. But this morning, she'd woken a hot mess of tears as thoughts of Dalton and Aunt Elise melded together. The grief over one fueled the other until Bria's trickle of tears had turned into heaving sobs.

She hated that. Hated the way her heart ached as if Deena DeMarco squeezed out the blood while cackling.

Deena was an easy target to blame based on the past. She never liked Bria. And Bria had a feeling Dalton's mom had added more to Molly and Paul's story, which was why he hadn't called. Was using Deena as an excuse easier than thinking the reason was Bria herself?

One hundred percent.

But what else could it be?

Dalton motioned to an empty park bench.

He lives.

Bria shouldn't joke, but at least he hadn't forgotten about her.

She sat. The bench was dry and hard against her bottom but not as uncomfortable as the tension crackling in the air.

He sat at the far end, leaving too much space between them.

A sign?

If so, this talk wouldn't go the way she hoped.

Bria crossed her arms over her chest.

Kids rode their bikes ahead of her, laughing and lifting their faces to the wind. Another group of kids around nine or ten years old kicked a soccer ball back and forth. Their carefree smiles and easy laughs brought a rush of envy. She wanted to be like that again.

Only you can make yourself happy.

Selena T had said that on her most recent podcast, and the advice was legit. But having Dalton in Bria's life made being happy that much easier. She wanted that to continue.

Did he?

Bria rubbed her fingers over her sweater. She debated asking him a question, but he was the one who wanted to talk, so she remained quiet.

Two kids rode by on scooters. Their parents, laughing, jogged after them.

Once upon a time, Aunt Elise used to bring Bria to the park. It was her third favorite place to go. The cupcake shop had been number one. School second.

Bria glanced at the gray clouds.

Wish you were here now.

Another glance showed Dalton staring off into the distance.

Bria's unease grew exponentially. Was fate against them the same way it had been with Molly and Paul? Or Molly and Dad?

A breeze toyed with the ends of Bria's hair and carried the scent of rain.

Bria couldn't take this any longer. She uncrossed her arms. "Are we going to sit here or talk?"

Dalton rubbed his palms over his jeans. "Sorry."

She didn't want to goad him, but he wasn't making this easy on her. "For?"

"Not getting in touch." The words rushed out. "I'm not ghosting you."

Bria expected a sense of relief to wash over her. It didn't. Her throat remained tight. "That's good."

"I needed...need time." His voice cracked.

"I understand." Her hand reached out to comfort him, but she pulled it back. She had no idea where things stood. "But you could've told me. Texted. I'll never force you to talk when you're not ready, but you left me second-guessing everything by going radio silent."

"It's a lot to take in."

"So much. I get it. There's no rush." Bria meant it. "I'm still processing everything."

He nodded.

Dalton still hadn't told her anything concrete. Was he having trouble with something she'd said, or that his mom told him? Bria's nerves ramped up. She didn't want to push him, but she feared they would sit there all day if she didn't.

"I mean it. Take your time. But I need to know something first." Her heart raced so fast she thought it might burst out of her chest. "Are we okay? Or is what happened between our parents going to change things?"

The words tumbled out, and Bria didn't care. She rubbed her neck to ease the tightness.

Dalton tilted his head but said nothing.

Maybe he needed time to answer her question.

Bria's palms grew clammy. She rubbed them together, but that only made it worse.

What had Selena said at the coffee shop about being patient?

Bria was failing. She pressed the toes of her boots against the asphalt.

"I don't want things to change," Dalton said finally, and a flash of relief came. "You must know how much I loved my father."

"You practically worshiped him."

Dalton nodded. "That's why this is so difficult for my family and me."

His family? That surprised Bria.

She turned to face him. "I never wanted to make things difficult, but I thought you should know."

"Knowing is one of those double-edged swords, but thank you for telling me." He scrubbed his face. "Have you spoken to your dad?"

"He's visiting Molly."

"Did you ask if he told you the truth?"

The question reverberated like a death knell. Bria's lips parted. They'd discussed this on Wednesday night, so why was Dalton bringing it up now? "No, because he told me the truth."

"Ask him." Dalton's voice sounded almost unnatural. "Your dad didn't tell you everything."

Uh-oh. Deena had said something to him. "What didn't my father say?"

Dalton's shoulders sagged.

"Hey, I said you could have time," Bria said. "I'm sorry if I pushed—"

"You're not pushing. I want to tell you. This whole situation is just so hard. I never thought Dad was capable of…" Dalton's voice was raw. "My dad had an affair with Molly, and my mother knew, but it wasn't his fault."

"Not his fault?"

"Molly chased after him, made it impossible for Dad to say no to her."

Bria wrung her hands. She hadn't expected Dalton to reason away his father's behavior. "I have no idea what Molly did or didn't do, but even if she threw herself at him, no one could force a person to have an affair. The other person must have agreed."

"She must have been relentless in her pursuit of him." A vein on Dalton's jaw twitched. "And Dad was only human."

Justifying his father's cheating sent red flags waving in Bria's brain. The words didn't even sound like Dalton. "Is that what your mom said?"

Dalton stiffened. "It's true. Dad wouldn't have gone after another woman. He loved Mom and me."

"Yes, but affairs happen."

"He wanted to stop this one. That's why he didn't ask Mom for a divorce." Each word came out faster than the last. Dalton took a breath. "He went to Hayden Lake to break up with Molly."

"That means your dad did the honorable thing again." Which Bria hoped gave Dalton, and even Deena, solace. But something niggled at Bria. There had to be more to the story because based on what Dad said Paul Dwyer appeared to be a man who not only wanted his cake but a dozen cupcakes, cookies, and brownies to eat, too. She hoped for Dalton's sake that wasn't the case.

"He was." Dalton's voice was firm. He loved and respected his father. That much was clear.

Bria didn't want to make Paul out to be a bad guy—his actions and lack of them had done that. But she wanted Dalton to accept the truth so that they could move forward. She scooted toward him, cutting the distance between them in half. He didn't move toward the bench's edge, so she moved even closer.

Dalton blew out a breath. "Except…"

The word hung in the air.

Her skin prickled. "What?"

He bit his lip.

Bria touched his forearm. "Please, tell me."

He took another breath. "There's a reason I haven't called you. I've been debating if I should tell you everything my mom said. She said it might hurt you or change things."

"You hurt me by disappearing without a word." Bria was channeling Selena T. "Might as well say it."

Still, he hesitated.

"I'm pretty sure I'm numb right now," Bria added. "You can tell me anything."

Dalton raised a brow. "Anything?"

"Relationships need open communication and trust, honesty, to thrive."

"True, but…"

"How bad can it be?" She meant that. Nothing he said would surprise her.

He stared at the asphalt beneath their feet before raising his gaze to meet hers. The turmoil in his eyes made her tighten her hand on him. "Mom said Molly was upset over my dad breaking things off. She was distraught."

Dad had never mentioned Paul breaking up with Molly. Only that he hadn't asked Deena for a divorce. It had sounded to Bria that Paul still wanted Molly, and she was the one who left. But Bria didn't want to interrupt Dalton. "Go on."

"Molly didn't swerve to miss an animal in the road."

Bria leaned closer. "Then how did she end up in the lake?"

Dalton covered her hand with his. "She drove off the road and into the lake on purpose."

Huh? Bria bit her lip. Replayed his words. That would mean Molly tried to...

Bria gasped. Everything in her recoiled. She pulled her hand from beneath his. "No! There's no way. That's just... Dad would've said something. He promised not to keep any secrets. He told me everything."

Dalton stiffened. "That's what my dad told my mom."

This made no sense. Bria rubbed her face. "Your dad told my father something different. One of them is lying."

"Not my mom. Dad didn't want to hurt Brian." Dalton finally looked at Bria. "They were friends. That's why he said an animal caused the accident."

"My dad said Mom was going back to Berry Lake. Home to us." Dad believed that. So did Bria. Otherwise... She shook her head.

Dalton's gaze narrowed. "My dad felt sorry for Brian. That's why he took a loan from his insurance money to invest in your father's deal."

"Is that what your mom said?"

"Yes, and it makes sense when you think about it."

Maybe if you're a Dwyer.

Bria clasped her hands on her lap. The gap between them grew, even though neither had moved.

"There are two different stories." Her gaze met Dalton's and pleaded with him. "Your dad's not here to tell us the truth, and Molly can't clear anything up. That leaves speculation, especially about her driving into the lake, unless she told your dad she would—"

"I believe my mom."

"I believe my dad."

Stalemate.

A Frisbee flew above them. Dalton didn't appear to notice it.

"Ever since you returned to Berry Lake, you haven't had anything nice to say about your family except for Ian. You told me you didn't trust your mother. So why do you trust her about this?"

A beat passed. And another. "Mom was different when I went over there on Wednesday night. She was like her old self when Dad was alive. She wouldn't lie to me about this."

"You're sure about that?"

"What she told me fits with the man who raised me." Dalton's voice cracked, hurting Bria's heart. "My dad made a mistake. His cheating is hard for me to accept. I'm not sure I have. But my mom wanted me to know Dad was righting the wrong and not continuing the affair. He never planned to run off with his lover. Everything she told me I'd bet my life on."

"I get it. I do. I feel the same way about my dad." There had to be some way to move beyond this. "So where does that leave us?"

Dalton's eyes gleamed. He rubbed them. "I'd like to say it doesn't matter."

She leaned forward. "You promised you wouldn't let your family get in our way again."

His expression tightened. "It's not *my* family getting in the way this time."

Chills skittered along her spine. "You're putting this on my father?"

Dalton nodded once.

Bria hadn't expected that, but she would stand up for Dad, the way she wished he'd stood up for her over the years. She squared her shoulders.

"My dad isn't perfect, but he's spent over thirty years taking care of a woman he loved, even though she loved another man." Bria tried to keep her voice steady. "No matter how Molly's car ended up in the lake, I'm proud of my dad for doing that."

"What about him scamming people out of their life insurance? You're proud of being the daughter of a con artist?" Dalton's voice sharpened. He sounded like a stranger. "Brian's playing you the way he has your entire life."

She shook her head. "He's not who we thought. Everything he did was for Molly."

"That's what he told you, but what if he's lying?"

"He's not."

"How can you be so certain when he's lied to you for over thirty years?"

"Stop." Her hands covered her ears. She didn't want to listen anymore. "Why are you saying this? I love you. I thought you loved me."

"I do." Dalton didn't hesitate to answer. "But you need to see the truth."

Bria's nerve endings twitched. Unable to sit, she jumped to her feet. "What truth?"

"Your father is a liar." Dalton's matter-of-fact tone belied the seriousness of the situation. "Get him to admit it to you. That's the only way you'll see the truth and my dad's reputation remains intact."

His dad? She balled her hands. "Forget about your father for a minute. What about us?"

Dalton took a breath and then stood. "As long as your father's lies continue, there can't be an us."

His words sliced into her heart. Her lungs seemed to implode. "I-I…"

She struggled to breathe. Her vision blurred.

Her fear about Deena had come true.

Trembling, Bria lifted her chin. "Love is supposed to be unconditional. It shouldn't have anything to do with my dad or your father's reputation or whatever your mom put into your head."

"Your dad could destroy my family's reputation."

"Your mother and sister already did that."

He stepped away from Bria. "That's unfair."

"But true. Your mom has never wanted us together. Not back in high school or now." Bria wasn't the same mousy girl who ran away the first time he'd broken up with her. "What did she say so you'd give me an ultimatum?"

"Your dad invested and lost my father's money. Made my mom marry…" Dalton wouldn't look at Bria. "Each time my mom sees your dad, it's a reminder of what happened."

A ball of fire lodged in Bria's throat, burning from the inside out. She moved in front of him, so Dalton had to look at her. "I have to choose between you or my dad?"

Dalton said nothing, but his jaw jutted forward. "My mom—"

"Hasn't been a part of your life since you left Berry Lake. I've spent more time with you than she has in the last fifteen years." Bria's hands flew to her hips. "This doesn't make sense."

"It's what my father would have wanted."

"Your dad didn't care about appearances, or he would have never proposed to Molly. How dare you ask me to choose between you and my father, Dalton Dwyer? That's not love. That's manipulation and has your mother written all over it. Never thought I'd say this, but goodbye, Dalton. And good luck. With a family like yours, you're going to need it."

Anger boiled in Bria's veins. Tears stung her eyes.

She forced her feet to move away before she lost it.

History was repeating itself. Once again, Dalton was Deena's pawn.

The worst part?

He didn't even realize it was happening.

chapter eighteen

SATURDAY EVENING, MISSY sat with her friends in her living room. They'd visited the kittens in the office, eaten fast food from The Burger Barn, and caught up. Bria told them about the heartbreaking conversation she'd had with Dalton in the park. Mario rested his head on Selena's leg. Peach curled up on Missy's lap. The only thing missing was Elise. But Missy wanted to believe their former boss and friend was there in spirit.

Bria reached for a Black Forest cupcake from the tiered tray in the center of the coffee table, but she didn't take a bite. "Dalton is in denial, so he's trying to beg a confession out of my dad or something."

Missy shivered. *Confession* reminded her of when the sheriff and fire inspector questioned her about the fire. She hoped they had more suspects and clues than when they'd spoken to her.

"I'm so sorry this happened to you. It's like your senior year all over again." Nell touched Bria's shoulder, her RN bedside manner coming to the forefront. "But you got through that then, and we'll make sure you do this time, too. How are you feeling about things, or is it too soon?"

"I've been trying to understand where Dalton's coming from. His loyalty to his father is driving this. The same way it did the first time." Bria's voice cracked. Her red-rimmed, puffy eyes gleamed. "The worst part is we'll never learn the truth about what happened that night in Hayden Lake. Even if my dad had proof Molly was coming home to us, it would still be his word against Deena's."

"I'm sorry, but this has Deena written all over it." Juliet's harsh tone surprised Missy. "The woman is a master manipulator with her kids."

"And men," Nell added. "What Sal has done to Sheridan defies logic. It's like she's the stepdaughter, not Remy."

Missy would go to the grave being Team Sheridan's loudest cheerleader. Despite the efforts of Sheridan's father and stepmother, things had worked out for the lovely young woman. She met a man in South Carolina and would marry him in Berry Lake come December. The wedding invitation had arrived yesterday.

"Oh, Deena's the ringleader of all of this." Bria's shoulders slumped, and Nell pulled her closer. "I thought now that we were older, she would be okay with us dating. That love was strong enough to see us through anything. It isn't."

Bria buried her face in her hands.

On the other side of Bria, Selena leaned into her. "Love can be the most powerful force in the universe, but love isn't always enough. Relationships come into your life for a reason, but not all of them last forever. That's not a failure on you or him or the love you shared. It's just what happens sometimes."

Bria lowered her hands. "I hate that this is happening. Hate, hate, hate it."

Juliet handed Nell the box of tissues. Bria took one and blew her nose.

"Part of me wants to fight for us." Bria grabbed another tissue. "Then the other part tells me it'll be futile."

Missy rubbed Peach. Running her fingers through the cat's fur soothed the hurt she felt on Bria's behalf. She wanted her friend to be happy, carefree, and in love. "You're a planner. You always have been, but you don't have to decide what to do tonight. Take your time. Nothing is ever set in stone."

"Missy's right." Selena shot a grateful smile her way that made Missy sit taller. "Even if you decide one thing, you can choose to do something different. People think they're stuck, but they choose to be stuck. You can always make a different choice."

Wait. Missy pressed her lips together to keep from crying out. Her hands balled. She didn't choose to be stuck. She loved Rob. What other choice was there?

She leaned forward and opened her mouth…

Bria drew her knees up and wrapped her arms around her calves.

Missy clamped her lips together again. Now wasn't the right time for her to ask when Bria needed their help more. She would have to ask Selena another time.

"Is it awful that I wish Dalton would make a different choice?" Bria asked.

"No," the four others said at the same time.

That brought a much-needed smile to Bria's face.

"But can I address the elephant in the room?" Nell asked. "I don't mean to diminish your pain, Bria, but I must ask. Do you really want Deena DeMarco as a mother-in-law?"

Bria's eyes widened, and then she laughed, doubling over, and dropped her cupcake. Only a quick save from Nell kept it from hitting the carpet.

"Your reflexes are on point, Nell." Bria wiped her eyes. "I never thought about it. I love Dalton, but his family didn't seem to matter to him, so it was a nonissue. But I was naïve about that, given what Dalton said about my dad today. The thought of Deena around my kids…"

Bria shuddered, and Missy didn't blame her for that. The Hanfords had been the best in-laws and would have doted on Briley or any kids Missy and Rob might have had. But like their son, they'd been taken too soon.

A familiar pang hit.

Missy held onto Peach, who then jumped off her lap.

Oh, right. Missy forgot the rules. Peach decided the amount love she received and when.

Silly cat.

Juliet raised her glass. "Well, they could call her Grandmanipulator."

"I don't have a proper answer," Bria admitted, her voice hoarse. "But I needed the laugh, so thanks."

Missy had rarely seen Sal and Deena since the cupcake shop fire. Sal had adopted his new wife's rudeness. Together, they'd become the customers no one enjoyed serving. Unfortunately, Owen and Remy took after their mom, but Ian seemed pleasant enough. Bentley usually took Ian's order, though.

Bria groaned. "I wish I could turn off my love. Dalton hurt me so much today, but I still love him. Why do I still have feelings for him?"

"Love isn't logical. Selena T has drilled that into all of us podcast listeners." Missy's love for Rob these past nine years hadn't been logical. But moving on from him had proven impossible.

Not that you've tried.

Not really.

Was that the choice Selena had mentioned before? Either way, this wasn't about Missy.

Missy shifted on the couch. "In Dalton's case, if he comes back—which I hope he does if that's what you want—make him grovel. I'm talking on his knees, groveling with a grand gesture."

"Would be nice, but I can't see that happening." Bria looked up. The whites of her eyes had reddened. "An apology would be nice."

"What's that saying from the podcast?" Nell asked.

"Forgiveness is key," Juliet said. "Is that the one?"

Nell nodded. "What Juliet said. Forgiveness is key."

"I'm just supposed to forgive Dalton? Not make him grovel?" Bria sounded confused.

"I'll take this." Compassion filled Selena's eyes. "Forgive yourself first. This isn't about who's at fault. It's loving all parts of you, including your heart, that love Dalton. No one knows if Dalton will apologize, but even if he doesn't, you can forgive him for hurting you. And that forgiveness—for yourself and him—will help you move forward when you're ready."

Missy didn't want Bria to be stuck. "With or without Dalton, your life will go on. But it's your choice how you move forward."

"My choice." Bria's voice sounded stronger this time.

Pride flowed through Missy. Bria might hurt for a while, but she would get through this. "And we're all here to support you with your choice or changing your mind or whatever."

"That's good advice for me, too." Juliet's voice was softer than usual. Her eyes appeared more serious. "Ezra texted me after he left the coffee shop with Grandma. He wants to meet."

No one said anything.

Missy bit her lip. Juliet was making so much progress in her life and with herself. Missy didn't want her to return to her horrible husband, but the choice was Juliet's and hers alone.

Nell scooted forward on the couch. "Did you reply?"

"Nope." Juliet's answer was short but spoke volumes.

Missy let out the breath she'd been holding.

"I'll call Tamika on Monday and ask what to do." Juliet's confidence wasn't as strong as usual, but Missy assumed a soon-to-be ex-husband had that effect on their wives. "My attorney is kind to me, but she's a bloodthirsty shark to Ezra."

Selena shimmied her shoulders. "Which is why I referred her to you."

"This isn't as big of news as Bria's or Juliet's, but I took a walk with Gage around Berry Lake earlier today," Nell said with a big grin. "It was so fun."

"Go, Gage," Juliet cheered. "I'm glad he came up with a tamer outing for you."

"He didn't. I did." Nell's face lit up. She grinned. "I invited him."

"Wait." Bria's forehead creased. She held her cupcake halfway between her lap and her mouth. "You wanted to do something outdoors? Where is my friend Nell, and what have you done with her?"

Missy scooted forward. "She looks the same, but the Nell I know would never willingly go on any trail or path unless there was a prize or reward."

Nell rose from the carpet onto her knees. "Oh, I got my reward at the end." She squealed. "He kissed me at the scenic view. Not a peck. A full-on movie-worthy kiss with a fabulous backdrop. It was so romantic. And the kiss was his idea. Not mine."

Bria's mouth slanted. She scratched her neck. "I still don't get why you suggested this."

"Gage did something I enjoyed. I wanted to return the favor by doing something more his style without the adrenaline rush. He was thrilled, and he didn't break any land speed records by turning the walk into a race."

Selena's lips parted. She studied Nell. "You really like Gage."

"What's not to like?" Nell asked. "He's gorgeous, fit, wants to spend time with me. His kisses curl my toes, and my mother loves him. If we find a happy medium between our interests, this might work out."

"I'm happy for you." Missy loved seeing Nell all bubbly, but she needed to speak up, even if it wouldn't make a difference. "But I still think Welles deserves a shot."

"I know you do, and I appreciate it." Nell's smile softened. "Welles is a great guy, but he's not my type. Firefighters are all the same, and he's one of the worst. He dates so many women. That's too big a risk for someone like me to take."

"Yeah, I can see that." Missy didn't want Nell to feel bad, even if Missy wasn't convinced about Gage being Mr. Right. "Just throwing it out there."

"I'm happy you did." Nell didn't quite have Juliet's princess sing-song voice down, but happiness brimmed. "I have lots to learn about Gage. Nothing's been mentioned about us being exclusive. And for all I know, he plans to return to the East Coast sooner rather than later, but I'm enjoying myself, and he's a safe option."

"Come on." Missy loved Nell, but she was deluding herself. "Safe is not the adjective I'd use when you thought you'd die on your outings."

"Did I mention his kisses? The man is a better kisser than a climber. And it's been how long since I've been kissed by a man like that?"

"Boston," they all replied.

"Exactly. I deserve this." Nell didn't back down. "We all do."

"One hundred percent," Selena agreed. "Though it sometimes takes a few times to get it right."

Bria's eyes welled again. Nell handed her another tissue.

"Be careful." Missy didn't want her friend to get hurt—her heart or her body. "Please."

"I will." Nell peeled away the liner from one side of the cupcake. "Gage, Welles, and I are going climbing next weekend. Gage said it was a route well within my skill set."

"We'd already planned to a Posse gathering tonight, but…" Bria sniffled. The puffiness around her eyes had only gotten worse. "I'm sorry I turned dinner into a Bria cryfest. At least Nell has happy news."

"Oh, no you don't, Bria." Juliet got off the couch and hugged Bria from behind. "The Posse doesn't believe in quid pro quo. But if you want to go there, we'll have to count all the Juliet cryfests we've had in the past few weeks."

The corners of Bria's mouth turned up. "There were a few, weren't there?"

"Uh-huh." Juliet grinned. "And each one helped me so much, so if you need another or several, just let us know."

"You'll have to video me in," Selena added. "Logan will be home tomorrow night, and I promised him I'd be there."

A knock sounded on her door.

"Dare must have seen all your cars in the driveway and realized there'd be cupcakes." Missy stood.

"Sit." Juliet stood. "I'll get the door."

Missy did. "You don't have to ask me twice."

Juliet opened it. "Sam?"

Missy's muscles tightened. Her hand flew to her hair, and she combed her fingers through the strands. She hadn't seen him since the other night, except in her dreams, but those didn't count, even if they'd been lovely.

Wait. Not lovely. Inappropriate. Because of Rob.

She glanced at Rob's framed photos on the mantel. That put her in the correct frame of mind. Except that didn't explain why Sam Cooper stood at her door on a Saturday night.

"Is Missy here?" It wasn't Sam asking but another male voice.

Juliet glanced at Missy with a worried expression. She clutched the doorknob so tight her knuckles turned white. "Yes."

The word came out strangled.

Something was wrong. Missy's pulse accelerated.

Her friends' faces paled.

Missy couldn't see the door from where she sat. She stood and limped over.

Sam and Sheriff Royal Dooley stood in their full uniforms. Both men wore poker faces.

"Hello." Missy's voice cracked. She forced herself not to stare at Sam and looked at the sheriff. "What brings you by tonight? Did you hear we were having a Posse gathering, and there'd be cupcakes?"

Sheriff Dooley's posture was bent, and he rubbed at his chest. Missy had never seen him do either.

The hair on the back of Missy's neck stood up. "Are Jenny, Dare, and Briley okay?"

The words came out fast, matching the rapid beat of her heart.

"They're fine," Sam answered so fast she almost missed what he said. He took a step forward, and Missy fought the urge to go to him.

Sheriff Dooley side-eyed his deputy. Sam didn't move any closer.

Selena stood behind Missy and Juliet. "If the O'Rourkes are fine, why are you here?"

She used her Selena T voice from the podcast.

The sheriff hunched, glancing at his feet before he straightened. "I have a search warrant."

"I don't—" Missy's legs weakened, and her head spun. She stumbled.

Sam stepped forward, but Sheriff Dooley held him back.

Juliet and Selena supported Missy.

"Missy needs to sit, Sheriff," Sam said.

Missy did, but no one moved.

Why isn't anyone moving? She glanced around, and her gaze met Sam's.

Regret and something else she couldn't define filled his eyes.

Her fingers itched to hold Sam's hand. "This isn't—"

"Do you give us permission to enter, Missy?" Sheriff Dooley asked.

Do I have a choice? Missy's mind went blank. She'd spoken to Elias after they'd released Brian on Thursday. Her attorney hadn't been concerned because they had no evidence. And now...

They need evidence to pin the arson on me.

The air whooshed from her lungs as a band tightened around her chest. Only it wasn't grief or loneliness. This was one hundred percent fear. Fear they'd arrest her the way they'd done to Brian Landon, who was as innocent as she was.

"Missy…?" the sheriff asked.

Missy's knees were still weak, her legs like boiled spaghetti, but she forced herself to stand straight. Though without the support of Juliet and Selena on either side of Missy, it wouldn't have been possible. "I have nothing to hide."

"Is Missy considered a suspect in the cupcake shop fire?" Selena asked.

"I'm here to search the premises. Missy was a person of interest before Brian Landon's arrest." Sheriff Dooley handed Missy the piece of paper. "This gives me permission to search the house, but I'd like you to agree before Deputy Cooper and I enter."

Missy looked at Sam, who mouthed, "I'm sorry." The emotion in his eyes made sense now. But the search wasn't his fault. He was only doing his job. She wouldn't hold that against him.

"Come in." Missy stepped out of the doorway. "But I'd prefer if Sam searches the room with the kittens. He knows the protocol to keep them safe. And please don't let Peach and Mario out. They are indoor-only cats, but if the doors open, they'll bolt."

Her voice was steadier than the way her insides quivered. Missy ran through a list of what they might consider evidence. She came up blank.

"We agree to your terms," Sheriff Dooley said as if Missy had a say in the matter. "Would you like to wait outside?"

The alternative—seeing the two men go through her things—made her nauseous. Not trusting her voice, Missy nodded.

"I can't believe this is happening." Nell joined them at the door. She got up in the sheriff's face. "Elise will haunt you for this, Royal. I hope she scares you so badly you wet your bed."

The sheriff's Adam's apple bobbed. "Just doing my job, Nell. I loved Elise. She, of all people, would understand that."

Bria strode up to the door. Her eyes and splotchy face were proof she'd had a terrible day that was only getting worse now.

"My aunt would *never* understand what you're doing." Bria's voice sharpened. "First, you try to pin the fire on my dad with no evidence. Now you're here on a Saturday night, trying to find something on Missy. This is the definition of ridiculous. I have no idea who's issuing the orders, but stop it and do your job. In case you forgot, that's finding the real arsonist."

Missy's love for her friends quadrupled. No matter what happened, the Posse would have her back. If anyone could keep Missy out of jail, these four women, Jenny, Dare, and Elias could do it. She trusted them with her life.

Sam stopped them as Juliet and Selena helped Missy out the front door. He touched Missy's arm and leaned toward her.

"I'm sorry," he whispered, his breath warm on her skin. His fresh soap-and-water scent tickled her nose. "This is wrong on all levels. I'll do whatever I can to help you."

Missy appreciated his words, but she didn't want him to get in trouble. "Do your job."

He nodded. "If that's what you want."

What she wanted was for him not to let go of her. His touch gave her strength and let her know he cared.

Missy wanted to return the favor. No words came, which was for the best with everyone surrounding them. She covered his hand with hers. Only for a second, but the flash of gratitude in his eyes was enough. Missy hoped he saw hers in return.

They continued staring at each other when her friends pulled her away. Missy forced herself not to glance over her shoulder.

Her front door closed.

Missy's energy drained. Juliet and Bria, who'd taken Selena's place, held Missy up.

"I didn't do it." Missy didn't know what else to say.

"We know." Nell typed on her cell phone. "I'll call Jenny."

"Th-Thanks." Missy shivered. She rubbed her arms. "If she saw the sheriff's car, she would have come over. I don't want her to freak out."

Probably too late.

"I'm calling Elias." Selena had her phone to her ear already.

Sam came out with Rob's old hoodie. It was one of her favorites and what she wore whenever she felt down. "Put this on, so you don't get cold."

As she took the sweatshirt from Sam, their fingers brushed. Tingles exploded.

She jumped.

Was it static electricity?

Sam jolted, but he said nothing. His gaze never left hers. "I'll do—"

The front door opened, and Sheriff Dooley stuck his head out. "Get in here, Deputy Cooper."

"I'll sort this out." Sam grabbed her hand, squeezed it, and headed into the house.

The door closed.

Missy waited for her friends to say something about Sam's actions, but no one spoke. She put on the sweatshirt. That took the chill away, but it didn't lessen the fear surging throughout her body. "I can't believe they think I did it."

Her voice trembled. She crossed her arms over her chest.

"We know you didn't." Nell's voice was raw. "You heard Sam. He knows it, too, and wants to help you."

Bria and Juliet hugged Missy.

As soon as Nell and Selena finished their calls, they joined in.

"Group hug," Selena said.

"We'll get through this," Bria added.

"That's right," Nell said. "They won't find any evidence."

"Of course, they won't," Juliet agreed.

"Thanks." Somehow, Missy had found her voice. There was only one more thing to say. "Cupcake Posse forever."

These women were all she needed. They were all she had besides Peach and Mario. They wouldn't let her down. They would help prove her innocence. Missy only hoped it didn't come to that.

chapter nineteen

A
S SOON AS Sam's shift ended, he texted Mom to tell her he would be late. That would stop her and Dad from blowing up his phone if they realized he hadn't come home after his shift finished. Then he showered.

From the time he met Sheriff Dooley, the father of the current sheriff, Sam had wanted to go into law enforcement. But times like tonight clashed with his idea of what his job should be and what the higher-ups ordered him to do.

Especially when no one in the state, let alone Berry Lake, would believe sweet Missy Hanford lit the cupcake shop she loved on fire.

The search warrant served tonight made no sense.

The hot water washed away the grimy feeling of having to search Missy's cottage for evidence. He scrubbed hard with the body wash as if he could remove the memory of his part in all of it.

Royal had been tight-lipped about the warrant, only saying justice would prevail.

Whose justice?

Sam wanted the answer to that question.

Before hitting the locker room, he'd casually asked about the arson at shift change. People mentioned that Reggie Lemond was leading the investigation and working with the DA. Given the false charges brought against Brian Landon, the fire investigator didn't impress Sam.

Sam didn't want the guy to blame Missy because they had no other suspects.

No matter the reason for the search warrant, Sam wanted to make things better for Missy—easier.

Tonight had been a mess. Literally, with the way Royal tossed aside her bedding and mattress, sure she'd hidden a smoking gun—a lighter or matches—on top of the box spring.

But the space was empty.

The entire cottage had been neat and tidy. The only signs of Rob had been a few pieces of clothing, photos in her bedroom, and the shrine to him on the mantel.

Thankfully, Royal left that stuff alone. He'd been looking for something, but he hadn't told Sam what. The only evidence beyond Missy's electronics appeared to be journals. Sam had bypassed the one on the kitchen counter because Missy had told him it belonged to Elise Landon when he'd had dinner there, but Royal had taken the journal and others from the bookcase.

Sam dressed quickly. It was getting late. The sheriff confiscated Missy's two phones, even though her old one still didn't work, and her computer, so Sam had no way to call her. That meant he had to drive by.

All he wanted to do now was apologize and make…amends— by helping Missy clean up the mess the sheriff had made.

Making amends had been one of Josh's steps on his journey to sobriety, and by doing a favor for Jenny, he'd met Hope and fallen in love.

Nothing like that would happen to Sam and Missy, but the fear in her eyes had struck hard. He needed to make sure she was okay.

When Sam arrived at Jenny and Dare's house, Selena Tremblay's expensive SUV crossover was no longer in the driveway, but Sam recognized Nell Culpepper's car.

Sam shouldn't have expected Missy's friends to desert her. The five women had been tight the summer they worked at the cupcake shop. Rob used to joke about being jealous of the women's time together and how he'd considered applying for a job there so he wouldn't be left out. All those years later, the friends seemed closer than ever. Guys were different. At least his friends. They only got together for weddings and funerals.

Sam parked and hurried along the side of the house to the cottage. Lights glowed from inside the windows.

At least he wouldn't wake anyone.

He knocked.

The door opened. Dare O'Rourke stood there. His neutral expression had a slight edge, as if weighing whether Sam was a threat. Not that Dare would be outmatched. The guy was solid and could still take anyone, even though he'd been medically discharged from the Army Rangers. "Can I help you?"

"I'm Sam Cooper. Josh's brother."

Dare relaxed. "Oh, right. Sheriff's deputy. Missy mentioned you."

Sam straightened. He hoped in a good way.

Dare's gaze narrowed. "This isn't another official call, is it?"

Sam peered around Dare but didn't see anyone in the living room. "Nope. I'm here as Missy's friend." Sam ignored how the last word tasted like chalk in his mouth.

"She's upstairs with Jenny and her friends, trying to put everything where it belongs." He motioned to a sleeping little girl in a portable playpen. "I'm on baby and kitten duty."

"I shouldn't have knocked."

"No worries." Dare sounded sincere. "The kid's used to the noise."

"Do you mind if I come in?" Sam didn't want to wait. "I know the way."

Dare hesitated.

Sam got it. The guy had no clue who he was. "If Missy doesn't want me to stay, I'll leave. I just want to check on her. She looked upset earlier."

Dare's eyes widened. "You were here with the sheriff?"

"Yes, please, let me in." Sam wasn't one for begging, but he would do whatever it took. "I want to apologize, too."

Dare sighed. "Okay, but it's your funeral."

"What?"

"Expect my wife and the Posse members to send icy glares your direction after the way you messed up the place."

"I tried to be neat. I can't say the same for the sheriff." Sam took a cautious step. "Can I…"

"Go."

Sam headed to the hall past the office on the right and the bathroom on the left. Straight ahead was Missy's bedroom. The door was ajar.

Female voices discussed something, but Sam couldn't make out the words, and he wouldn't eavesdrop.

As he raised his arm, his stomach churned. Leaving might be the smarter move, but he was committed.

Sam knocked.

"Dare?" a woman whose voice Sam didn't recognize asked.

"No, Sam Cooper."

Silence. Whoever had been talking stopped. It reminded him of the time he'd been at the symphony. The performance was so mind-blowing that the audience sat for several seconds in awe before clapping.

The door opened. A woman with a big grin stood there. "Hey, I'm Nell Culpepper. Come in."

This must be how Daniel felt entering the lions' den.

Sam stepped inside. Nell, Bria Landon, Jenny Hanford O'Rourke, and Missy, who held on to a squirming Mario, stood there. The other women stared at him with various degrees of curiosity and suspicion. But Missy...

She came toward him with red eyes. "What are you doing here?"

"Are you okay?" The words rushed out. *So much for being smooth.* "I'm so sorry about tonight."

"It's okay."

The mattress was in place, and someone had put on new bedding. Various items from the dresser and the closet were no longer on the floor. "It's not. I tried to be neat."

Jenny stepped forward. "Not sure if you remember me, but I'm Rob's sister."

Sam shook her hand. "I remember you."

"We can tell what you went through versus Royal."

"That's right," Nell added.

Elise's niece came up to him. "I'm Bria Landon."

"I remember you, too."

"I was out of high school when you started, so that's why you don't remember me," Nell joked.

Sam didn't want Nell to feel bad or old. Ava hated when that happened. "You worked at the cupcake shop with Missy that summer, right?"

Nell nodded. "Excellent memory."

"Well, our work is done here. Come on, Bria and Nell." Jenny motioned to the door. "It's getting late."

As Missy cringed, her cheeks turned a pretty shade of pink.

"See you for brunch," Bria said.

"Bring nothing." Nell's glance traveled from Sam to Missy. "We've got it covered."

"Thanks." Missy placed Mario on the ground. "Tell Dare thanks."

"I will, but it's unnecessary." Jenny hugged Missy and handed over her phone. "Keep this until you get a new phone, or they return your others."

Missy held on to it. "Thanks."

"Pleasure meeting you," Nell said as she headed out of the room.

Bria passed by him. "Nice to see you again, Sam."

"Let me know if she's not doing okay when you leave," Jenny whispered to him on the way out.

"I'm fine." Missy set the phone on her nightstand. "Thanks for everybody's help."

No one shot icy death stares Sam's way. He should be relieved, but the exchange with her friends left him thinking he'd been missing part of the conversation or something.

Mario rubbed against Sam's leg. "Hey, big boy."

"Wow." Missy sounded surprised. "Mario's usually not so friendly with people."

"He has good taste." Sam scratched behind the cat's ear and then moved closer to Missy. The sadness in her eyes told him she needed a hug, but did he dare? "I'm sorry."

"You had a job to do."

"You're not an arsonist."

Relief flashed in her eyes. "I'm not, but I'm so happy you believe me."

Her eyes watered. She blinked.

Oh, no, she's going to cry.

Sam wrapped his arms around her. "Hey, tonight must have been scary."

"I was terrified." Her arms slipped around him.

He tightened his arms, pulling her closer, soaking up her vanilla scent, which was more delicious than the cupcakes she'd made him.

Holding her felt both right and wrong. The need to comfort her battled with what he should do. But he couldn't ignore that standing there would be a dream come true under different circumstances.

Except they weren't.

Now wasn't the time to get all creepy by thinking about how natural holding her felt and how perfect they fit together.

Even if they did.

She didn't let go, so he didn't either.

Missy rested her head against him, and his hand traveled up to her hair. The soft strands slid between his fingers.

Flutters exploded in his stomach.

Focus, Cooper.

"You're not alone," he said. "Whatever's going on, we'll figure it out. No matter what it takes."

She didn't drop her hands, but she tilted her head to look at him. "You mean that."

It wasn't a question.

His heart pounded in his throat. He swallowed. "I do."

"Thank you."

"Whatever you need. I want—"

Missy's nose wrinkled. "What do you want?"

You.

Forever and always.

But he couldn't say that.

Why not?

The male voice seemed to come from outside of Sam. But no one was there except Missy, the cats, and the kittens.

Ya got nothing to lose, Sammy.

Whoa. That sounded exactly like…

No, it couldn't be.

But Sam glanced over Missy's head to the photograph of a smiling Rob Hanford, sitting on the dresser.

This is your shot, dude. Go for it.

"Sam?" she asked.

Sam thought he must be more tired than he realized, or he was hallucinating. But whichever, the advice sounded better than making up a polite half-truth about why he'd wanted to be with Missy tonight.

He took a breath. "I want this. You."

Her lips parted, but she said nothing.

"I've been crazy about you forever."

"Forever?" Missy sounded surprised.

"So long, but you were with Rob, and he was a friend and teammate, and…" Sam lowered his arms and stepped away. "I'm sorry this is so awkward. I didn't plan on saying all this tonight. I only wanted to check on you, and now I've blown it."

"Blown what?"

"My shot." Sam forced the words out. "With you."

Missy froze. She didn't blink or breathe.

Oh, well. He'd tried. "I'll go."

"Stay."

"What?"

She looked around the room. "I, um, want you to stay. You didn't blow anything."

Sam shook his head to make sure nothing was stuck in his ears, impeding his hearing. "You're sure?"

Missy nodded. "I, um, like you, too. But I'm not used to feeling like this about anyone…"

"But Rob."

Another nod. "I haven't dated anyone else. Ever. I-I need to go slow."

Joy bubbled inside him. "How does glacial-slow sound?"

"Maybe a little faster than that."

He laughed, and so did she.

Sam leaned forward, placing his forehead against hers. "Never imagined tonight would turn out like this."

"Me neither. Though, I might still freak out."

"Same." He ran his finger along her jawline. "It's late. You must be tired."

Missy nodded. "And you worked all evening."

"I did, but I can sleep in tomorrow." Sam didn't want to leave. He still couldn't believe this was happening. "One pro to swing shift."

"I have brunch with my friends. Selena is driving home tomorrow. But if you want to visit the kittens…"

"I want to see the kittens *and* you."

Missy inhaled sharply.

Sam waited for her to freak out, whatever that meant for her.

"Okay. I have Jenny's phone, but I don't go out much," she said instead. "You'll know I'm home if my car is in the driveway."

His heart swelled. "I'll stop by."

"I look forward to it."

Sam stared at her lips. A kiss wouldn't be taking things slow, but he'd waited over half his life for Missy. Yes, he'd dated women, some seriously. Those relationships, however, had gone nowhere, and now he knew why.

How hard could waiting a little longer be?

What did you do?

Missy stared at Rob's photos on the mantel. She was ready to ask Sam to leave when she thought she heard Rob.

Take a chance on Sam. Please.

The words had been so clear—as if he'd been in the room with them.

Had that not happened, who knew what she might have said to Sam? But now…

Peach and Mario followed them. *The cats must remember Sam from his other visits.*

They reached the front door.

Missy looked at Sam.

He stared at her with a goofy grin.

Tingles filled her stomach. She felt like she was twenty years younger. "Thanks for stopping by."

"I'll be back."

She laughed. Sam was so cute. "Can't wait."

That much was true. Who knew what would happen by taking a chance? But Missy was happy she had. No matter the catalyst.

"Can I give you a goodbye hug?" he asked with a hopeful tone.

"Yes." She hugged him. "Drive safe."

"Always."

Kiss him.

Ugh. Really?

Yes, please.

Missy lowered her arms. "Here goes," she mumbled.

His brows drew together. "What?"

She tapped her lips against Sam's. Nothing more than a peck, but those same tingles from before danced around her mouth.

Sam's smile lit up his face. "I should probably go."

She nodded, forcing herself not to touch her lips. "Good night."

He kept glancing at her as he headed out the door. It was so adorable.

"Remember to lock the door," he said.

"Always." Missy closed and locked the door. She went to the fireplace and picked up Rob's photo. "Was it you or my subconscious?"

She waited for an answer.

None came.

Had she pushed herself to do that? Maybe Selena would know, but…

Missy set the photo in its place. She kissed her fingertips and put them on the glass where his mouth was. "I have no idea what's happening with Sam. But if this goes south, I'm blaming you."

chapter twenty

JULIET PULLED THE egg strata out of the fridge, where it had stayed overnight. That had let the mixture soak into the French bread at the bottom. She'd added marinated artichoke hearts, sun-dried tomatoes, and parmesan cheese. The red and green were more Christmas colors than Halloween, which was less than a week away, but none of the orange and black ingredients appealed to her.

At least the upcoming holiday meant she had this weekend off from hosting kids' birthday parties. Parents didn't want to spring for a princess tea party when they would get double usage out of their kids' costumes by throwing a Halloween-themed birthday instead. She had to work at a barbeque tonight—a charity event—with Charlene.

Selena poured herself a cup of coffee. "That looks amazing."

"I hope it tastes as good." Juliet glanced at the temperature of the oven. Right where she wanted it to be. She opened the range, slid the casserole pan onto the middle rack, and closed the door. "Did you get a text from Jenny?"

"Yes." Selena held her cup in front of her. "Under no circumstances are we to mention Sam Cooper to Missy."

"Do you think anything happened last night?"

"No idea, but I can't believe he came over after searching her house and Dare didn't punch him. He considers Missy his fourth sister."

"I wish we had stayed up so we could ask Bria when she got home."

"Ask me what?" Bria rounded the corner into the kitchen. She wore patterned leggings and a matching burgundy sweater that fell past her hips.

Selena reached for another mug, poured Bria a cup, and handed it to her. "About Sam Cooper and Missy."

"He came to apologize for searching her things." Bria blew on her coffee. "I think he was worried Missy might be upset with him."

Juliet grabbed a glazed doughnut hole from the box she'd picked up yesterday. "Was she?"

"Not at all. Missy knows Sam was just doing his job, but—"

Selena leaned closer. "Don't leave us hanging."

Juliet nodded. "Please. I had nightmares about the sheriff searching Missy's house."

Bria took a sip.

Seriously? Juliet groaned. "Bria."

Bria lowered her cup. "Well, me, Jenny, and Nell might as well have been invisible last night."

"Was Sam rude?" Juliet asked.

"Not at all," Bria clarified. "But he only had eyes for Missy."

Selena grinned. "Aww."

Bria nodded. "Watching those two was like being back in high school. That first blush of love. Given Rob and Missy became a couple before they were old enough to date, that's probably the best thing for her."

"And what about Sam? You think he'll be okay with going slow?" Juliet asked.

Bria nodded. "The poor guy has it so bad. Heart eyes, puppy dog eyes, goo-goo eyes. If Missy asked him to paint the sky purple, he'd try to do it. Missy would have to be blind not to see how much he likes her."

"Did you get Jenny's text?" Selena asked. "I don't understand why she wants us not to ask Missy about Sam."

"Jenny's being cautious," Bria explained. "Something was happening between the two of them, and I'm guessing Jenny fears whatever progress Sam might have made last night will get wiped out if we push Missy too hard."

Selena feigned shock. "Us push?"

Juliet laughed. "The Posse can be a *tad* overzealous."

Bria nodded. "I believe the term you're looking for is *extra*."

"True, but anything we do is with love." Selena took a sip. She sighed as if tasting the sweetest ambrosia. "I get Jenny's point, so Missy should be the one to bring up Sam."

Juliet set the oven timer. "And if she doesn't?"

Selena stared over her cup with a mischievous gleam in her eyes. "We give Missy until after Halloween, and then we pounce."

Bria sighed. "A whole week? I need some *good* news."

"This isn't as good as Missy and Sam, but I have something almost as sweet." Juliet picked up the box she'd purchased yesterday and handed it to Bria. "Doughnut holes."

Bria's smile returned, and she took two. "This will tide me over. Thanks."

"If Missy doesn't mention Sam today, promise to video call me when she does." Selena ate a doughnut hole, too. "I can't wait for Logan to get home, but I'll miss you all."

"Come back when he goes on another road trip," Juliet suggested.

Bria nodded. "And think how great it'll be when they finish the remodel of your lake house, and you can live here in the off-season."

"And move here permanently when he retires," Selena added.

"Did he announce his retirement?" Juliet asked surprised.

"No, but this season has been harder on his body." Selena refilled her cup. "It might be time."

Bria grinned like her old self. "I won't root against Seattle, but I hope this is Logan's last season. The Cupcake Posse together in Berry Lake again."

"And this time as co-owners of the cupcake shop," Nell added.

Selena raised her mug. "It's going to be awesome."

The doorbell rang.

"I bet that's Nell or Missy." Juliet wiped her hands on the front of her apron. The tiaras and roses pattern in pinks and purples was one of her favorites. "I'll get it and tell Nell we're going along with what Jenny texted."

Juliet opened the door and gasped. "Grandma? What are you doing here?"

Grandma wore one of her Sunday best dresses. Juliet thought she must be on the way to, or coming home from, church. She stared down her nose as if Juliet were an ant to be stepped on or brushed aside. "In case you've forgotten, I disowned you. Please call me Penelope. Or better yet, Mrs. Jones."

The words sliced into Juliet with razor-sharp precision. She'd known her grandmother was a harsh woman, but until recently, Juliet had never experienced that side herself.

No wonder Mom and Dad preferred traveling to living in Berry Lake. If only they'd taken me with them.

And then Juliet remembered.

If they had, she would be dead, too.

"Marc Carpenter is working on my new will. I'm leaving my entire estate to my darling Ezra. You remember your husband, don't you? He's trying to work things out with that sweet young woman named Remy, since you won't return his calls."

Juliet balled her hands. It was that or scream in her grandmother's face. Juliet didn't want to lower herself to Ezra's level. "My lawyer will reach out to his lawyer on Monday."

"Go home to your husband. You might need to beg, but Ezra is a forgiving man. He will take you back."

Unbelievable. The woman still lived in another era when husbands did whatever they wanted, and their wives looked the other way. "Is there a reason for your visit, Penelope?"

Grandma startled. She took a breath, and then she squared her shoulders. "I heard Lulu is ill."

"She's doing better now."

"I want to see her."

"Did Mrs. Vernon ask you to look at her?"

"No, but as one of her oldest and dearest friends, I want to make sure you're not being neglectful of that poor dog."

The dog that Grandma forced Juliet to take.

The woman might have raised her, but she'd gone too far. "No."

Grandma's nostrils flared. "I beg your pardon?"

"No, you may not see Lulu."

Grandma harrumphed. "I never—"

"You never have to think of me again. You disowned me. I hope you and Ezra and whoever he ends up with live happily ever after. But as soon as you die, he will sell the Huckleberry Inn to the highest bidder and not think twice. You might want to pre-plan your burial arrangements because he can't even be bothered to buy toothpaste or make any food that requires heat."

Grandma's mouth gaped.

"Please don't bother me again, Mrs. Jones."

Juliet slammed the door. Her heart pounded so hard, she touched her chest.

Selena and Bria clapped.

"I know how much you loved and respected your grandmother." Selena wrapped her arms around Juliet in a big hug. "But I'm so proud of you for standing up for yourself. No one has the right to hurt you like that."

"They don't." Bria joined in on the hug. "And I need to follow your example."

The three stepped back.

Juliet's eyes watered with sadness, surprise, and relief at finally not taking what those who supposedly loved her said. Her heart hurt, but she would no longer tolerate that kind of behavior.

"I thought we'd be able to go back to the way things were, but what she said, I snapped." Juliet still couldn't believe it. "I knew things had changed forever. And that was okay. I was okay. And I deserve better."

"You deserve the best," Selena agreed. "We all do. And you took a gigantic step to find out who Juliet Jones is beyond a wife and granddaughter."

"Missy and Nell will be here anytime, so we'd better set the table."

Selena laughed. "Always the hostess with the mostest."

Juliet rubbed her eyes and beamed. "Which is why I'm an awesome event planner."

Bria grinned. "One thing you don't have to find out is the type of friend Juliet Jones is. She's an amazing one."

"I'll take amazing." Juliet couldn't wait to see what else she would discover about herself.

Brunch at Elise's house meant eating more sweets than savories, but those were Nell's favorite, and she'd had two slices of bacon and a serving of the egg strata, so those counted as protein. She popped a glazed doughnut hole into her mouth. Not as tasty as a cupcake, but a satisfying sweet.

She had agreed with the others to leave Sam and Missy out of this morning's conversation. But Jenny was a spoilsport. Still, Nell knew Jenny had Missy's best interests at heart.

One thing about last night remained on Nell's mind. She'd forgotten to ask Selena about the call she'd made last night. That should be a safe, Sam-free topic. "Did you ever get hold of Elias last night?"

Missy shook her head. "Brunch has been so lovely. Do we have to ruin it by mentioning the search warrant?"

"Only this part about Elias," Selena assured her. "And only because I'm leaving soon."

A resigned expression settled over Missy's face. "Fine."

Except Missy sounded anything but fine. She was probably worried they would bring up Sam.

"Elias and I spoke this morning. He was stunned by the search warrant. He mentioned how everyone knows Missy doesn't even like it when people light candles on their cupcakes."

"They might hurt themselves," Missy added.

Nell smiled. "That sentence alone should be enough to prove her innocence."

"I wish it worked like that." Bria sounded almost breathless.

Bria was putting on a good front, trying to hide her heartbreak. Nell understood because she'd done the same thing after getting dumped. Seeing Bria now was almost enough to make Nell happy she'd turned down hiking with Gage today and told him to ask Welles instead. Her friendships were as meaningful—no, more important—than a burgeoning relationship.

"Is Elias worried?" Nell asked.

Selena shook her head. "Elias says Reggie Lemond is under pressure to find a new suspect now that Brian is free. But he's not worried about Missy. I'm not, either."

"You said worry is a four-letter word," Nell reminded them.

"It's a waste of time. None of us should worry about Missy." Selena pointed at Missy. "That includes you."

Missy laughed.

"Just so everyone knows, I told Elias if he needs to bring in a big-gun criminal lawyer, I'll cover the expense."

Missy stood. "Selena—"

"I said 'if,' and we all know you're innocent." Selena spoke in a matter-of-fact tone, as if she hadn't pledged to spend tens of thousands of dollars if need be. "Now, sit. Your foot is still healing."

Nell laughed. "Better do it before she goes all Selena T on you."

Missy sat.

"You covered Lulu's vet bills, you figured out a way to help Brian pay Molly's bills, you're loaning me my share of the money for the cupcake shop at zero interest, and now this." Juliet threw up her hands and bowed to Selena. "I'm not sure if we should call you Saint Selena or Bank of Selena."

"Oh! I like the ring of both." Selena laughed.

Nell shook her head. "Is anyone surprised by this?"

Selena brushed her hand as if waving a magic money wand, which it was in Nell's mind.

"Money isn't to be hoarded. What you put out returns to you, especially when you help others, whether your friends, family, or strangers," Selena explained. "In Missy's case, it's also business related. She's the heart of the cupcake shop. We can't run the place without her, so the sooner she's cleared as a person of interest, the better. That way, we can reopen our remote location with no distractions when the cottage food permit arrives."

Missy sniffled. "You're going to make me cry."

"Don't because then we'll all start crying, and we did enough of that with me yesterday," Bria said.

Selena nodded. "That means no crying when I leave. I'll be here again before you know it."

Brunch with the Posse was the perfect way to spend a Sunday morning, but Nell knew one thing that would make it better. "That's the cue to break out the cupcakes that Missy wasn't supposed to bring."

Juliet brought the box from the counter to the table.

Missy looked smug. "And you told me not to bring anything."

"I was wrong." Nell pulled out a chocolate cupcake. "We always need your cupcakes, and we always need you."

Nell bit into the cupcake and nearly sighed at the chocolatey goodness.

She hoped Elias would get all suspicions surrounding Missy cleared up this week, so she could concentrate on whatever was happening with Sam.

Sam hadn't slept so well in… He couldn't remember. He hadn't thought he stood a chance with Missy, yet she'd kissed him good-night. Okay, it wasn't a passion-filled goodbye, more like a chaste peck, but lips had made contact, so that counted in his book.

He parked and entered the sheriff's office through the employee door. Two steps inside, he felt eyes on him. A glance around showed gazes staring his way with laser-beam intensity and questions—lots of questions and curiosity.

He remembered those same looks from people in town when his brother's alcoholism was no longer a secret.

Josh was doing well now. The rest of his family, too.

What's going on?

He tried to ignore it.

Murmurs sounded, replacing the usual background noise of the department, but he heard someone mention his name.

This wasn't about his family but him.

That had never happened before.

Sam's breaths came faster. An urge to run to the locker room ASAP struck, but that would only draw more attention to himself. He quickened his pace, keeping his gaze on the floor in front of him.

The entrance beckoned like a lighthouse in dense fog. *Almost there...*

"Sam," Mary, the admin, called out his name.

So much for making a clean getaway. Sam stopped and turned toward Mary's desk. Forcing a smile made the muscles around his mouth hurt. "Hey."

Mary barely raised her head from her computer monitor. "Sheriff Dooley wants to talk to you, Deputy Cooper. Now."

She usually reserved her dismissive tone for non-department folks. This was the first time she'd directed it at Sam.

"Thanks." Sam forced the word from his dry throat. A run-through of his calls didn't suggest he'd done anything wrong. He'd had no write-ups in Seattle to follow him to Berry Lake. Even though he felt responsible for Ritchie's death, an internal investigation showed no fault on Sam's part. He'd even been given a commendation for the incident.

That still burned.

The office door was open.

Sam glanced inside.

Royal sat behind his desk, a stack of files in front of him. He paged through a familiar-looking journal.

Sam squinted. That was Elise's old journal. The one he'd put in the evidence bag at Missy's house.

Why was Royal going through it and not wearing gloves?

Sam moved into the doorway. "You wanted to talk to me, sir?"

Royal didn't look up. He shoved the journal underneath the top file. "Come in and close the door."

A closed door equaled wanting privacy.

Sam's shoulders tensed. A frisson of worry shot through him, but he stepped inside and shut the door behind him, anyway.

The click of the latch sent a punch to his gut.

Royal motioned to the chair opposite the desk. "Have a seat, Sam."

Sam had only been sent to the principal's office once in high school. This was a hundred times worse. Not even after the investigation following Ritchie's death had Sam's stomach been tied up in enough knots to vie for a place on his grandma's wall of macrame hangings the way it was now.

Sam sat and placed his clammy hands on his legs, mindful he didn't rub his palms. A deputy should be calm and collected, not show nerves. He didn't want to disappoint.

Royal leaned back in his chair. "Most people expect me to be a throwback to my father."

A history lesson. Not what Sam expected, but he would go with it. "I remember your dad. He was an excellent sheriff."

"People liked him. That's why he ran unopposed for decades. Same for me, though I'm not part of the good-old-boys' club like he was. I'm more progressive than that."

Berry Lake progressive, maybe. Not anywhere close to Seattle progressive, but Sam kept his mouth closed.

"Through all the years, whether a sheriff or a deputy, this department has had one job. To keep Berry Lake safe."

Sam had no idea where his boss was going with this, but he nodded. "Yes, sir."

"When I hired you, I said, 'Royal, Sam Cooper's what this town needs. Not only now but in the future. Especially after I retire.'"

Whoa. Back up a minute. Sam's throat tightened.

"That's right, son. I can picture you as the next sheriff of Berry Lake."

Sam swallowed. "I'm honored. That would be a dream come true."

"You've always wanted to be a police officer or sheriff's deputy." Royal's lazy grin spread. "I remember when you were about six or seven. My dad gave you a tour for your birthday. Stuck a sheriff's badge sticker over your heart. Showed you things we never show outsiders."

"Best birthday ever, sir."

Royal steepled his fingers. "I imagine it was. You caused quite a commotion when you turned on the sirens in one of the patrol cars. Mary spilled an entire pot of coffee."

"I remember the siren, but not the other part."

"You were in the parking lot. You wouldn't have known. When Dad found out, he laughed. Said, 'that Cooper boy will work here one day, and after you retire, Royal, he'll be the next sheriff of Berry Lake. Mark my words.'"

Sam's breathing stilled. He'd dreamed about that as a kid. To know both sheriffs recognized that potential floored him. He hadn't been on the job long enough for a promotion, but maybe there was a class they wanted him to take to prepare for the future.

Sam sat taller. His chest puffed. He wanted to tell Missy. "I had no idea."

Royal nodded. "That's why when your resumé came across my desk, I remembered what my father had said about you and took it as a sign of fate. You've got big-city experience and special training that others don't."

Despite everything Royal said, the tension in the air sharpened. That was strange, but Sam might be reading the room wrong since he still didn't know why he was there. "I'll do whatever it takes, sir."

"Glad to hear it. We need team players in Berry Lake. So far, you fit right in. Gained the respect of the department fast. We've only had compliments since you started."

"Thank you, sir."

"But something's come to my attention."

Sam's heart gonged in his chest. "Sir?"

"Did you go to Missy Hanford's house after finishing your shift?"

Sam had, or Royal wouldn't have asked the question. "Yes, sir."

"Are you and Missy friends?"

The innuendo in those words nearly knocked Sam over. *Yes* sat perched on the tip of Sam's tongue. Who was he kidding? He would marry her tomorrow if he thought he had a chance of her saying yes. "Yes. We've known each other for a long time. I was friends with her husband, Rob."

"You're not dating?"

"I don't—"

"Answer the question."

"We haven't had an official date yet." The pizza dinner sort of counted. "But, yes, we're dating."

"I appreciate your honesty. And I'll return the favor." Royal straightened in his chair. "Appearances matter in this town, especially in the sheriff's department. We can't keep the town safe if people don't respect us, or if there's talk about a conflict of interest. Do you understand what I'm saying?"

"Am I in trouble, sir?"

"Not yet." The yet floated between them. "But you can't see Missy Hanford again until the investigation finishes."

"She's innocent." The words flew out.

"That's for the legal system to decide. She's a suspect in a felony and off-limits for the foreseeable future. I won't have you putting the department in jeopardy because you want to hang out with your late friend's widow."

Every nerve ending went on high alert. When had Missy become a suspect? And Sam had taken a huge step forward with her. No way was he stopping. "But—"

"This isn't up for discussion." Royal's face reddened. "Stay away from Missy Hanford. And remember, you're still on your ninety-day probation. I can fire you without cause. Understood?"

All that future sheriff talk had been to soften Sam up. Royal hadn't been serious.

"Understood?" Royal repeated.

Sam nodded. "Anything else, sir?"

"No."

He left the office, bypassed the locker room, and headed outside. No way would Sam leave Missy hanging without a word. He didn't think Royal would pull phone records, but he wanted to be smart about this.

For Missy's sake and his own.

Sam scrolled through his contacts until he came to someone who wasn't part of the Posse or involved in Missy's case. Hope was the ideal person. She was family and would help him out with no one suspecting anything.

Sam called her.

Hope picked up on the second ring. "Hey, I thought you had a shift today."

"I'm at work, but something happened, and I need your help. I wouldn't ask, except it's important. My future happiness depends on it."

"Whatever you need," Hope said, her voice full of the same kindness she'd shown Josh and his family from the beginning. "Just ask. That's what family's for."

chapter twenty-one

SUNDAY NIGHT, SELENA unpacked her suitcase and tossed the dirty clothes into the washing machine. She watched the clock as if waiting for quitting time on a Friday. The minutes passed like hours, and soon, she yawned. The days in Berry Lake and the drive home to Seattle were catching up with her, but...

Nope.

She wouldn't go to bed, even if the thought of the luxurious sheets against her skin made her heart sigh, strumming through her like a well-tuned violin. Wanting to make the most of the moment, she pictured each of the Posse members and visualized their lives the way they wanted.

Her life, too.

Health, wealth, success, love, peace.

The feelings erased the emotions from the weekend.

So much was waiting for each of them. Unfortunately, the timing was unknown.

The front door opened.

Her heart soared.

Selena ran to the foyer.

Logan wore a suit, but he'd loosened his tie. His hair looked like he'd run his hand through it a few times. The messy style was super sexy. He'd let his beard grow, too, no doubt because of their winning-streak superstitions.

He held his arms out for her.

She launched herself against him, and he lifted her feet off the ground.

Selena nuzzled against his neck, inhaling his scent, a mix of spicy, earthy aftershave and sweat. "Missed you so much."

"Missed you more." He lowered his mouth to hers.

He tasted like peppermint—the flavor of gum he chewed to keep his ears from clogging up while flying.

Logan placed Selena on the ground and let go of her. "I'd love to keep holding you like that, but I need a day or two to let my body recover."

Selena rubbed his shoulders. His moan of satisfaction kept her going. She found a knot and pressed, hoping it would release. "Were all the games that rough?"

"Yeah, but the pain level seems based on age." Logan shrugged. "Sucks to get old."

Old? She stepped away and studied him. "You *look* like my hottie hockey-playing husband, but you sure don't sound like him. What's going on?"

"We're not a month into the season, and I'm hurting worse than I have in the past. This might be it."

Anticipation buzzed through her. "*It*, it?"

"You want me to say it?"

"Please." She held her breath.

"Retirement."

Yes! But Selena controlled her excitement. "You'll be in the Hall of Fame so fast."

Logan laughed. "You're my number one fan, so you have to say that."

"You're one of the top defenders in the league today, and you could go up against any of the greatest who ever played."

He swooped down and kissed her. "You're okay with all this?"

"More than okay. We've discussed your retirement. Planned what that would be like for us."

"Yes, we have." He sounded more content than she thought possible.

"Does the team know?"

He twirled a strand of her hair. "No. I haven't mentioned it to Ted, either. I wanted to talk to you first."

Ted, the agent who'd talked Logan into playing year after year. Ted, the agent who didn't care about his clients. Ted, the agent who was only interested in how much money said clients brought him.

Ted disliked Selena. The feeling was mutual, but Ted had been a part of Logan's life before her. Her husband had a strong sense of loyalty and believed Ted was more like a surrogate dad than a money-grubbing agent. But retirement meant Ted would no longer be a part of their lives. That was something else to celebrate.

She kissed Logan. "I won't say a word, but you need to plan this out when you're ready. Get the team and their PR department involved."

"And you."

"That's a given." Selena wanted to scream and dance.

"Will the lake house be finished by the end of the season?"

"I'll make sure it is." She would offer a bonus to make sure it happened.

"It'll be better when we live in Berry Lake, and you don't have to keep driving back and forth." Logan held Selena close. "I'll have to share you with the Posse, but I'll get you most of the time."

"Nearly all the time." She shimmied against him. "I can't wait for that. I know you love hockey, but each season seems longer and gets harder."

"Won't be for much longer."

Selena yawned.

"That drive from Berry Lake must have worn you out again." Logan swept her into his arms. "It's time for bed."

"Bed, huh? What about sleeping?"

He kissed her again. "That will come. I need to make up for the time I was away. Hate these road trips."

"Me too. And I'm not *that* tired."

Logan winked. "I was hoping you'd say that."

As he carried her up the stairs, joy pulsed through Selena. Her patience was paying off. Soon, that something-was-missing feeling would be a thing of the past. She and Logan would live the life they'd dreamed about in Berry Lake with each other. And she and her friends would run the Berry Lake Cupcake Shop.

What more could she ask for?

Bria slept in on Monday morning, staying under the covers until her stomach growled. Hunger was a good enough reason to get out of bed. She glanced at her cell phone.

No texts.

Not surprising.

Yesterday, everyone headed home after brunch, including Selena, to catch up on what they had put off all weekend. Bria had binged a series, cried, reviewed her meetings with clients, cried some more, and slept.

Her plan for today was to cry less.

So far, so good.

Bria climbed out of bed. The house was quiet, something it hadn't been this weekend with Selena staying there, too.

She peeked in on Lulu crated in Juliet's room. The little dog didn't even raise her head.

Lulu's sad eyes tugged at Bria's heart. "You know you're stuck in there until you heal. But soon you'll be running around and annoying Butterscotch."

If a dog could speak, Lulu would have said, "Whatever."

Bria headed into the kitchen with her cell phone. The coffee pot was on and full. Juliet must have made it before she left for work.

Best housemate ever.

Bria poured herself a mug and sat at the table.

And brave.

Juliet is so brave.

Bria wanted to be the same. She hit her contacts and called Dad.

One ring, two…

"Good morning, baby doll." Dad sounded so cheerful. "Everything all right?"

A lump formed in Bria's throat. "Are you with Molly?"

"I am. She loves the unicorn you gave her."

"I'm glad."

"Guess what she named her?"

Bria took a wild guess. "Rainbow?"

"Nope. She named her Bria."

Her jaw dropped. "What?"

Dad laughed. "Sometimes things like this happen, and I love it when they do. Hold on a moment."

Silence.

"What did you name your unicorn?" Dad asked.

"Breeeee-a," a voice answered.

Not a voice.

Molly.

My mom.

Something inside Bria's chest swelled. Her eyelids heated. She blinked.

"Did you hear that?" Pride filled Dad's voice. "Molly's the one who came up with your name, but it still surprised me."

"M-Mom named me?" Bria took a breath.

"She took the first four letters of my first name," Dad said. "I was so touched then. I still am now. You're the best of us, baby doll. The very best."

Bria's throat burned. "Thanks."

"How's Dalton?"

Oh, boy. How did she answer that? Might as well tell the truth. "I talked to him about what you told me. He didn't want to believe that about his dad, so he went to Deena."

"And Deena told him that Paul wasn't planning to divorce her, and Molly drove into the lake on purpose."

Bria sat stunned. "Exactly that."

Dad sighed. "It feels so good not to be living with this secret. The secrets killed Paul, not cancer."

"Who did Paul lie to?"

"Everyone. The truth of what happened between Paul and Molly probably lies somewhere in the middle of what he told Deena and me."

Sighing, Bria slumped in her chair.

"That isn't the answer you wanted," Dad said.

"No. Dalton believes Deena, who blames Mom for the affair and you for them losing all their life insurance in poor investments."

"I never invested a penny of Paul's money. It all went directly to Molly's care. There are no records. I'd give them to you if I had any."

"I believe you, Dad."

"That means everything to me." The love in his voice stretched from Wishing Bay to Berry Lake and embraced Bria in a gentle hug. "Even though I have no proof, your mother was on her way back to us, and Paul wanted to stop her."

"Did she call you?"

"No, I drove to Hayden Lake after the accident. I asked around. She'd stopped for gas at a convenience store and bought two things: a can of pop and a toy. The clerk remembered her because of the light-up wand. Molly had told her it was for her two-year-old daughter. When the police finished their investigation, they gave me everything they'd found in the vehicle. The toy was soggy, but it was there. If what Deena says is true, I doubt your mom would have stopped to fill up her car or buy you a toy."

"I agree." Bria stared into her coffee cup. "But Dalton won't."

"If it'll bring you two back together, I can stay away from Berry Lake."

"No." The word shot from Bria's mouth. "We're family. And this is your hometown. I won't ask you to stay away. I need you, Dad."

"And I need you, too. In her own way, so does Mom."

"I know." In her heart, Bria did. "I'll find a long weekend where I can visit Wishing Bay."

"We'd love that. But what about Dalton?"

"I can't give him the proof he wants, so he either changes his mind or he doesn't."

"Will you be okay if he can't?"

The burning in her throat and behind Bria's eyelids returned. "Not right away, but I will be."

Eventually.

"We Landons love with all our hearts, but we haven't been so lucky in love. I want that to change for you, baby doll."

She wondered if he meant all Landons, including Aunt Elise. She'd dated Sheriff Dooley for years, but they'd never gotten a happily ever after. Bria rubbed her eyes. "Me too, Dad. Me too."

Pulse racing, Missy entered the Carpenter Law Office on Main Street. She was there to meet with two different people. Her lawyer, Elias Carpenter, made sense. But Hope Ryan Cooper asking to see her didn't.

The receptionist greeted Missy. "Go on back. Elias's office is the second door on the right. It's marked."

Missy headed to the hallway. Her foot was a little better. She didn't know if that was because of more healing or anticipation of seeing Sam again. Perhaps a combination of both. He must have worked late or been tired when he got off work last night. She hoped that meant he would visit her today.

Elias's door was open.

Hope sat inside. She stood. "Do you need help with your foot?"

"I'm good." Missy took a seat. "Though, I'm curious why you want to see me."

"Elias said we could talk privately in here." Hope closed the door and sat. "Sam asked me to speak with you."

Missy's body tensed. "Sam? Is he okay?"

"Physically, he's fine, but the sheriff threatened Sam's job if he sees you during an active investigation."

Seriously? "This sucks."

"Yes, it does. Sam wants you to know how much he cares about you and is sorry, and he already misses you. But he doesn't want you to worry or get upset."

"Tell Sam he has nothing to be sorry about and not to worry about me. I'm okay." Missy rubbed her forehead to stave off a headache. "Elise will haunt Royal for sure now."

Hope laughed. "I'm sorry, it's just—"

"This whole situation is ridiculous." Missy's arms plopped to the side of the chair. "I'm guessing you're here because he can't talk to me either."

Hope nodded. "No calls or texts. Sam didn't want you to think he was ghosting you."

Missy blew out a breath. She'd finally taken a chance, but she'd also wanted to go slow.

Be careful what you wish for.

"Thank him for me. Tell him I understand. And when he can finally come over, the kittens will be bigger and more fun to play with, and he'll have new cupcake flavors to try."

Hope grinned. "I'll tell him that."

"I'm not guilty, so the investigation can't last that long." Missy rubbed her chin. "But no matter what happens, Sam's job is the important thing. I'll do whatever it takes to make sure he doesn't suffer."

Hope did a double take. "You're taking this better than either of us thought you would."

Missy had been through the highs and lows of life. A few days or weeks apart was nothing in the grand scheme of things. No way would she jeopardize Sam's career for a few dates. That would be stupid. "Sam has wanted to be a police officer for his entire life. I won't stand in the way."

"Sam hates that this is happening."

The situation reminded Missy of saying goodbye to Rob when he deployed. At least the stakes weren't as high this time, but... "Me, too. We only just got together, but we'll figure it out once the fire is behind me."

"I'm impressed."

"Don't be. It's all stuff I learned from Selena T's podcast. She deserves the credit."

Hope's expression turned thoughtful. She reached into her pocket, removed a business card, and handed it to Missy. "If you need anything or want to get a message to Sam, please contact me."

"Thank you for playing go-between."

"Sam and his entire family played a huge role in Josh's recovery. I might not have ever met him if they hadn't done that." Hope grinned. "Plus, I'm a sucker for romance. And the way Sam talks about you is the definition of adorable."

Missy's cheeks heated. "Well, he is adorable."

"And so are you. I look forward to..." Hope's complexion turned green. "Oh, no. Where's the bathroom?"

Missy rushed Hope out of the office and into the bathroom.

Hope barely made it to the toilet before she threw up. She flushed the toilet and washed her hands. Tight lines formed around her mouth. "I'm so sorry."

Missy handed Hope a wet paper towel. "How far along are you?"

Hope's eyes widened. "How—"

"Jenny had terrible morning sickness with Briley. Except it hit around the clock."

"Same." Color returned to Hope's cheeks. "I'm eight weeks along, but no one knows. We're waiting until we get past the first trimester. The h-C-G levels are high enough to suggest twins. Given I'm a twin—"

"That's wonderful."

Hope touched her stomach. "Except for this part, it is."

"Your secret's safe with me." Missy winked. "Not that I could tell Sam, even if I wanted to."

Hope laughed. "He'll give my brother, Von, a run for the best uncle award."

"He will." But Missy had a feeling Sam would be an awesome dad, too.

On Wednesday, Dalton sat in the stands watching football practice. He hadn't expected to be at the high school today, but Tanner needed him to meet a surveyor in Berry Lake at noon. The entire time, Dalton had searched for Bria.

Not that he knew what he would say if he bumped into her. But he missed her.

A week ago, he would have visited her as soon as he finished working. Now he watched Ian prepare for a big game coming up. The team had a bye this Friday.

Breaking up this time around had been worse than in high school because they'd been kids then, unsure of their feelings and what life had in store. He had a better handle on the the feelings part now, but the same uncertainty existed with life.

Maybe it always would.

A whistle blew.

The players on the team lined up in formation. The positions of the two wide receivers suggested a pass.

Once upon a time, Dalton had played on the same field. He'd been in the shadow of Josh Cooper until the guy graduated and played college ball. Even as Dalton took his turn in the spotlight, the Cooper legacy lived on. Not that Dalton had been the same caliber quarterback as Josh or Ian.

Ian ran to his left and threw a forty-yard pass to a receiver, who caught the perfectly placed pass with little effort. Ian was destined for the pros with a big-league arm, an eye for the game, and two fast legs.

Dalton was so proud of his youngest brother. Dad would be, too.

A familiar pang struck Dalton's chest.

Would Dad have really hated Brian Landon after being such good friends for so long?

A whistle blew.

As the team ran off the field, Dalton stood. He shouldn't second-guess himself. His mom had been so supportive since

303

his talk with Bria. It was as if they had turned the clock back, and Dalton wanted it to stay that way. He missed his family. He couldn't bring back his dad, but he could stop avoiding his mom and siblings.

Ian yanked off his helmet and jogged to the bottom of the stands. "I thought you were in Portland this week."

"Tanner needed something done in Berry Lake, so here I am."

"Will you be at the game on Friday?" Ian asked, the hope in his voice matching his eyes.

"Wouldn't miss it!"

"Are you staying to have dinner with us tonight?"

Ian might be the next college superstar, but he was still a kid at heart. Dalton was a big brother/surrogate dad rolled into one. "Yes, I am."

"Good." Ian squinted. "You don't look so good, bro."

Dalton ran his fingers over his face. Whiskers scratched his fingertips. "Been a rough couple of days."

"Sorry about you and Bria."

"How'd you hear?"

"Mom mentioned it to Sal. She said it's for the best."

Mom had said the same thing to Dalton. He wanted to believe her, but he wasn't there yet. A part of him kept waiting for Bria to tell him her dad lied, so they could return to the way they were.

"It might be." Dalton hated the constant ache in his chest that wouldn't go away. "Did Mom say anything else?"

Ian waved to a student who was walking around the track. "That our family would finally be the way it was meant to be." Ian gulped from his water bottle. "No idea what that means. But Mom's been busy with some fundraising thing for the town's first responders."

"I had no idea."

"Yeah." Ian wiped the sweat from his forehead with the bottom of his practice jersey. "Sal invited the fire department and the sheriff's office staff over for dinner on Friday. Not that Mom cooks, and Charlene Culpepper won't work with her after how they treated Sheridan, so she hired someone from Hood River to cook."

Mom wasn't much into charity unless the funds came her way, but she seemed to have turned over a new leaf in a big way. "Sal seems to be good for Mom."

"He's okay, except you'd think a man his age wouldn't be all puppy dog eyes and yes, dears." Ian shrugged. "That's why Mom tolerates Sal more than her other husbands, but she flirted big-time at the dinner. Never knew Mom had a thing for first responders. Sal laughed about it the next day."

"He must not be worried about being replaced."

"Few in Berry Lake can afford the lifestyle Mom's grown accustomed to."

That was true. "Are things good with you?"

"Football's great. School's going a little better."

"You mentioned that Bentley's tutoring is helping."

"Yeah. Wouldn't be getting the grades I am without him." Ian smiled. "That reminds me. Whatever you do, make sure things are cool with Bria. I don't want to be banished from the cupcake shop when it reopens."

"Priorities."

"I've got them."

Dalton laughed. "I'm sure you'll be welcome to spend your money there. Elise Landon was a hardnose, but Missy Hanford's a total softie. You'll be fine."

"Missy always let Bentley give us free cupcakes when we won a game. But when she's arrested…"

"What are you talking about?"

"At that dinner, someone said Missy was the arsonist since Brian Landon went free. It would suck if they charged a Gold Star widow for something she didn't do."

"Yes, it would." And that didn't seem like an appropriate dinner topic, given it was an ongoing investigation. Especially with people like his mom, Sal, and Ian there. "Do you remember who said that?"

"Nope." Ian took another sip. "I need to shower. See you at home."

With that, Ian headed inside.

Dalton remembered Missy being questioned before they arrested Brian, but something about an arson suspect being discussed at a private dinner sounded sketchy. And Ian was correct about Missy Hanford not being an arsonist.

Dalton would bet the last cottage on Pinewood Lane on Missy's innocence. As he walked to his car, he couldn't stop thinking about what Ian had said.

Something wasn't right.

And though he'd left the ball in Bria's court, this wasn't about them. It involved her aunt's estate, of which Bria was the personal representative for. She was also Missy's friend.

Good job rationalizing getting in touch with Bria, Dwyer.

He ignored the voice in his head.

Dalton needed to tell Bria. He only hoped she hadn't blocked him.

chapter twenty-two

W*HY IS THIS happening?*

Bria paced the length of her living room.

After talking to Dad on Monday, Bria had been doing so well. For two whole days, she'd only cried a few times. She'd focused on her clients and finding new ones. And then Dalton texted her.

A groan escaped.

Maybe it was petty, but she'd wanted to be the one in control of the situation.

Not reacting to his text.

But that was exactly what was happening.

So much for being brave like Juliet.

Bria had dumped her cup of coffee as soon as the text arrived, but now she wished she hadn't. That would give her something to do other than reread his text for the hundredth time.

Which was what she did again.

DALTON: *Important. Need to talk to you. Not about us, but Missy and the fire. Please.*
BRIA: *I'm at home.*
DALTON: *I'll be there in ten.*

Ten minutes.

As Bria continued to pace, thoughts swirled in her mind.

The text had nothing to do with them—he'd made that clear. She placed her free hand over her heart.

Still beating.

Of course, it was. But her heart must be sporting a new bruise or two from his text.

What had Selena suggested when stuck on a train of thought that wasn't good for her?

Oh, right. She needed to put her thoughts on something else.

On the corner of the couch, Butterscotch stretched so one paw touched Lulu's crate. Much-needed warmth balled at the center of Bria's chest. Last night, Juliet had found the cat sleeping next to the crate. That was why she'd put Lulu in the living room this morning before leaving for work.

Who would have guessed the dog and the cat weren't mortal enemies but best buddies?

If only Dalton and I…

Oops. Bria hadn't meant to go there. Thinking about something else had worked.

Until it didn't.

No matter.

Dalton's not coming to see me about our relationship.

Bria glanced at the clock on the mantel—almost time.

Her pulse galloped as fast as the underdog winning the Kentucky Derby.

A part of her—a large part—still hurt. She wouldn't get over it quickly. How could she? They would never agree on the truth, and Dalton would never accept her father.

A hopeless situation.

Yet, she wanted to be the reason Dalton reached out. Her heart didn't want to let go.

Stupid.

The doorbell rang.

A shiver ran along her spine.

He's here to talk about Missy. Nothing else.

Resolve in place, Bria opened the door.

Dalton hadn't shaved in days, but the beard looked good on him. Though, his complexion appeared duller and the light in his eyes had dimmed.

That didn't make her feel any better, because she looked the same only without the beard, though don't ask her to show her legs where a forest grew.

"Hey." Dalton brushed his hand through his hair. "Thanks for seeing me."

She clutched the doorknob as if it were the only thing keeping her upright. "Hi."

"Can I come in?"

So much for pleasantries. She motioned him inside and then closed the door behind him. "Your text said it was important."

"Yeah." He headed to the opposite end of the couch from Butterscotch and Lulu. "It's more of a hunch, but I strongly feel something's not right with the arson investigation."

"Okay." But she was far from okay.

Bria sat in the chair, even if she wanted to sit next to him. She needed to focus on why Dalton stopped by. The rest had to wait.

"Remember what Selena T says about trusting your gut?" Bria asked.

Dalton nodded. "That's why I'm here. My instinct tells me Missy will get blamed for the fire the same way your dad did."

"She's innocent." *Just like Dad.*

"They might blame her, anyway." Dalton's tone was firm, adamant.

Bria leaned forward. "Why would they do that?"

"I don't know the reason, but Ian overheard someone say Missy was most likely the arsonist. The person is with the fire department, but Ian didn't know who said it."

"Wait." Bria thought about the search warrant. "This was discussed at a dinner?"

Dalton nodded. "At Sal and Deena's house on Friday night."

"That makes no sense."

Dalton sat forward on the couch. "You lost me."

"They released my dad early Thursday morning. The sheriff didn't serve Missy the search warrant and go through her house until Saturday night."

Dalton drew away. "They *what*?"

"Sheriff Dooley showed up with a search warrant on Saturday night. We were all there having dinner. He made a mess of the place. It seemed unnecessary. I mean, it's Missy."

"Exactly."

"What evidence would they have to say she's the arsonist on Friday? And if they had enough to say that, why did they need a search warrant?"

Dalton shrugged. "They could be using something she said when they questioned her the last time."

"I don't think so. They harped on her lost keys so much Elias had to cut off Reggie Lemond. The guy was fishing for something."

"Someone could have just been gossiping."

"Or they have inside info."

Dalton stroked his beard. "It makes no sense to me. You?"

His gaze met hers, and Bria's heart bumped.

Traitor.

She forced her attention away from him and onto Missy. "Something's definitely sketchy."

"Glad you agree."

Bria did, and she was concerned. "Missy is meeting with Elias right now. Do you think—"

"Let's go." Dalton stood and pulled his keys out of his pocket. "I'll drive."

"Thanks." Bria grabbed her phone and purse. "And I don't just mean about driving."

The corners of his mouth lifted slightly. "I know. We make a good team."

She nodded. They made a good team, but as Selena had said, sometimes love wasn't enough. Bria only hoped their teamwork helped Missy.

That was the most important thing right now.

Entering Elias's office on Wednesday afternoon gave Missy a sense of déjà vu. She'd been there two days ago to meet with Hope, and being back brought the feelings of missing Sam to the front and center of her mind.

Until now, Missy had been able to push aside thoughts of Sam to focus on the kittens, Mama Cat, Mario, and Peach. She'd also baked cupcakes. Lots and lots of cupcakes. More than she or the Posse could eat unless they wanted to make themselves sick.

But baking took Missy to her happy place—the spot where everything was sunshine, rainbows, and flowers. She'd never expected to find room for anyone other than Rob there. Yet there was space for more.

For Sam.

Realizing that gave her all the feels, but was it too soon to be thinking this way?

Maybe, but Missy didn't need to make any decisions right now. And when she did, she could always change her mind. Missy liked the idea of having a choice. Even if choosing to move on from Rob terrified her.

You've got this, babe.

Missy hoped Rob was right, but first, she needed to clear her name so she could see Sam again. That was why she asked to meet with Elias. "Thanks for seeing me today."

Elias stood. "I'm always here to help you."

He was younger than Missy, but the skinny kid with perpetually skinned knees and hair that always fell into his eyes was all grown up. He looked every inch a successful attorney in a crisp dress shirt and tie.

He motioned to a chair, and Missy sat. Elias came around the desk and leaned against the front of it. "What can I do for you today?"

"I need to clear my name. Prove I shouldn't be a person of interest. Or a suspect. Whatever they think I am."

Elias crossed his right ankle over his left. "Would this have to do with a certain sheriff's deputy?"

Heat rose up her neck. "Our lives would be easier if I wasn't part of the arson investigation."

"Since no charges have been filed, there's not much you can do."

Missy slumped in the chair. That wasn't what she wanted to hear. "What if I find my set of keys that are somewhere inside the shop? That was a sticking point for Reggie, right?"

"I wish it were that easy."

She fidgeted in the chair. "What's difficult about going into the cupcake shop and using a metal detector to find my keys?"

"The cupcake shop is still considered a crime scene. That means no trespassing."

"I watch every crime show on TV." She also enjoyed listening to true crime podcasts. "I know how it works, but this should clear me, given Reggie made such a big deal about my lost keys when they questioned me. Have they even searched for my keys?"

Elias scribbled on a notepad. "I haven't received an answer to that question yet. I'll call Reggie again."

"I just want this to be over with." She blew out a frustrated breath. "They took all my journals. I didn't think about what I may have written, but now I cringe to think anyone is reading them." She rubbed her neck. "Some were from high school and filled with nothing but pages of me handwriting Mrs. Rob Hanford. Others I used for journaling. It was part of my grief counseling. The depression was bad."

A few times, things had been bleak. But Mario and Peach had needed her. Jenny and Elise, too. They'd kept Missy from giving up.

"I have ups and downs. That might never change, but I'm so far above those low points now."

Elias wrote more on a yellow legal pad. He'd used one before, which cracked her up. She'd never thought the name may have come from lawyers using the pads.

"I understand. I have a call into the DA because the search seems unreasonable," Elias said. "Yes, you were at the scene, but the timestamps on your calls have been verified. And what you said happened matches with Welles's report."

"Will your call get Sam in trouble with the DA?"

Elias smiled. "Not since he works under the direction of the sheriff."

Missy blew out a breath. She didn't want the investigation to affect Sam. "Thank goodness."

Elias studied her. "You like Sam a lot."

"Maybe. Yes." She took a breath. "It's new."

Elias laughed. "I'll do my best to make sure you see him soon."

Excitement shot through her. "Thank you."

The phone on the desk rang.

"Excuse me." Elias picked up the receiver. "Yes, please send them in." He hung up the phone. "Bria and Dalton are here."

Say what? Missy leaned forward. "Together?"

"Sounds like I missed the latest round of the Berry Lake gossip train, but you can see for yourself in a minute."

Given what had happened since Saturday, nothing would surprise Missy.

The door opened. Elias straightened.

Bria entered the office, followed by Dalton, but the two didn't hold hands as they usually did when they were out. And the distance between them wasn't normal. They usually walked so close together they almost bumped into each other.

Bria rushed to Missy's side. "Dalton's younger brother heard something. It might be important or just a hunch."

Elias shook Dalton's hand. "Owen or Ian?"

"Ian." Dalton told them about the dinner party. "Something's off. Someone was saying Missy was the arsonist on Friday when they didn't serve the search warrant until Saturday night."

Weird, but...

"I don't have any enemies." Well, except her parents, but they'd left town when she was eighteen. And that was on them. No one knew where they'd gone. "No one is out to get me, if that's what you're worried about."

"Everyone loves you." Bria held Missy's hand. "But Dalton felt so strongly about this that he reached out to me. We both agreed you and Elias needed to know."

Elias scribbled notes. "Thanks for bringing this to our attention. I'm hopeful no charges will be filed, but I'll keep this in Missy's file."

It was impossible to miss Bria and Dalton's shared glances. It was clear the two still loved each other. Missy hoped they figured things out or moved on.

"The person who called Missy the arsonist might not be involved in the investigation," Elias continued. "Many people in town have their opinions on who set the fire."

"I hadn't thought about it only being someone's opinion." Bria crossed her arms over her chest. "I'm sure a few still think my dad did it, even though he was in Wishing Bay."

Dalton leaned against the wall. "It still feels off to talk about at dinner. Are there confidentiality rules for investigations?"

"Police and fire investigators can discuss cases to find information, but a subject has a right to privacy. Can you ask Ian if he remembers who said it? And who was at the dinner?"

"I'll ask him tonight at dinner," Dalton said.

Missy had hoped Dalton and Bria had something concrete, but Elias was treating this as nothing more than a hunch.

Oh, well. Missy would have to figure out a way to search inside the cupcake shop. She didn't want to trespass and get into more trouble. That wouldn't be good for Sam or her. Welles might know a way or…Bentley. The kid was smart and used drones. Maybe one of those could do a search.

"I gotta admit it's more fun watching crime drama than experiencing it," Missy joked.

The others laughed, lessening the tension in the office.

The phone rang again.

"Excuse me," Elias answered. "Denise…" His face paled. "Stall. Give us a few minutes if you can."

Elias's voice sounded unnatural. He hung up. "The sheriff is here with a warrant for Missy's arrest."

What? Missy's heart slammed against her chest. She struggled to breathe.

This can't be happening.

"No!" Bria covered her mouth with her hand. "They can't do this."

Dalton straightened. He took a step toward Bria before retreating. "There must be something we can do."

Panic flashed in Elias's eyes. He took a breath, and the calm lawyer returned. "I'll do whatever I can."

Tears stung Missy's eyes. The worry on the three others' faces only reaffirmed this was really happening. "I didn't do it."

"Of course, you didn't." Bria hugged her, holding on tightly, as if she were afraid to let go. Missy didn't want her to.

"We'll find out the truth," Dalton reassured her. "Do whatever Elias needs us to do."

Elias came up to her, so Bria let go of Missy.

Missy hunched her shoulders, but she couldn't hide from this.

"Say nothing, Missy. Promise me." Elias's eyes implored her. "Not one word. In this office. In the jail. Anywhere. Unless I'm with you. Got it?"

As Missy's vision blurred, a lump in her throat grew. She nodded.

"We're here for you," Bria said.

And then Missy remembered the others counting on her. "Oh, no. Someone needs to tell Sabine to get the kittens and Mama Cat. And Jenny will need to feed Mario and Peach. They'll be so scared when I don't come home."

"I'll take care of it." Bria patted Missy's back. "We've got you."

"I'll call Jenny," Dalton offered. "Don't worry."

"Thanks," Bria answered for Missy.

The door opened.

Sheriff Dooley entered, followed by Sam, who looked as pale as Elias had. Only Sam's eyes were sunken and appeared haunted.

She wanted to kiss away his pain and make everything better.

Sam stared at her with a mix of regret and something else. Affection, maybe.

Love.

The voice in her head was as clear as the sound of her breathing.

Missy wanted to cry out to Sam, to reassure him the same way he would her if he could, but the stakes were too high not to do what Elias said.

She blinked to keep the tears at bay, but warm tears slid down her cheeks anyway. She clung to Bria's hand like a lifeline.

Bria sniffled. Tears streamed down her face, too.

Dalton's hands alternated between balling and flexing. He looked like he wanted to punch someone.

Sheriff Dooley cleared his throat. "Missy Hanford, you're under arrest. Turn around and place your hands behind your back."

No! This wasn't fair. Wasn't right. Missy took a step back and bumped into the wall.

She didn't want to be handcuffed and dragged down Main Street like a criminal for all to see. She wasn't an arsonist.

Someone else set the fire. Someone who almost killed her. Someone who was still out there.

She glanced at Elias, his jaw jutting forward, and Sam, who mouthed, "Sorry."

Elias held out his hands. "Is this necessary, Sheriff? I'll escort my client to your office, and you can book her. She's not a flight risk."

Of course, she wasn't. Where would she go? Missy wanted to cheer on Elias for stopping the madness.

A vein ticked at the sheriff's neck. "Cuff her, Sam."

She gasped, or Sam did. Maybe both had.

Sam remained in place.

"Don't make me ask you again, Cooper," the sheriff ordered.

What had happened to Royal? Missy didn't recognize the man she'd seen almost daily until the fire. He'd loved Elise so much. He'd been as sweet as a confetti cupcake. Had her death changed him that much?

Sam came closer to Missy. He held a pair of handcuffs.

She stepped away from Bria, who ran to Dalton. Missy didn't blame her friend for that. She would have loved to find security— sanctuary—in Sam's arms.

Would they ever get the chance to be together?

More tears fell. Missy's chest heaved, but she wouldn't lose it. Not yet anyway. That would make the situation harder on Sam.

He faced her and mouthed, "I'm so sorry."

Elias didn't want her to talk, but…

"It's okay." Missy spoke as softly as she could without only blowing air.

Gratitude flashed in Sam's wet eyes.

He'd heard her. He had to have heard her.

Metal clinked against metal.

That erased any relief she might have had.

As Missy turned and placed her hands behind her, a shiver ran along her spine. She closed her eyes. Not that she could see anyone facing the wall. But her hearing sharpened.

Bria cried, and Dalton calmed her with soft murmurs.

Someone typed on a computer or phone. Most likely Elias.

A foot tapped on the floor. She guessed that must be the sheriff.

Sam touched Missy's hand gently. His fingers were warm, and he squeezed.

Missy squeezed his. That was all she could do without speaking. It wasn't nearly enough.

"Hurry up," the sheriff spat.

The first cuff went on Missy's right wrist and clicked as he slowly tightened it. When Sam let go, a rush of ice shot through her.

Sam took her other hand, but this time, his fingers shook.

Arresting her was killing him. And she hated that. Hated that this was happening to him.

To them.

Hang in there.

Missy didn't know if she could. Her knees were ready to give out. But Sam seemed to know that because he pressed a leg against her on one side and supported her as he put on the other handcuff.

"Step away from her, Cooper."

A beat passed. Then his body heat was no longer near her, and a chill skittered across her.

"Turn around," Sheriff Dooley said in a monotone voice.

Missy opened her eyes and faced them. It was as she'd imagined. Dalton held a crying Bria. Elias typed on his phone. Sheriff Dooley's ruddy face appeared impatient. And Sam.

Sweet, dear Sam wiped his red eyes.

A sob escaped. Missy pressed her lips together.

He took a step toward her until the sheriff side-eyed him.

Sam stopped, but that took effort.

Missy was going to get him in trouble if she didn't do something. She closed her eyes and tried to still the fear grabbing hold of her.

She focused on Dalton's soft voice trying to comfort Bria, and Elias who now seemed to be speaking to someone on his phone.

All she wanted was to hear—to feel—Sam's heartbeat against hers. But he was too far away. And he had to stay even farther away. For his own good.

And for hers.

Missy sniffled.

That wouldn't help Bria or Sam, so Missy raised her chin and opened her eyes.

She gazed into Sam's eyes. Finding strength in them.

In him.

"You have the right to remain silent," Sheriff Dooley said until the words faded into nothingness. She thought they must be planning to interrogate her right away. Otherwise, they would have waited to read the Miranda Rights. "Let's go."

Sam rushed to Missy, but the sheriff pushed him away. "Stay in line, Cooper. I've got her."

Sheriff Dooley led her toward the door. Missy nearly stumbled, but she managed to right herself. The entire time, the sheriff kept moving.

As Dalton smoothed Bria's hair, Bria wiped her eyes. "I texted everyone. We'll be right there. I promise. I love you, Missy."

Missy promised not to say a word, so she nodded.

But when she looked at Sam, she puckered her lips, kissed the air, and tried not to bawl her eyes out.

Help us, Rob. Please.

No voice or feeling came.

But Rob was there. Somewhere. He would do what he could to get her out of this mess. So would Elias, Sam, and her friends.

chapter twenty-three

AS SAM STATIONED himself in the hallway next to the booking area, his insides burned. He'd pressed his fingernails into his palms so hard they'd left an indentation. That was nothing compared to what Missy was going through.

His stomach churned.

He should be in there, but Sheriff Dooley forbade Sam from going in. It was killing him to be apart from her.

Missy had been so scared, but she put on a good front. Sam had a feeling that had been for him, and it made him love her even more.

Love.

He loved Missy Hanford.

He had since that first day of high school. It was just too bad Rob had fallen for her in middle school. Even though Sam had moved on and away from Berry Lake, his love had remained, lying dormant. Now that it was back, stronger than ever, he would hold onto Missy with both hands.

She was his future.

Seeing the fear in her eyes had made him want to punch Royal. More than once, Sam almost had, but then Missy would look his way, as if knowing she needed to rein him in, and then he regained control of his temper.

If not for Missy, he would be being booked into jail himself for assaulting the sheriff.

Not that anyone who cared about Missy would blame Sam. He thought Dalton and Elias both wanted shots at Dooley. Bria, too.

Sam ran his fingers along the brim of his deputy hat. Wearing the hat had filled him with such pride only weeks ago. Now, he only felt shame. Shame for how Sheriff Royal Dooley had treated Missy in Elias's office. Shame for the way the sheriff dragged her along Main Street in handcuffs so all could see. Shame that someone must be paying off the sheriff for him to do this.

Sam's muscles might not ever relax after the disgusting display.

That was the only way to describe how the sheriff acted with Missy.

Everything had been unnecessary, too.

Only a dirty cop—or sheriff—would turn an arrest into such a spectacle. It was as if the sheriff had one mission in his life—to hurt and embarrass Missy Hanford.

The original Sheriff Dooley must be rolling over in his grave at his son's actions.

Royal didn't deserve to be Berry Lake's current sheriff. His treatment of Missy had destroyed any respect Sam had for the man or his position.

And Sam didn't know what to do next. The idea of working for a crooked cop...

"Sam." Mary's guarded expression told Sam his troubles today likely weren't over. "I have a message for you."

He straightened. "Yes, ma'am?"

"Sheriff Dooley wants you to wait for him in his office."

Sam tightened his grip on his hat. He glanced at the booking room's doorway.

"It's not a request," Mary said.

Sam nodded, but he didn't want to be that far from Missy. He looked at the doorway again. Not that he could see her from where he stood. The sheriff had made sure of that.

Mary's eyes softened. "Would you like me to go in there with her?"

Tension released from Sam. Not all of it, but enough. He rocked back on his heels.

"Please, Mary. That would be so kind of you." The words rushed out of him. "I—"

"No need to explain, Deputy Cooper. But you'd better go before you get into more trouble."

Mary entered the booking area with a glance back.

Sam trudged away. Each step he took away from Missy felt like a mile.

The sheriff's door was open.

He went inside, sat, and pulled out his cell phone. A message from Hope appeared on the screen.

> **HOPE:** *What's this about Missy getting arrested for arson?*
> **SAM:** *It's true. I put the handcuffs on her myself.*
> **HOPE:** *Oh, Sam. I'm so sorry. Where are you?*

SAM: *Missy's being booked. I'm waiting in the sheriff's office. He wants to talk to me.*
HOPE: *Does Missy need anything?*
SAM: *I'm sure she will. Jenny is on her way so reach out to her.*
HOPE: *I will. What are you going to do?*
SAM: *Don't know.*

Heavy footsteps sounded in the hallway. Sam knew who they belonged to, unfortunately. He typed quickly.

SAM: *Gotta go.*

He tapped *send* and shoved his phone into his pocket.

The sheriff walked in and kicked the door closed. His nostrils flared. "I told you to stay away from Missy Hanford."

"I haven't seen or spoken with her until today."

"Didn't look like it to me."

"I did exactly what you ordered me to do." Sam removed his phone. "Want to check my calls, sir?"

Sheriff Dooley sat behind his desk. "You were crying, Cooper. I saw you wipe your eyes. Be a man. Deputies aren't supposed to cry like that."

Sam wanted to remind the sheriff that not all deputies were men, but this probably wasn't the right time. He wouldn't apologize for letting his emotions get to him. He was human, not Robocop. No reason to be embarrassed.

He held his head high. "Missy's innocent."

"She set the fire." The sheriff touched his nose. "The DA will prove it."

The words didn't match Dooley's actions. Based on a tell Sam had learned at the police academy, the sheriff was lying.

Sam's breath hitched. Something more was going on, but he didn't know what.

The sheriff's gaze narrowed. "Which leaves you in a bit of a pickle, doesn't it?"

Sam considered the question. He had one of his own. "What do you mean?"

"A sheriff's deputy can't exactly date a convicted felon."

Sam's spine went ramrod stiff. "What happened to innocent until proven guilty?"

"Some cases are more open and shut. If Elias Carpenter is as smart as he thinks he is, he'll convince Missy to plea bargain."

Wait. She was just arrested. How was this even being discussed?

"At least there are other single women in Berry Lake for you to choose from. I'd recommend a hometown girl. That'll help you get elected when the time comes."

What? This conversation made zero sense. But Sam knew one thing. "The only woman I want is Missy."

"Then you'll never be sheriff."

Surprisingly, that didn't seem like the worst thing in the world, even though it had been Sam's dream. "I guess I won't then."

Saying the words should've hurt more. Or perhaps his dream had changed. There was one thing he wanted more, one thing that mattered most to him.

And Sam knew what he needed to do. He stood.

Royal drew his brows together. "I'm not finished talking to you, deputy."

"Too bad. Because I'm done with you." Sam removed his badge and holster. He placed both on the desk. "I'll save you the effort of firing me. I quit."

🧁 🧁 🧁

Sam texted his family to tell them he'd quit before the Berry Lake rumor mill beat him to it. He also mentioned Missy getting arrested and told them Hope could fill them in if they had more questions. Then, Sam turned in everything that hadn't belonged to him, much to Sheriff Dooley's dismay.

"You made your point, Sam." Sheriff Dooley followed Sam to the locker room. "Please reconsider. Resigning isn't necessary. I'm sorry."

That was his second apology.

Too little too late. And the words held no sincerity.

Sam left the sheriff and headed to the locker room, where he cleaned out his locker and dressed in jeans, a T-shirt, and tennis shoes.

As he carried his assigned gear to Mary's desk, he noticed the curious stares. He set the items in the box she'd motioned to.

She sorted through everything and handed him a piece of paper. "Sign this."

Sam read over the separation paperwork and then signed it. Since he was still on probation, two-weeks' notice wasn't required. A good thing because he wouldn't have wanted to work there one more minute. "Thanks."

Mary leaned closer. "When things settle, apply to the surrounding towns. They need someone like you. I'll be your reference."

Her offer floored Sam. "Thanks."

A new law enforcement job, however, wasn't on the horizon. He would stay with his parents and do whatever he could to support Missy.

Mary handed him a receipt. "Good luck, Sam Cooper."

"Thanks." As he walked to the public entrance, he waited for regret—or *something*—to hit.

Nothing did.

Sam opened the door and stepped outside.

"Sam!" Dad waved and hurried toward Sam. Mom, Ava, Josh, and Hope were there. They must have all seen his message, but he hadn't expected them to come to town.

Mom hugged Sam. "Quite a day you've had. Are you sure about this?"

Sam nearly laughed, but Mom would be the one to ask. "Better be sure since I burned all my bridges. But I'm positive I made the right decision."

"I'm trying to decide whether to yell at you or hug you, little bro," Ava said.

Sam grinned. "Hugs are much better than yelling."

The two hugged.

Hope touched his arm. "I guess you figured out what you wanted to do."

He hugged her. "Yes, thanks."

Josh stepped up and hugged Sam. "Something tells me I'm missing something."

Hope laughed. "Sam needed help, and I was available."

"It was more than that. Your wife went above and beyond. I owe her."

"Anytime." Hope smiled. "I miss Von, and this made me remember the times we helped each other out."

Sam appreciated everyone coming, but he itched to get back inside. No, he wouldn't be with Missy, who would be in a holding cell, but he wanted to be closer to her. "Do you mind if we go into the waiting room?"

"That's why we're here, Son." Dad clapped Sam's shoulder. "Missy has Jenny, Dare, and Briley, but we want Missy to know the Coopers stand with her. We're all family now."

Sam's eyes watered. He rubbed them. "Thanks, Dad. That means so much to me. To...us."

In a jail cell, Missy stood with her arms crossed in front of her orange jumpsuit. It wasn't cold, but this place gave her the chills. The air smelled funny, as if someone had tried to hide mildew with an air freshener.

She still wore her own shoes, but one deputy said she would be issued a new pair of shoes when they transferred her to the county jail in Klickitat.

When she'd met with Elias after being booked, he told her a judge would arraign her tomorrow. That meant she would have to spend the night there.

If only Sam could be assigned to this part of the sheriff's department. Just for tonight, so she wouldn't be alone.

Except for all she knew, deputies on patrol weren't allowed in the holding block. Not that anyone who didn't have to be there would want to visit. She wouldn't.

At least she was alone.

Missy still might sleep, but she doubted she would close her eyes if someone else were in there with her.

The cell was small, with a pair of bunks and thin mattresses she wouldn't let her cats sleep on. A sink and toilet were in the corner.

No stall or door, but out in the open.

Missy shivered. Maybe she could hold it.

Elias didn't think she would be considered a flight risk, and Selena offered to post bail.

Bail.

Missy rubbed her arms. "Why is this happening?"

She doubted if she would want to watch another crime drama in her life after this. The reality was nothing like what they showed on TV.

The bad guys didn't always wind up in jail.

And whoever set the fire was walking free while they'd locked her up in there.

Her chest tightened once again, making it difficult to breathe. The stinging in her eyes told her what would come next.

Tears.

Nope.

She squeezed her eyes tightly shut to keep the tears from falling. She'd cried so much her head hurt.

Footsteps echoed in the aisle outside the cell.

Missy didn't know what to hope for. She backed into the far wall, away from the bars, but anyone who looked in would see her. There was no hiding there.

Mary, who'd been a regular and a friend of Elise, came up to the cell. "I won't ask if you're okay because I know you're not. Do you need anything?"

Sam. But Missy couldn't ask for him, no matter how much she needed him. She rubbed her arms. "No, thanks."

"I brought you something that might cheer you up."

Missy bet Jenny delivered a box of cupcakes to the town jail. But the last thing Missy wanted to do was eat or drink anything. She didn't want to need the toilet. "Thanks."

Mary smiled at her. "Don't stop believing justice will prevail."

Easy to do from that side of the bars, but the woman had been nice to her. The least Missy could do was play along. "I won't."

"You have five minutes. Not a second longer," Mary said to someone Missy couldn't see. "Don't waste time."

Mary hurried away.

Sam took the spot where she stood.

Am I dreaming? Missy blinked. He was still there.

He smiled at her. "You're not dreaming, sweetheart."

Missy ran to him. Her hands curled around the bars. "You're here. I can't believe you're here."

"The waiting room is full of all your friends and family. My family, too."

She didn't understand. "Yours?"

"They're now your family, too. They're here to support us, just like the Posse."

Her heart swelled. "I like the sound of us."

"Same." Sam glanced to his right and left. "I don't have much time. But Mary got me in here."

"I'll make her dozens of her favorite cupcakes when I get out, but what will Sheriff Dooley say if he catches you?"

Sam blew out a breath. "It doesn't matter now."

"Wait." She took a closer look at him. "Your shift isn't over. Why aren't you in your uniform?"

He swallowed and gazed into her eyes.

The only thing she saw was affection in their depths, but that made no sense. The sheriff had threatened him before.

Missy tightened her fingers around the bars. "Sam?"

He patted her hands. "I resigned."

She startled. No way had she heard him correctly. "You what?"

"I quit." He smiled, which should have been the last thing he did. "I'm no longer employed here, but Mary saw me in the waiting room and snuck me in."

Missy understood how he stood in front of her. Nothing else, however, made sense. "But you always wanted to go into law enforcement."

"I want you more."

Her heart wanted to believe him, but it made little sense. "But being a deputy is your dream."

In the same way being a Marine was Rob's.

"You're my dream, Missy." Sam pressed against the bars as if they would disappear by sheer willpower. "I love you. I never want you to think my job is more important than you. Nothing will ever be more important."

Her lips parted. She stared at the affection in his eyes, but... "You love me?"

"So much."

The familiar stinging returned to her eyes, but this time, her heart soared. The last thing she expected to happen today, but... "I can't believe you quit. Not even..."

She glanced down.

"What?" Sam asked.

Missy's gaze met his. "Not even Rob did that for me."

"I know how much you loved him, how much that love still lives in your heart, but I'm not Rob."

"You're not. And I'm good with that." She swallowed. "I love you, Sam. I love you."

He laughed. "That sounds even better than I thought it would."

"Just wish we weren't here saying it."

"We'll get through this. Figure this out. Don't give up hope, okay?"

"I won't." She hoped he heard the resolve in her voice. "No giving up."

"No giving up." There wasn't much room, but he came closer to the bars and kissed her lips.

Missy enjoyed the unique taste of Sam, with a bit of heat and salt added in. As sensations pulsed through her, she waited for memories to swamp her.

None came.

She kissed him again and again. A sense of something—contentment, maybe—settled over her.

Be happy.

Live out our dreams.

He's yours. And you're his now.

I love you, but he can give you what I can't.

You deserve this and more, babe.

Missy drew back. "Did you hear anyone?"

Something sparked in Sam's eyes. "Not this time, but before. At your house on Saturday night and another time…"

She didn't know what the future held outside of this jail cell, but it didn't matter. Love would see them through.

Somehow. Someway.

"I love you." Missy spoke the words for Sam and Rob, the two men who meant the world to her. One stood with her, and the other lived in her heart and memories. And for the first time in nearly a decade, she felt at peace.

Thank you, Rob, for bringing me Sam.

You always knew what I needed before I did.

I'll always love you.

chapter twenty-four

HOW MUCH FARTHER to the top?

The question looped through Nell's head until she might scream. Okay, the lactic acid buildup in her muscles made her want to yell, but swallowing her frustration was easier than being a total wimp. Gage and Welles waited above for her to climb the pitch, but she kept thinking about being out of shape.

Stop.

Her gut had been telling her to stop before they'd started to climb. It might be because Missy was stuck in jail for a crime she didn't commit. Sure, Bria was helping Missy, so she didn't have to think about the unresolved issues with Dalton. And Juliet would do what she could between hosting parties for Charlene and waiting for the divorce from Ezra to be finalized. At least Selena looked happier, so things must be going better with Logan, and she would make sure everyone took care of themselves while being there for Missy.

Yet, Nell had nothing happening in her life like her friends. That was why she was rock climbing with two handsome guys on Halloween day, even though she still had to buy another bag of candy for the trick-or-treaters and carve her pumpkin.

Yeah, going out today hadn't been Nell's brightest idea.

The Posse was supposed to stick together. And she wasn't there. That must be why she couldn't shake off the feeling she shouldn't be on the climb.

But then she remembered how Gage had taken her to dinner and a movie earlier in the week. They'd also eaten with Mom last night. Nell hadn't wanted to cancel on climbing. Not that she owed him. But the outing with him and Welles had been on her calendar for a week, so she shouldn't feel so guilty for being there and not with her friends.

An idea formed. A good one.

Nell would visit Missy as much as possible next week. That would make up for not being there today.

A rock dug into her fingers. She gripped it tighter so she wouldn't fall. She must be improving at climbing because she didn't go second this time. The guys had climbed before her, and Gage belayed her from above. He kept the rope tight, which she appreciated. His send-off with a kiss had provided extra encouragement.

Her leg scraped on something, most likely a rock, but she knew better than to look down—fear of heights. The first-aid kits she and Welles brought would come in handy later.

Nell pushed herself up, one move at a time, one appendage at a time. Arm-arm-foot-foot-repeat. It sounded easier in practice. Neither Gage nor Welles yelled encouragement, so she must be doing okay or was too low to hear them.

Please don't be the latter.

Sweat dampened her hairline. Add in her helmet, and she would give Medusa a run for her money.

The worst part?

She didn't care.

Gage had seen her like this or worse, yet he still wanted to go out with her. Welles didn't seem to care about her looking disheveled. His constant flirting didn't have an on-off button.

Good.

One shouldn't have to worry about personal grooming when doing outdoor activities. She would die on that sword.

Get out of there.

Nell didn't understand where the sense of doom came from, but she kept going.

Mind over matter, or in this case, gravity.

She reached up for the next hold. The hard rock cut into her fingertips—one more to add to the dozens of others. At least pretty hands weren't a prerequisite for nurses.

Her left foot found a hold, and she pushed herself up.

Stood.

When all she wanted was to sit.

Oh, and not die up here.

That was a distinct possibility, and she tried hard not to think about it.

Gage called the climb easy for her abilities. Welles had warned the section she was on now was the most challenging part.

Nell hoped it didn't get more difficult. She took a breather.

Talk about tough.

Not tougher than me, she hoped.

"You're doing great, babe," Gage yelled down. "You're almost there."

She'd also learned not to look up, so she waved, uncertain whether they would see her.

Tell them it's time to go.

That odd sensation reappeared.

She must be more worn out than she realized. But the sooner they got to the top, the sooner they could come down. The descent always went faster.

Her legs shook—they'd only trembled on the lower pitches of rock.

As if sensing her struggle, Gage tightened the belay rope. She got a short lift, just enough to reach a hold.

Maybe he was mellowing and forgetting his *no pain, no gain* motto.

He'd made her earn every inch in the past, but she would happily take the help.

"You've got this," Welles shouted, who was always the cheerleader, which was why she enjoyed it when he joined them. If he weren't there, she might have anchored to a clip below and watched Gage do this himself.

He probably would have.

Climbing without a rope on a sheer rock wall wouldn't faze him.

Unlike her, the guy had nerves of steel.

Or a death wish.

Each time she tried to decide which, he kissed her, wiping the question from her mind.

Where was she? *Oh, right. The climb.*

Nell reached for a handhold, but she couldn't quite touch it. She tried again.

Nope.

It was too far away.

"Angle the shoulder of the arm you're reaching with toward the rock," Gage yelled.

Why? This is futile.

"Try it, Nell," Welles called out.

Nell blew out a breath, put her left shoulder toward the rock, and reached up with her right arm.

Wait. She reached higher. An inch or two more. All she needed.

Nell gripped the hold. "Got it."

Gage was skilled, but she slowed the other two down. They should go out next time without her.

Welles and Gage cheered.

That part didn't suck.

The guys' handsome smiles might have motivated her, but fear kept Nell staring at the rock in front of her. As Nell climbed, she pretended to be encased in a bubble that started at her fingertips and ended at her toes. That way, if she fell, she didn't have far to go.

A total delusion, but hey, whatever worked.

"Keep going, babe."

Something in her stomach fluttered. *Guess I liked the endearment more than I realize.*

She climbed, working her way up the rock. Shaking limbs and straining muscles slowed her ascent, but she had to almost be at the next stop on the route.

Please let me be close.

She reached up, found her footing, and pushed herself up. Two sets of dirt-covered climbing shoes came into view.

Relief flooded her.

I made it.

She manteled herself onto the ledge. A move made easier by whoever helped her up. She glanced at Gage, gathering the rope as if ready to go again. It must be Welles with his hands on her, but more climbing?

Please, no.

Nell needed to rest. A nap sounded perfect.

Hands touched her shoulders. "Clip in."

She clipped onto the climbing bolt.

Better safe than sorry.

As tired as she was, slipping would be easy to do.

Welles glanced at the climbing bolt before lifting his hands. "You're getting better at this, Nurse Nell."

"Self-preservation instincts help, Paramedic Welles."

Welles aimed a charming grin her way.

This one, however, was less flirty than usual. Had he finally given up asking her out? The workday would be more boring, but it was for the best, given Gage.

Nell undid the figure-eight knot on the rope to hand it off to whoever climbed next. She'd learned to belay but preferred to do it on the ground, not halfway up a mountain.

"Let's keep going," Gage said.

Welles handed her a water bottle. "Let's take a break. Have a snack."

Give Nell time to recover was unspoken but implied.

If only she could ask Missy to make Welles a dozen of his favorite cupcakes, but she should be out of jail soon. And the baking would begin. No one believed Missy was the arsonist except Reggie Lemond, and his so-called evidence was a big stretch.

"I don't want to wait." Gage was fully cloaked in his weekend warrior persona. The only thing missing was a cape. "We've had a break."

"I haven't," she reminded. "I need a minute."

Or ten.

Gage handed the rope out to Welles. "Belay me."

Welles kept his arms at his sides. "We've got plenty of daylight. What's the rush?"

Gage shrugged. "Don't like standing around."

"Why not?" Welles motioned toward the horizon. "It's gorgeous up here. Why not enjoy the view and a snack?"

Welles understood the importance of snacks and rest. Nell liked that about him.

"We'll eat at the summit." Gage shoved the rope into Welles's hand. "This next part won't be hard for Nell. Lots of bigger rocks to hold on to."

Something flitted across her skin. She slapped her arm, but no smushed bug appeared under her hand. *Strange.*

Welles leaned back and studied the route. "A couple of those rocks look sketchy to me."

Gage rolled his eyes and tied in, still clipped to a bolt. "You sound like a dad. I researched the route. It's well-traveled and tested."

Welles shot her an *I-tried* glance.

She smiled at him. "Belay him, Welles."

Nell wanted to get out of there. She kept getting weird vibes. Ones that didn't seem related to her guilt at not being with the Posse. She would ask Selena about them.

It wasn't Gage. The guy had two speeds, fast and faster—when they were doing something physical. He was different when they weren't outside. Something about this place left her feeling unsettled. "I'm ready to get to the top."

So we can go home.

She wouldn't move from the couch all day long tomorrow.

A smile spread across Gage's gorgeous face. "Now that's my Nell."

His Nell?

That was new, but she had no complaints. Especially when he happily played the dedicated boyfriend in front of her mom, but...

She shook the thought from her head.

Climb first, think later.

As Welles prepared to belay, Nell grabbed her water bottle from her pack and drank.

"On belay?" Gage asked.

Welles held the rope. "Belay on."

"Slack," Gage called, and Welles let out the rope. Gage moved closer to the rock. "Up rope."

Welles stood with his legs apart and his hands on the rope threaded through his belay device. He was strong and solid, especially with his tight shirt showing off his muscles. He called himself a paramedic, but he had to pass all the firefighter training first.

Why was she staring at Welles?

Nell focused on the water bottle's logo. Not as interesting, but better.

"You'll enjoy this pitch," Gage said.

She assumed he was talking to her and glanced up.

Gage stared at the hold above him. "Climbing."

"Climb on," Welles said.

The physical part of climbing didn't appeal to Nell much, but the partnership aspect of the sport did. The forced intimacy and trust of your safety in someone else's hand brought her and Gage closer. Welles, too.

Gage headed up the next pitch of the climb, what Nell hoped would be the last part. A glance around the summit, a snack, and a photo if Gage's MO continued. Then, they would rappel down. Not her favorite part, but if she closed her eyes, she could almost believe she was on a carnival ride.

"Gage was over at your place again." Welles kept his eyes on Gage. "Things getting more serious?"

"We're doing more things that don't require a helmet and nerves of steel."

Welles laughed. "Good for Gage, trying something new."

"Trying is a good word. I consider walking from a restaurant to the movie theater an extreme sport, but he's not complaining too much. We even had dinner with my mom."

"Meeting the family already?"

"He met her before our first date. The same day as the cup-cake shop fire."

"Oh, right. I remember that."

"Slack!" Gage yelled.

Welles let out some rope. "Gage is a nice guy. An adrenaline junkie, but..."

"We're nothing alike."

"Opposites." Welles peered up. Squinted. "Stay on the route, Gage. You're way off to the right."

Gage laughed. "Yes, Dad."

"As long as you're happy." Welles's expression grew more serious. "*Are* you happy?"

Nell nodded. "I am."

"Good." He glanced up. "I just never imagined you with someone like him. But you're happy, so—"

"What would make me happier is a bag of peanut M&Ms."

Welles laughed. "Front pocket of my backpack."

"I love you."

"If I'd known candy was all it would take for you to admit that, I would've locked you down years ago."

She laughed and reached for his pack.

"Off belay," Gage called.

Welles took the rope out of his device. "Belay off."

Nell removed a familiar yellow package. "He climbed that fast."

"It's the easiest pitch on the climb. But be sure not to go off route like he did. You don't want…"

Something popped from above.

Nell froze.

Welles's face paled.

Dust fell.

"Rock! Rock! Rock!" Gage screamed.

Huh? The popping turned into cracking.

"Nell!" Welles grabbed her, and as if time slowed, he pushed her against the rock.

Her helmet hit something, and the jolt shot to her toes.

He covered her with his body. His arms tightened around her. "I've got you."

A roar filled her ears.

Something hit Nell, and pain ripped through her. She cried out.

Dirt coated her mouth, filled her nostrils…

Welles gasped.

A weight pressed against her. She couldn't breathe…

🧁 🧁 🧁

Thank you for reading *Kittens & Kisses*. If you want to know what happens next to Nell, Selena, Bria, Juliet, Missy, and the Berry Lake Cupcake Shop, read *Wedding & Wishes*, the fourth book in the series. For more info, visit melissamcclone.com/berry-lake-cupcake-posse/weddings-wishes.

Missy Hanford first appeared in the book *Jenny*. Sam Cooper made his first appearance in *Sweet Beginnings*. Sheridan DeMarco, Sal DeMarco and Sabine Culpepper's daughter, is in *Sweet Yuletide*. To learn more about those books, check out my Beach Brides/Indigo Bay miniseries which contains prequels to the Berry Lake Cupcake Posse series, visit melissamcclone.com/beach-brides-indigo-bay-series.

Join Melissa's newsletter to receive a FREE story and hear about new releases, sales, freebies, and giveaways. Just go to www.subscribepage.com/w9w0y1.

I appreciate your help spreading the word about my work. Tell a friend who loves friendship women's fiction about this book and leave a review on your favorite book site. Reviews help readers find books!

Thanks so much!

about the author

USA Today bestselling author Melissa McClone has written over fifty sweet contemporary romance and women's fiction novels. She lives in the Pacific Northwest with her husband. She has three young adult children, a spoiled Norwegian Elkhound, and cats who think they rule the house. They do!

If you'd like to find Melissa online:
melissamcclone.com
facebook.com/melissamcclonebooks
facebook.com/groups/McCloneTroopers
patreon.com/melissamcclone

other books by melissa mcclone

The Beach Brides/Indigo Bay Miniseries
Prequels to the Berry Lake Cupcake Posse series…
Jenny (Jenny and Dare)
Sweet Holiday Wishes (Lizzy and Mitch)
Sweet Beginnings (Hope and Josh)
Sweet Do-Over (Marley and Von)
Sweet Yuletide (Sheridan and Michael)
Indigo Bay Sweet Romance Collection (Box Set of all five books)

The Berry Lake Cupcake Posse Series
Can five friends save their small town's beloved bakery?
Cupcakes & Crumbs
Tiaras & Teacups
Kittens & Kisses

Silver Falls Series
The Andrews siblings find love in a small
town in Washington state.
The Christmas Window
A Slice of Summer
A Cup of Autumn

347

For the complete list of books, go to
melissamcclone.com/books